FOUR DEGREES NORTH

Confronting Terror in Central Africa

Ken Kerkhoff

Andrew Benzie Books
Martinez, California

Published by Andrew Benzie Books
www.andrewbenziebooks.com

Printed in the United States of America
First Edition: April 2020

10 9 8 7 6 5 4 3 2 1

Kerkhoff, Ken
Four Degrees North: Confronting Terror in Central Africa

ISBN: 978-1-950562-18-3

Cover and book design by Andrew Benzie
www.andrewbenziebooks.com

To my wife Dee.

CONTENTS

Map of Cameroon and Nigeria

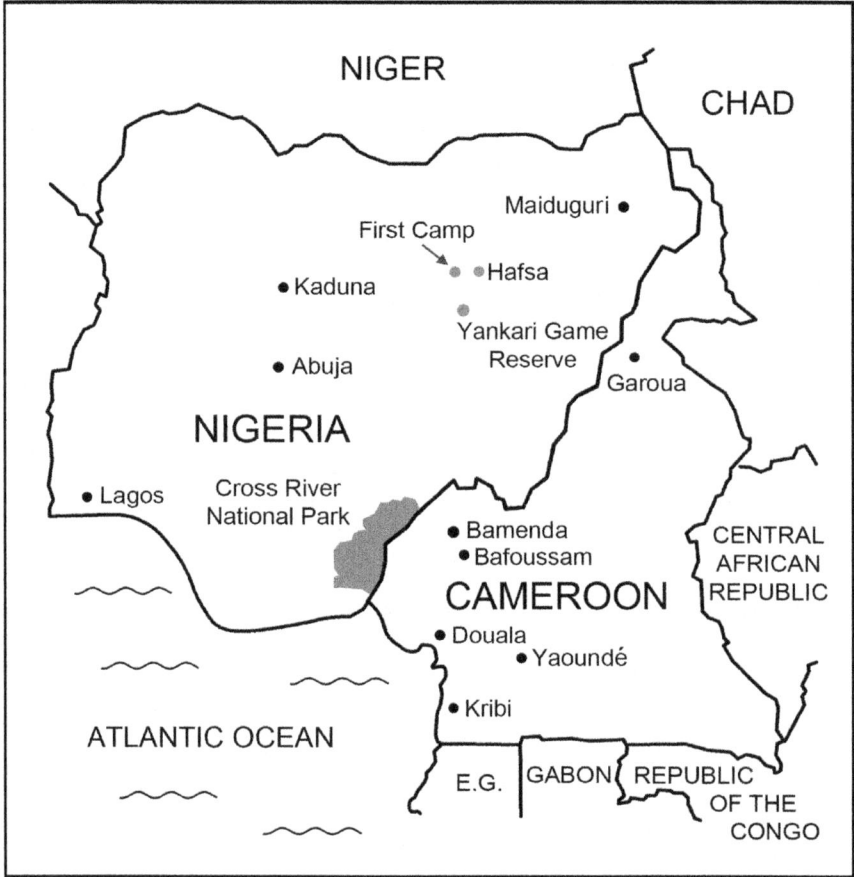

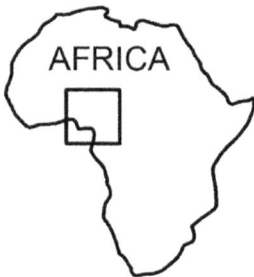

NIGER

CHAD

Maiduguri ●

First Camp

● ●Hafsa

● Kaduna

●
Yankari Game
Reserve

● Abuja

Garoua ●

NIGERIA

● Lagos

Cross River
National Park

● Bamenda
● Bafoussam

CENTRAL
AFRICAN
REPUBLIC

CAMEROON

● Douala
● Yaoundé

● Kribi

ATLANTIC OCEAN

E.G. GABON REPUBLIC
OF THE
CONGO

AFRICA

NOTE: *The city of Douala lies
4.05 degrees north of the Equator.*

Drawing not to scale.

FOREWORD

This fiction narrative is set in the African countries of Cameroon and Nigeria. The story begins early in December 2017. The names of places, except for the village of Hafsa, are factual, but the names of all the characters are the creation of the author.

The jihadist terrorist organization called Boko Haram exists in fact. Based in northeastern Nigeria it is as deadly ruthless as portrayed herein. Organized in 2002, Boko Haram was ranked as the world's deadliest terrorist group by the Global Terrorism Index in 2015. One of the goals of this novel is to expose the violence Boko Haram employs to instill fear in infidels, thereby encouraging them to follow the precepts of sharia law.

Boko Haram may also be called Islamic State in West Africa (ISWA) or the Islamic State's West Africa Province (ISWAP). The leader as of this writing is Abubakar Shekau. The size of the organization is not easily determined, but membership estimates range from three hundred to twenty thousand jihadists.

Over 230 distinct languages are spoken in Cameroon, and more than 520 vernaculars in Nigeria. European colonization and international economic intervention over several hundred years have influenced communication patterns.

Speech in countries like Cameroon often reflects a tendency to blend sounds that foster oral efficiency. Pidgin English evolved from the need to communicate amidst the presence of multiple tribal and foreign languages. Pidgin in Cameroon and some neighboring countries includes English and French vocabulary employed with indigenous grammatical construction.

Cameroonian pidgin is easy to learn and understand. The reader can get an idea of some of the common terms and phrases in the appendix titled *Kamtok* at the back of this book. Nigerian pidgin is somewhat similar to Cameroon Pidgin English. The author has avoided making any distinction as the story crosses the border. There is no precise spelling for most pidgin vocabulary, and pronunciation varies in different regions and from person to person.

Many Cameroonians prefer to speak in pure English or French, using pidgin only where necessary. A negative stereotype exists among those who consider pidgin a poor man's communication crutch. However, many visitors to Cameroon enjoy the rhythm of pidgin, and quickly learn to speak it when shopping in the open markets or when dealing with domestic employees and local tradespeople.

Today's Cameroon was influenced by events following World War I, where Germany's Cameroon colony was divided between England and France. That apportionment resulted in two systems of government and two official languages, English and French.

At the time of this writing, the Republic of Cameroon is experiencing disenchantment over the precarious balance between the Anglophone and Francophone elements of language and governance. The author has intentionally avoided dwelling on the ensuing conflict.

CHAPTER 1
MOUNT CAMEROON

Yaoundé had been quiet that Sunday forenoon while two gray cargo vans silently motored past Cameroon's National Assembly Building, charred from a fire the previous month. The vans turned onto a tree-lined boulevard that housed several governmental, ministerial, and law offices. The crunch of rubber on pavement provoked little attention. The calls of wild guinea fowl scratching for edibles the only other discernible sound. There was no visible security presence in front of the aging government building. The vans stopped under the shadows of a purple-flowered jacaranda tree.

The first-floor assembly room was filled with high-ranking government officials, including a number of cabinet ministers who had come for an extraordinary Sunday meeting called by the president to deal with civil unrest in the west.

At eleven a.m., a dozen figures burst from the vans and ran toward the entrance. Military-style *shemaghs* or scarves wrapped around their heads disclosed dark, menacing eyes. The cuffs of their camouflage cargo pants were stuffed into heavy boots. Bulky green shirts partially concealed weapons.

Sunday morning amblers stared in confusion, unsure if they were witnessing a national army exercise or a terrorist attack. Moments later they scrambled for cover as shots were fired. Two surprised security guards near the door had no chance to warn the assembled government leaders. The guards died before they could unlock their weapons.

The attackers mounted the steps and flung open the doors. Nine terrorists rushed inside the hall. Three others turned their weapons outward to discourage interference.

Automatic gunfire clattered inside the large room. Smoke bombs sent thick clouds of haze, stifling resistance. A woman's scream pierced the clamor as the attackers pulled two government ministers from their seats and forced them toward the door. A third security officer inside the chamber fired a pistol at an assailant. His bullet missed. A fusillade of return fire ended his stand.

The intruders fled the building, dragging one official and pushing another terrified minister before them. Someone shouted a command in an unfamiliar language, and bystanders dove for cover behind concrete barriers and metal hydrants. A militant waved a black flag with Arabic script. Terrified citizens later described it as no Cameroon Army *guidon*, but definitely a terrorist's banner.

A captive minister spotted the pennant, his eyes reflected absolute terror. It was the banderole of murderous Islamic terrorists known as Boko Haram. The minister grabbed for his captor's weapon and nearly succeeded. He was savagely clubbed by another attacker. The minister fell but continued to struggle. For his effort he received two high-caliber bullets to his head.

Within ten minutes of stepping out of their vans the attackers sped away with one hostage.

*   *   *

In the sky above Cameroon, Alan Burke adjusted his glasses once more, and stretched his six foot-two-inch frame to ease the kinks in his muscular body. He felt tense, still stoked by yesterday's meetings in Paris, anticipating his new job, and thinking about his wife travelling alone in Nigeria. *I wish Mona had traveled with me. I could use her support.* Alan and Mona planned to be together in two days. Five hours ago, he kissed her goodbye at *Aéroport de Paris-Charles-de-Gaulle*, where they boarded separate airplanes.

U.S. State Department training had begun six months ago in Washington D.C. Alan's head was crammed with a myriad of details about Africa and Cameroon. He learned about Cameroon's history, her culture, her economy, her major trading partners, her friends, and her enemies.

In a matter of hours Alan was expected to begin his diplomatic career as a U.S. Embassy attaché in Yaoundé. He pondered his future as he reached again for the *New York Times International Edition* and tried to focus. He glanced at the headline, "Nigerian Army Begins New Initiative to Control Boko Haram Terrorists." He stuffed the newspaper back into the seat pocket. *I can't concentrate now, too worked-up. Anyway, the* Times *is two days old.*

Boko Haram? Nigeria? Crap. He grabbed the paper again. *Boko Haram is that violent Nigerian organization that kills and rapes. They are the ones who kidnapped 276 girls from a school in Chibok.* Alan felt his body tense up. *I hope Mona's escort met her at the Lagos airport as planned.*

The *Times* article stated that the Nigerian Government established a Terrorist Special Forces Unit, and that a General Rasaki was placed in charge. *Hmm, Rasaki's name wasn't on my influential persons list.*

The memory of his beautiful wife boarding a Lagos-bound plane in Paris filled him with trepidation. He had wanted her to travel with him, but she was determined to complete an assignment for her employer. *I guess she wants to demonstrate her independence. I'm proud of her desire to be her own person.* Alan had always encouraged her professional work, but now he worried for her safety.

Past Mount Cameroon, Alan glanced out his starboard window to see the Gulf of Guinea, south of the Cameroon Coast. Remembering some of the history of the country, he recalled that in the 15th Century, Portuguese explorers on the Gulf gave Cameroon its name. Then, the mountain erupted red hot lava in the distance, while the continental seafarers caught a bounty of shrimp just off the coast of what is now Cameroon. They named the river, *Rio dos Camarões*, or, River of Shrimp, later called Cameroon in English.

This was one of those moments Alan wished he could be sharing with Mona. *She's probably in Lagos now, meeting her guide.* Mona had insisted that she would serve legal papers at several businesses, then catch the next flight to Douala. The *Times* headlines made him wish he had insisted that they travel together. His only consolation was that Mona's law firm was arranging for someone to meet and accompany her while in Nigeria. *At least she'll be with me in Yaoundé for Christmas.*

Mona's assignment would complete her intern responsibilities for the Maryland law firm she worked with during her graduate studies. That mission involved contacting a Lagos company regarding consumer product fraud. Since Nigeria bordered Cameroon, and since the assignment was expected to last no more than two or three days, the state department allowed her to travel there, provided that she be accompanied by someone from her firm.

Alan and Mona had met in graduate school and found they shared a love for adventure and travel. They married shortly after Alan secured his state department job. Together they looked forward to exciting careers working and living overseas.

Alan's plane touched down on schedule and taxied toward the terminal. The ear-splitting sound of reversing jet engines brought Alan's focus back to the present as he prepared himself for the hot Douala air. Nevertheless, the humid furnace-blast shocked him when he stepped off the plane into a stifling-hot breeze. Douala, at four degrees north of the equator, has an average daily temperature around 27.8 degrees Celsius (82F). Daytime temperatures in December and January, however, easily reach 35 C (95F), and, because of the high temperature and the city's proximity to the Gulf, the humidity could reach one hundred percent. Alan's shirt was sweat-soaked in seconds.

From an air-conditioned shuttle bus Alan scrutinized his surroundings. Douala's aging airport with its two-story rectangular terminal appeared gray and devoid of charm or remarkable architecture. The Air France jet he arrived on, a Kenya Airways 737, and an Ethiopian Airlines jet were the only planes on the tarmac. People standing on the terminal's top floor deck waved at the bus as though they could see inside the smoked windows.

Slow lines of arriving passengers inside the non-air-conditioned terminal sweltered as they presented immigration documents. Alan observed that most of his fellow passengers appeared to be Africans, but with varying languages and colorful dress styles. Several Asian and European travelers also shuffled in the line. Alan was not surprised to see travelers from other nations. Douala was the main commercial center for Cameroon and a major regional shipping port.

A babble of languages permeated the scraping of luggage and rustling of documents. The rhythmic chords of Pidgin English contrasted with local dialects, as well as traces of French, Spanish, German, and Swahili.

Alan's diplomatic passport cleared immigration quickly, and his baggage escaped scrutiny. For some other travelers, customs officials wanted to inspect everything. The customs offices pushed their hands through neatly folded clothes and personal belongings, opened toilet caddies and even inspected toothbrush holders. They probed the bottom of every briefcase, looking for false bottoms hiding drugs, weapons, currency, or other contraband. They demanded an explanation about any unusual object and were generally capable of doing so in both French and English.

In one European man's backpack an inspector spotted an old copy of *Penthouse Magazine*. When the official demanded an explanation, the indignant traveler created a scene. Two customs officers in starched khaki appeared and hustled the unfortunate traveler to an interview room.

Alan thought about the horror stories he had heard about perplexing regulations in certain countries. And that money spoke louder than regulations. Bribes were common.

His duty-free Johnnie Walker Black Label survived customs, so Alan moved toward a large, open area that contained ticketing booths, baggage handlers, and taxi drivers. Shouting men bellowed the merits of hiring their services. The mass of humanity moved through the lobby toward the brilliant sunlight beyond.

Scanning over the heads of the milling crowd Alan spotted a large sign held high by a Caucasian man wearing a flamboyant Hawaiian shirt and a floppy tweed ivy flat cap. The man behind the BURKE sign was someone Alan hadn't met but assumed was Dr. Leonard Watson. He fit the description of the thirty-something U.S. diplomat who worked out of the U.S. Embassy Branch Office in Douala and monitored a large, American construction company in Cameroon.

"Alan Burke?" the man shouted over the din of the surging crowd of humanity as Alan waved at him.

Len, a rather stocky, five-foot-nine-inch Midwesterner, was dressed in loose-fitting khaki pants despite the high temperature, probably because of the blistering sun and the nasty mosquitoes.

"Hello. You must be Dr. Watson."

"You betcha. That's me," said Len in his best Minnesotan as the two shook hands, "at your service. Call me Len. I trust you had a pleasant flight?" Looking over Alan's shoulder Len added, "Where's your wife?"

"My wife will be here in a couple of days. I'll update you on her travel, but can we get out of this suffocating heat first?"

"Absolutely. I have an air-conditioned car waiting just outside. Let me carry one of those bags." Len introduced Alan to the Cameroon driver who popped out of the SUV. "Alan, meet Eric. Eric, Alan Burke." Conspiratorially to Alan he added, "Don't tell him but this man is the best driver in the country. He works for USAID. This car is one of theirs, but we are borrowing it and Eric. His shift is just about over, so we'll drop him off. He'll drive us tomorrow."

"Happy to greet," Eric said cheerfully offering his hand. "Listen," he said as he reached into the vehicle and turned up the volume on the radio.

A French-speaking newsman was completing an emergency bulletin. When the announcement ended, Eric summarized, "They *git* some *kayne* accident today in Yaoundé. I did not catch details, but I hear something '*bout* murder."

"Yeah I caught the tail end," Len commented, "something about a government building in Yaoundé. Hope it wasn't a coup attempt."

"Great." Alan said, "My first day in Cameroon, and I'm welcomed with a coup."

"For now," Len concluded, "we'll stay tuned and alert. It's probably nothing, but I'll check with the embassy."

Alan watched Eric place the baggage in the back, noting the respectful smile and warm, friendly eyes. The driver's English was understandable and he seemed strong and agile. Having worked part-time for the U.S. Agency for International Development while in grad school, Alan knew about its efforts to end extreme poverty and improve food production in developing countries. USAID, like many expatriate organizations, preferred to employ local drivers, thereby creating indigenous employment as well as allowing foreign diplomats and businessmen to avoid the hassles of maneuvering through dense traffic and searching for parking.

The embassy staff had arranged for Alan's stay in Douala's Pullman Douala Rabingha, one of the finest western-style hotels. Alan would fly to Yaoundé tomorrow evening. The short flight east would only take an hour.

As Eric maneuvered the car through traffic, Alan was struck by the contrasting images along the crowded roadway. Hundreds of people hugged the sides of the dusty road, many were barefoot or clad in flip-flops. Bicycles, motor scooters, and various animals and carts moved in all directions, clogging the roadway. Trucks and taxis parted the waves of the masses by blasting their horns. These were forced to give way to luxury sedans carrying single passengers dressed in business suits or the attire of the well-off. On his left he saw makeshift shelters of tin and cardboard. To his right stood modern high-rise buildings that reflected sunlight off glass and steel, some surrounded with manicured lawns.

A dusty haze filtered the sunlight, and scraps of garbage obscured the paved roadway, concealing potholes that jarred vehicles and passengers. Most pedestrians solemnly stepped aside to let vehicles pass. Others bayed at the encroaching vehicles, either to claim their share of the road or to advertise goods or food for sale.

Alan felt embarrassed that the outside dust, noise, and heat did not penetrate the closed windows of the SUV. He wondered if this barrier between him and the Cameroon people was destined to distance diplomats like him from the native population.

CHAPTER 2
WILD BIF

An hour before the sun dipped below Cameroon's namesake mountain, Len drove Alan to *Restaurant Palmiers*, an eating establishment favored by intrepid diners. Alan let the warm evening air caress his face as they passed through an area of gated homes interspersed with foreign commercial businesses represented in Cameroon. A small neon sign marked the entrance to a narrow driveway which wound for a hundred meters around tall palm trees and lush vegetation. A gentle ocean breeze rustled the rose bushes bordering the drive.

Strains of loud but infectious music emanated from the building. Alan swayed to the bold rhythm of Cameroon's home-grown makossa music.

A young woman greeted them at the entrance to the Palms. She was dressed in a richly-patterned Nigerian wrapper with a matching head piece. Her captivating smile enchanted Alan and warmed his spirits. With a slight bow she said in a husky, feminine voice, *"Bonsoir. Bienvenue aux Palmiers,"* Followed with, "Good evening. Welcome to the Palms." Her English was as fluent as her smooth, African French. She led them to a table inside with a view toward the Gulf. She

9

introduced their *serveuse*. A tantalizing blend of food aromas from the kitchen greeted them. Open bamboo shutters allowed salty breezes to waft through the large room.

Before Alan could open the proffered menu, Len ordered two Beaufort lager beers. Surprised at Len's quick maneuver, Alan asked, "What are you doing?"

"I assume you drink beer. Thought I'd get you started on the common man's beer. Once you get into your diplomatic circles you'll have to order only the imports."

Alan closed his menu, leaned forward and said, "I don't follow."

Len accepted his Beaufort from the young lady, eased the top off the cold, 650 milliliter bottle and explained, "There's a kind of pecking order in libation. You see, a lot of Cameroonians judge a man by the beer he drinks. They consume a lot of beer but most of it is stuff like this, or Guinness. Observe. Some locals take note of what you drink and make assumptions. The more expensive the beer you drink the higher your apparent status."

"So, what do you drink when you want to impress your counterparts?"

"Well, at the higher end of the scale are your European imports, like Becks, Heineken, and Saint Pauli Girl. But any imports rate high if they're expensive. Some people will feel insulted if you offer them something less than the best."

"Thanks, Len. I'll remember that." As an afterthought, he added, "Should I feel insulted because you ordered a working-man's beer for me?"

"Not at all. Unless you're a beer connoisseur, you probably won't taste much difference between that and the most expensive imports. I just want you to experience both ends of the spectrum. Next we'll try an import." Lifting his glass to toast, Len added, "Welcome to four degrees north of the Equator."

Alan smiled, took a swig of Beaufort, and nodded. "Not bad." He reached for the menu, and scrunched his brow at the entrees. After skimming, he asked, "Could you recommend something? My French is not that good."

"Sure," said Len, "each line is a different animal. You have your croc steak first, next is the broiled monkey, and the third line down is the stewed turtle cooked in a wine sauce, which I plan to order. Cameroonians refer to this type of food as *bush meat,* simply called *bif,* as in beef. *Bif* covers a wide variety of wild game, including gorilla, crocodile, snake, monkey, hedgehog, deer and all forms of animals that crawl, swim, walk or fly. However, gorilla and some other bush meats are protected. It's illegal to hunt those species, so I'd avoid ordering them if they were on the menu."

Skewered rabbit on couscous seemed least disagreeable to Alan. After ordering his turtle, Len said with a mischievous smile, "It's really good. You should try it."

"I'm sure it is," Alan said rolling his eyes and feeling queasy. "Most anything could be palatable when it's cooked in wine sauce."

Alan took another gulp of Beaufort and excused himself. "I've got to call my wife." He stepped into the warm evening air and found a spot away from the loud makossa. After two buzzes Mona's familiar voice said, "Hello."

"Hi love, how are you?" Alan was happy to finally contact Mona. "How was your flight?"

"Hi, sweetheart," Mona breathed excitedly, "It's so great to hear your voice. I miss you so much. My flight was fine, but the person who was supposed to meet me never showed up. I waited an hour before calling my boss. Ben Warner said that my escort has some sort of visa problem. They're going to work it out and call me tomorrow. I took a taxi from the airport, and I'm in my hotel now. How was your flight?"

Is Mona making a special effort to sound brave? "My flight was good. Dr. Watson met me at the airport as planned. We just ordered dinner in an ocean-side restaurant in Douala. I wish you were here." Alan could not hide his concern. "What kind of visa problem? How could a law firm mess up something so simple? Where was this person supposed to be coming from?"

"Before we left D.C., Ben said that an attorney would meet me and would engage a driver. I don't know the person. I only have a name, Pail Okeke. They didn't tell me where he's from. Supposedly, this Okeke guy is associated with my firm's Paris office, but that wasn't made clear."

Alan sighed. "Listen, honey, don't go anywhere until that escort shows up. If that doesn't work out just catch the next flight to Douala. Call me and I'll be here to meet you." They talked for a few more minutes before Alan said goodbye and promised to call the next day.

Walking back to his seat, Alan noticed several groups of excited people in animated conversations. He ignored them, as he did not know the local dialects or the African French. *What are those people so worked up about?*

"Everything okay?" Len asked.

"Oh, yeah. I guess. Just a small matter of travel arrangements."

"Good," Len said. "You never told me why your wife is not traveling with you."

"She is in Lagos. She'll be in Yaoundé within the week."

Raising his glass of beer, Len stopped mid-lift. He looked sharply at Alan. "What? What is your wife doing in Nigeria? For Christ sake, I hope she didn't go there for a vacation. That's not the choicest place to go for a fun-filled weekend."

"Oh, no. She is finishing up an assignment for a law firm. It's a firm she interned for while doing her masters studies. She is currently on a short-term contract. Mona will be with some other attorneys, and they're staying in the safest places. At least that's what she was told. Now, you have me worried."

"Sorry," Len said, "it's just that I don't relish traveling there by myself." Len shrugged, and added, "Even though I plan to attend a conference in Nigeria next week."

"Well," Alan said jokingly, "maybe if you go early you can help Mona find her way around."

Len ordered more beer and produced some scribbled notes on a paper napkin. Over cold Heineken, he talked about Alan's new host country. He described the oil fields off the coast of Limbe, and the commercial rubber and palm plantations in the Southwest Region. He talked about the large pineapple and banana farms that marketed produce to Europe and other parts of the world.

Alan looked forward to seeing the big plantations, but found it difficult to get his head into the conversation, thinking about Mona's predicament. Cameroon's oil and commercial crops represented major portions of the country's wealth. Len emphasized the plantations likely because his background included a prominent reputation as a wildlife and forestry advocate. Alan abruptly changed the subject. "I was told that this country was once considered one of the world's largest per-capita consumers of beer, wine and champagne, second only to France. Is that true?"

"You betcha. Cameroon is not considered a wealthy country, but somehow, Cameroonians manage to consume a lot of alcohol."

The turtle and the rabbit arrived simultaneously and were appropriately appraised. Alan absorbed the appetizing aroma of his sizzling skewers with delight and consumed the couscous with gusto.

While the two enjoyed their meal, Len discussed their itinerary for the next twenty-four hours. "Ambassador Morrison asked me to give you a tour of several projects in the Littoral and South Regions before you catch tomorrow night's flight to Yaoundé. You know, as the officer for the Douala branch of the embassy, my function here is mainly to assist U.S. citizens with passport issues and clearing of goods for U.S. businesses operating here. However, because an American company is involved in a major development in Kribi, and because of my background in forestation, I spend a great deal of time in Kribi."

"Yes. I was briefed in D.C.," Alan said, nodding.

"I don't work for USAID," Len said pointedly, "I am like an independent contractor, with limited State Department responsibilities. I manage to stay off the Ugly American list. My main function is to study the use of forest land and to report on the influence of development on Cameroon's southern forests. I studied forestry at the University of Minnesota with Richard Alquist, the USAID Mission Director in Cameroon, and he's buddy-buddy with your new boss Tyler Morrison - excuse me, Ambassador Morrison." Len smiled and whispered conspiratorially, "State department people take titles very seriously."

The attractive *serveuse* who had brought their food stopped at the table and asked if the two men were interested in dessert, coffee, or an after-dinner liqueur. Len ordered liqueurs.

"I've met Richard," Alan noted.

"As you know," Len went on, "Ambassador Morrison won't be back from vacation until after Christmas. He wants me to show you the Kribi project while you're here. The deep-water port project near Kribi is important to Cameroon's future development, and your diplomatic endeavors will involve Cameroon's increasing commerce with her neighbors."

"I appreciate your doing this, Len. It's nice to have a friendly face to introduce me to my new home. I'm still a bit nervous. This is a big change for me. Morrison informed me about the U.S. involvement in the region. I definitely want to see whatever I can while I'm in the south. Maybe you could even pass along some of the unofficial things you've picked up on the local culture and customs."

"Love to. It's an interesting country," Len said. "She comes with exploding lakes, great makossa music, exotic fruits, rubber, coconut and palm trees, and even some nice beaches. As delightful as that may sound, this country has its share of corruption, poverty and hunger."

Worry wrinkles formed on Alan's brow. *Of course, if there were only positives everyone would want to live here.*

Barely stopping for a breath Len continued, "Of course, you'll need to be proficient in French, and maybe I can teach you some Pidgin English. It would help in communicating with the villagers."

"I want to learn pidgin. People tell me it is a very fluid and easy-to-learn method of communication. But, what's this about exploding lakes? I don't recall anything about exploding water features in the tourism guides."

Len smiled. "People tell me that it happened at least twice. Some kind of volcanic action underneath bodies of water caused gases to explode. The most recent was in 1986. A large lake near the Ring Road, in the Northwest Region, exploded and emitted a cloud of poisonous gas. I read an article in *National Geographic* stating that the escaping CO_2 rolled down the hillside and instantly suffocated over

1700 people. Those people never knew what hit them. The gas killed every animal in that valley."

"Damn. That's a bit daunting. They didn't tell me about the hazards of working here."

"Oh, don't worry, my man." Len countered, "This thing is very rare. Anyway, you'll be stationed in Yaoundé, far from that region. Lake Nyos is way out in the remote cattle country."

Len sipped his Grand Marnier, leaned back in his wickerwork chair and continued. "This country contains many of the geographical features found throughout Africa. Some people refer to Cameroon as Little Africa. It has mountains, rainforests, grassy plains, sparse desert, and an ocean coastline. Its cultural diversity is extraordinary. There may be as many as 250 indigenous populations, with different cultures, customs and languages."

"Yeah, I read that too. But, I was also told that you can get along with a combination of French, English and Pidgin English."

"Cameroon's constitution," Len added, "provides for multiple political parties as well as freedom of religion. Much of the Cameroonian population is Christian, but a smaller portion is Islamic. Some people practice various indigenous religions. It is challenging for expatriates to work with a French-based system of government administration in one part of the country and a British-based system in the Anglophone regions. That's due to the country's colonial history. This country has survived Portuguese, Dutch, German, French, and British colonialism. Just be glad you only have to work with French and English."

Alan smiled, sipped his Grand Marnier, and reminded Len, "They briefed me on the current political situation here, but what do you know about Cameroon's history?"

"Here's my short, un-edited version," Len began. "After World War I, the Germans were forced out, and their colony was partitioned between the British and French. The British received control over the western portion of the country and France got the larger, eastern portion. The administrative and linguistic division of the country has been the cause of tensions since about 1919."

Alan relaxed, as large ceiling fans whisked a lazy, salty draft throughout the restaurant.

"After the Second World War," Len continued, "a Cameroonian named Ahmadou Ahidjo tried to unite the two parts of the country and gain independence from France. A United Nations-supported referendum allowed the northern part of British Cameroon to join Nigeria, while the South preferred to join the French-speaking area. Unfortunately, there are still disagreements about that arrangement today."

"I understand," Alan cut in, "that Cameroon became a shining example of African progress under President Ahidjo."

"True," Len said, "however, the president kept adding to his powers, and was reluctant to let other political parties challenge him, so the country never became a true democracy. Then, around 1982 Ahidjo abruptly handed the government to his Prime Minister Paul Biya and departed for France. Something about needing urgent medical care."

"Doesn't it seem a bit unusual," suggested Alan, "for the president to abdicate and turn his country over to someone else?"

"Yes." Len replied, "People say that after becoming president, and shortly after Ahidjo left Cameroon, Biya and Ahidjo had serious disagreements. Ahidjo accused Biya of turning the country into a police state, and Biya supposedly refused to allow Ahidjo to remove a massive fortune from the country. Some suspected that Ahidjo's wealth was actually the country's petroleum revenues that he had secretly diverted into a foreign bank account. Paul Biya sentenced Ahidjo to death in absentia."

Loud, animated discussion near the restaurant entrance distracted both men momentarily. "Something's going on," Alan observed, "but I can't make out what those people are excited about." Eventually, ignoring the distraction, he asked, "What happened next?"

"There was a coup attempt around 1983 or 1984, supposedly staged by military forces loyal to Ahidjo. It failed, leaving a chaotic political scene. President Biya survived the coup attempt and consolidated his power by becoming the president of the country's main political party. He named it the Cameroon People's Democratic

Movement. He has ruled Cameroon with a steel grip for some thirty-five years as president."

"Interesting," Alan said. "The two styles of administration and the two-language education and legal systems make for a sensitive political situation."

"You betcha." Len said. "And, you should be aware that there are rumors of massive fraud and corruption. In 1999 Cameroon was named the most corrupt country in the world by Transparency International, a global anti-corruption coalition. Some say the government was run like a kleptocracy. Since then Cameroon's ranking has improved a bit. Anyway, judging from what I see, industry and commerce seem to have survived. It's just hard to get anything done without greasing palms." Len went on with a sly smile, "Just between us fence posts, I looked up a lot of history on the internet when I heard you were coming. Oh, and incidentally, the version I just gave you about the politics might not appear in the Cameroon *pikin's* school books."

"What's a *pikin?*"

"Ah, your first lesson in local Pidgin English. A *pikin* is a child, and Cameroonians love *dey pikin* and *dey ol folk.*"

"Great. I now have a starter vocabulary."

The volume in the *Palmiers* grew louder and the hour approached eight p.m., so they split the tab and left. As they crossed the parking lot, Len's pocket emitted strains of Beethoven's Fifth Sympathy. He pulled out his cell phone, scrunched up his face and mumbled, "Hmm, I wonder what the chief wants at this hour. Hello, Tyler." Then he listened for a minute. His forehead wrinkled slightly, and his eyes widened as he glanced in Alan's direction. He emitted a muffled, "Shit. I thought that was over with. Yes, I will do that. I understand. I'll get him on his way there first thing tomorrow morning." Stuffing the cell phone back in his pocket and moving quickly toward the car he said, "Come on. Let's go."

"That sounded ominous. I assume Tyler is Ambassador Morrison, right? Something bad must have happened. What is it?"

Len cleared his throat and mumbled, "We're gonna hafta change our plans a bit."

CHAPTER 3
ZEBRAWOOD

Len confirmed that earlier in the day there had been a murder and a kidnaping in Yaoundé. Buckling his seat belt as the car raced up the driveway, Alan asked, "What happened? What did Tyler say?"

The SUV zigzagged through traffic toward Alan's hotel. "Yes. The ambassador's in Washington. He said a dozen militants attacked some Cameroon officials in Yaoundé this morning. The minister of the interior was shot and killed. Two security guards were also killed and several military and private citizens were injured. The minister of the treasury was abducted.

"What?" asked Alan, gaping in disbelief. "When? When did this happen?"

"Late this morning. It's already on the international news. According to reports, the Cameroon president was not harmed. The Cameroon Army attempted pursuit but the attack was well-planned, and the offenders got away during the confusion."

"Whoa." exclaimed Alan. "An attack on the capital? By soldiers? Was this a coup? Is there a state of emergency?" After a pause he added, "I'm supposed to be in Yaoundé tomorrow night.

"I know, I know. However, Morrison advises that you not go

there until we get assurance that it's safe, maybe in a day or two. It appears that whoever staged this raid did not target foreigners, however, we have to be careful. Normally, the Presidential Palace and government buildings are well-protected, and there are military installments throughout the city. They don't think this was a coup attempt. There have been no indications of further hostile actions. The attackers were wearing some sort of uniform. They may have been Nigerians. Witnesses heard them speaking Hausa. Some suspect these kidnappers might be either from political opponents in the Northwest Region or part of a guerrilla organization from Nigeria. We need to wait to see if there are any demands."

"Why didn't the ambassador call me? Alan asked. It would have been nice to get this straight from the horse's mouth."

"The horse tried to call your cell phone," Len responded. "Something about phone security."

Alan shrank into his seat. He was aware of the 1984 coup attempt, and that some political factions have been at odds with the ruling party, but those opponents were not known to be violent. "Was this an action related to the language issue?" Alan asked.

Before answering, Len parked in front of the entrance to Alan's hotel. "It appears more like an invasion of a foreign terrorist group. The few facts they know suggest something bigger than a local dispute or crime. Go grab your things and check out."

"Where will I go?" Alan pushed his glasses up onto his nose.

"Morrison wants you to stay out of both Douala and Yaoundé for a day, but to remain in contact with the embassy and the USAID Mission. As a U.S. diplomat you and I could also be targets, so we must stay out of harm's way until this thing settles. I have a place in Kribi. Come there with me now. You can use this USAID car for several days. I will arrange someone to drive you to Bamenda in the morning. You'll get to know the Northwest Region."

Alan shook his head. "No. I need to be with the embassy staff. Especially now that the ambassador is not there. Plus, I'm supposed to be in Douala to meet my wife when she flies in. I don't feel right about your plan."

"Don't worry. I'll see if the mission can spare Eric Mbando, the driver you met this afternoon. He is a good driver, speaks English, French and pidgin, and he knows the country. If your wife arrives in the next day or two we'll have someone meet her and make sure she is safe."

Alan retrieved his luggage and checked out. Len contacted the USAID office to arrange the continued use of the mission car and get permission for a driver. Eric was available to travel immediately.

"Where to next?" asked Alan, closing the rear boot and sliding into the passenger seat.

"We pick up Eric now so you don't have to come back to the city. Then we drive to Kribi, where you can stay in the guest bungalow. It's a long drive but at least you'll be out of the city. You can leave for Bamenda first thing in the morning.

Eric Mbanda stood near Douala's Roundpoint Deido, a central taxi hub. Alan spotted him clutching a document purse and a small duffel bag. Eric appeared bright-eyed in spite of the late hour and greeted the Americans with a smile and a cheery, *"Ashya."* He slid into the driver's seat as Len and Alan moved to the rear.

Alan guessed that the Cameroonian was in his mid-thirties, but the man evinced the innocence of a younger man. His round face with its attentive smile suggested wisdom of an older person. At about five-feet-six-inches tall Eric was compact, and appeared to be eating well on his USAID salary. As Eric placed his stubby hands on the steering wheel, Alan noticed the darkened crevices and cuticles, telltale signs of a mechanic's fingers.

"Eric," Len said, "I hope you got some rest. Tonight, we go to Kribi. Early tomorrow you will take Mr. Burke to Bamenda. You must bypass Douala, and go directly to the Northwest Region. Understood?"

"Yes sir."

Turning to Alan, Len said, "Bamenda should be the safest place to hold out for a day or two. The ambassador said there are some relationships there that you will need to cultivate eventually, and according to him, it's okay to use the USAID car and driver for the trip. He wants you to contact Mr. Marcel Ndobe when you get to Bamenda. Marcel is a Cameroonian who works for USAID."

Alan felt overwhelmed. The events of the day stifled his enthusiasm. He mumbled, "Okay, What about tomorrow's plane reservation for Yaoundé?"

"I'll take care of that," Len responded.

*   *   *

The terrain changed dramatically as the lights of Douala faded. Buildings and street lights were replaced with dense vegetation and rolling hills. Forest canopy occasionally opened to reveal a nearly full moon. Alan saw red African soil for the first time.

As a forestry expert, Len's excitement about trees bubbled into a monologue. "We are in a small timber conservancy left intact at the request of the United Nations," said Len. "The logging industry is up there with oil exports as one of Cameroon's biggest foreign exchange resources. Foreign timber companies compete fiercely for Africa's timber. The trees on our left and right are remnants of the African zebrawood species. They are among the most valuable of all the tropical trees. In front of us is an example of the *prunus africana*, also called red stinkwood, or African cherry. It is being studied for cancer treatment possibilities."

"You really take trees very seriously," Alan commented, "I had no idea you could get medicine out of a log."

Len seemed to enjoy demonstrating his scholarly knowledge so he continued. "Just as precious is the *lophira alata* species, which once grew in this area, but now is nearly extinct. Its hard wood is highly desirable for construction. The exploitation of the species is devastating to local villagers. Extracts from the bark are used by local women as a cure for menstrual problems. Extracts are also good for kidney ailments, headaches and stomach problems. So, you see, we are losing some valuable social and cultural history when these trees are exploited."

The dark canopy of zebrawood trees was replaced with open plains in less than fifteen seconds. "Pretty small conservancy," Alan observed with a hint of distraction.

"I'm afraid it's the best the United Nations could do to get the local government to protect some critical timber growth. Zebrawood is an endangered species." Len lowered his voice and leaned a little closer to Alan. "Local officials are suspected of accepting bribes in exchange for awarding choice parcels of timber."

"You did mention something about corruption earlier," Alan said.

"For example," Len offered. "Two years ago, authorities became aware of a large quantity of zebrawood being trucked to Douala. Local villagers stopped two of the trucks and alerted the gendarmes. The villagers were angry because the logging company broke a promise to build a community meeting hall in exchange for the right to harvest the trees. The local forestry office had taken a bribe, which allowed the company to bypass the Ministry of Forestry and Wildlife. That kind'a stuff goes on all the time, and that's why the forests need protection."

"Yes, but isn't that kind of thing present in every country?" suggested Alan.

"Over the past hundred years," Len went on, "German, British, French and other nations profited from cutting and exporting mahogany, ebony, iroko, zebrawood and bubinga trees. A few very rare endangered species, such as zebrawood and ebony, were reduced to small groves and are now officially protected. The world has an insatiable appetite for natural timber, especially the prized species that grew only in certain regions of Africa and Asia," Len suggested, "That puts a lot of pressure on honesty."

Alan leaned back in his sear, staring into the distance and becoming ever more aware of the fallibility of human nature.

Len continued, "Too many young diplomats come here without fully understanding what goes on in the real world. Did they tell you back in Foggy Bottom that this country was rife with corruption? Your mission in Cameroon is going to be directly affected by the fact that nations are sometimes led by people whose first thoughts are to rake in the spoils of industry and commerce before looking after their people. You gotta learn that success as a diplomat relies on a good understanding of more than just diplomatic protocol."

"Well, where do you fit into this stark picture you're painting?" asked Alan.

"I'll be as clear as I can," Len said. "I have an unusual assignment for a diplomat. I spend a great deal of my time with Massy Construction, the U.S. sub -contractor for the Chinese company that is funding the Kribi port project. New roadways are being constructed through the forests to move sea-borne goods to and from the Central African Republic, Gabon and the Congo."

"Guess that means this port will serve more countries that just Cameroon," Alan said.

"Yes, and Massy has to report to the Ministry of Forestry and the international oversite community. Those roads will certainly impact Cameroon's precious natural habitat as well as the people who live there." Len continued, "Can you imagine how those ribbons of high-speed highways will forever alter the lives of thousands of natives who now hunt and farm here? What will happen to the already endangered wildlife? The United Nations and the international community expect Cameroon to prove that those impacts will be minimal."

"Am I to understand," Alan said with a quizzical look, "your job includes preserving not only the trees but the social and physical well-being of the people who live there?"

"There is also a serious matter of local discontent. Developers destroyed a village to make way for this project, and jobs that had been promised to locals went to more qualified workers from outside, including foreigners."

Alan looked warily at his travel companion. He cleared his throat and asked. "Len, what is it, exactly, that you do?"

CHAPTER 4
LEN'S ANSWER

Alan studied his reflection in the car window as he waited for a response from Len, who was silent for a long while as they drove through the darkened forest. Alternating forest canopy and moonlit meadow mesmerized Alan. *Had Len not heard my question?*

Finally, Len said, "Me? I should tell you that I am not particularly enamored with my work with Massy Construction. As a U.S. diplomat, my primary objective is to represent Americans in Cameroon. My time, however, has become devoted to protecting this country's natural resources. Unfortunately, Massy Construction doesn't care diddly about trees. To them, trees are obstructions to be moved in order to get projects completed. Fortunately, international agencies placed conditions before approving this project. Massy puts up with saving trees as a necessary evil, due to a clause in their multi-million-dollar contract."

Alan's mood changed, as he began to see Len not as that happy-go-lucky guy in the Hawaiian shirt, but as a serious, well-intentioned professional. Len was only 38 years old, but he held a PhD in forestry and was already considered an international expert in tropical forestation and deforestation. Len worked for the U.S. state department primarily because of international interest in preserving Cameroon's forests. *I had thought that work was the bailiwick of USAID, not the state department.*

"Cameroon needs a shipping port that can accommodate deep-draught ships," Len continued, "I know nothing about building ports. Hell, I don't know the difference between rebar and a large nail. My challenge is increasingly more difficult because of global warming, which creates more pressure to save the world's forests. Without expert management and governmental protection, the forests will disappear quickly."

Alan's eyes lit up as though he finally made a connection. "So, your position with the state department is a dual role: assist the U.S. Embassy with diplomatic duties on the one hand and act as the guardian of the forests, the savior of Africa's timber resource, and the eye watching over the developmental impact to the native community on the other hand. I think I finally understand where you fit in. You're a diplomat with an unusual functional assignment."

"Yeah," Len added, "I couldn't have said it better." After a moment, Len said, "And just to be clear, although USAID and the U.S. Embassy are two totally different entities, they are both American, and they often share resources. That's why we are in a USAID car being driven by a USAID employee, while you and I are being paid by the state department.

They smiled as Eric drove through the dark forest.

CHAPTER 5
BONNY DOON

The SUV continued bouncing over the pitted road toward Kribi. In the silence of the backseat Alan was distracted and worried, concerned about his conversation with Mona.

He mumbled, "How could intelligent professionals be so irresponsible as to mess up something as important as my wife's safety?" Alan said out loud, as much to himself as to Len, "When we get a telephone connection I will insist that she forgets that assignment, and tell her to fly to Douala immediately."

After a minute or two of riding in silence, Len asked, "So, Alan. What about you? What's your story? Where did you grow up? What are your hobbies?"

Feeling anxious about the trouble in Yaoundé and his wife in Nigeria, Alan was annoyed at the questions. He pushed his glasses back up onto the bridge of his nose, ran his fingers through his straight, brown hair, and reluctantly launched into a brief summary. "Well, I'm from California. I grew up with my parents on the West Coast, in a town called Bonny Doon."

"Whoa." chuckled Len. "I never heard of that place. Is it an Irish settlement? Do your parents still live there? Sorry. Didn't mean to laugh. Please, go on."

"It's a small community near the coast, south of San Francisco. My parents were educators. It's a serene place, nestled in coastal redwoods. Bonny Doon began as a lumber camp in the mid-1800s. When the lumber industry gave way to tourism, the area became a popular get-away retreat for the upper crust from San Francisco. The area later became a haven for hippies and yuppies. The pristine beauty of the rolling hills facing the Pacific Ocean enticed my mom and dad to locate there when they got teaching jobs in Santa Cruz."

"Must be great living with the coastal redwoods," chortled Len.

"I loved it there. We were close to nature. My parents excelled in hiking and climbing. We traveled a lot. Spent most of our summers crossing the country looking for new adventures. My parents instilled a love for both the outdoors and for being aware of other cultures."

"Do your parents still live there? I mean, with my background in forestry, I'd be interested in visiting those forests."

"No. Unfortunately, my parents died when I was thirteen." Alan's gaze drifted away for a moment, then he continued. "They died in a car accident." Alan looked down.

"My parents met as Peace Corps Volunteers and had traveled much of the world before they settled down. They spoke often about interesting cultures and geography. They influenced my career choice by teaching me to respect and appreciate other cultures. They stimulated my interest in working in foreign service."

Troubles momentarily forgotten, Alan launched into memories of his past. "We made an overseas trip when I was twelve. For two weeks we hiked and climbed through the hills of southern France, and from Portugal to Spain. One day, while touring an ancient castle in Spain, I attended a presentation by a British author. The man told marvelous tales of places he visited in China, Russia, India and Africa. He related in detail the customs, dress, foods and cultural practices of people in those places. That's when I resolved that my mission in life was to work with people from all over the world."

They rode along in silence for several minutes. Finally, Len asked, "What about your wife? How did you meet?"

Alan thought for a minute as he considered Mona possibly sitting in a hotel room in a strange city far from home afraid to go out to the streets. "It's a long story."

"We have a way to go before we reach Kribi."

Alan shifted in his seat, leaned back, and began, "I met my wife, Mona, at Georgetown University. She's from Iowa. Her dad's a lawyer, and her mom teaches. Mona earned her undergraduate degree at Columbia University, became interested in international affairs. She entered the McCourt School of Public Policy at Georgetown. She also wants to work overseas."

In sweet reflection Alan remembered the day they met. "She's a beautiful person in many ways. Very intelligent, very giving. Maybe trusting to a fault. Almost too innocent that way."

Alan smiled as he recalled memories of his infatuation. "Before the Thanksgiving holidays shortly after we met, Mona told me that her parents sent her a ticket to fly home. I was saddened to think about not seeing her for a week. Impulsively, I asked if I could join her."

"What, you asked this girl you just met if you could meet her parents? Incredible. I don't believe this."

"Mona was initially taken off guard, but, to her credit, she recovered quickly. She simply smiled, thought for two seconds then her eyes lit up. Without waiting, I whipped out my phone and booked a flight to Omaha. I blew a month's living expenses on that trip, but I'd do it all over again. She's the most wonderful person in the world."

"That's a great story, Alan. I look forward to meeting her."

"That reminds me, I do need to get in touch with her soon."

CHAPTER 6
TROUBLE IN THE CAPITAL

"Len," Alan said, "is it really necessary to travel to Bamenda? The U.S. Embassy staff expects me to begin work tomorrow. I'm needed there. I know nothing about Bamenda, only that it is in the English-speaking part of Cameroon, and closer to the Nigerian border. Isn't it dangerous to drive there now because of civil unrest?

State department trainers had taught Alan to adapt to change and to think on his feet, but he was falling apart in the midst of his first crisis. *Come on, Alan, get a hold of yourself. You've got to calm down.* He wiped his glasses with his shirt and blurted out, "I need to get in touch with my wife, and my phone is out of juice. I need to make sure Mona knows what's going on. We're supposed to meet in Douala in a day or two."

Len said nothing. A diplomat's job carried many responsibilities. Len's far-away look indicated a need to address other issues soon.

"Look, Len. I appreciate your meeting me in Douala, but I feel a bit lost going to an unfamiliar place where I'm not expected. How am I supposed to find this guy Marcel? And, who is my American contact at the U.S. embassy? How will I get back to Douala?"

"Relax, Alan. I'll call Marcel. You'll be fine with Eric and the

USAID car. Eric is from the Northwest Region. He speaks pidgin, and he knows enough French to get you through the francophone regions with no problem." Glancing toward Eric Len added, "*est-il vrai?*"

Eric turned back toward the American and answered with a sheepish smile.

"Yes sir. I mean, *oui, monsieur.*"

"You can call your wife from Kribi. In several days all this will blow over, and she can meet you as planned. Also, as you probably know, a year ago the Cameroon government asked the U.S. for limited military assistance. They wanted some level of protection against potential terrorist incursions. The U.S. approved 300 military personnel to assist Cameroon in training and surveillance. They are currently in Garoua in Northern Cameroon."

"Thanks. Yes. I'm aware of that, and it's somewhat comforting, but that's a long way from Yaoundé. Anyway, who was responsible for this morning's attack?"

Len was slow to answer. A nervous eye twitch and a furrowed brow betrayed his uncertainty. "I don't know. There is a revolutionary group causing trouble in Nigeria that has crossed into Cameroon on occasion…"

"Do you mean Boko Haram?" Alan said. "I read about them. They ravaged several villages in Nigeria, murdering villagers and kidnaping hundreds of school girls. I thought they had been defeated and were no longer a threat."

"That's what I thought," said Len. "Richard said that according to witnesses, the attackers carried a flag similar to that of ISIL. Boko Haram made agreements with the Islamic State and with al-Qaeda. If it was Boko Haram we have a big problem."

Alan cringed at the mention of those violent organizations. His concerns multiplied as he realized he was going to be working in a city that had its share of violence. *Where is Mona? She could be in danger.* Mona had never traveled on her own, and her family was accustomed to traveling in places like San Francisco, Paris and London. *What have I gotten her into?*

At eleven p.m., the SUV approached the edge of a large

construction camp near the shores of the Gulf of Guinea, on the Atlantic Ocean. The streets were quiet. The stiff, salty breeze off the ocean cooled Alan as he, Len, and Eric approached the offices of Massy, Inc.

"There's a phone you can use to call your wife," offered Len pointing toward a cubicle. He reached into a small fridge to retrieve three bottles of water. "Good luck getting through, though. Sometimes communications are down for several hours at a time."

Alan's call to Mona's cell phone connected successfully but went to voice mail. "Hello, honey. It's Alan," he said after the tone. "I miss you. I'm calling from a place called Kribi, on the southern coast of Cameroon. Just want to say hi, and I hope you are doing well and staying safe in Lagos. I'll call you again in half an hour. I'll be on the road tomorrow, and may not be able to get in touch until late. If you get a chance to call back in the next thirty minutes call this number." He read out the number and closed with, "Love you, honey. Bye." He intentionally did not mention the trouble in Yaoundé.

The second attempt to reach Mona was again futile. This time he was unable to even reach her message box. After several more unsuccessful tries, Alan slammed down the phone. "Damn. What the hell is wrong with this country's telephone system?"

Len grilled hamburgers on the patio of his bungalow, and tossed a salad for the three men. Alan enjoyed a midnight dinner in the comfortable ocean breeze. In the local tradition, Len presented a collection of his favorite liqueurs. "Eric, I need your assistance to teach this man something about your country, as well as some rudimentary Pidgin English."

Eric rubbed his hands together and smiled. "*Yessah.*"

"Villagers here are always friendly," Len said. "People in the large cities, not so much. City folks are good people, just a little warier, and some can be predisposed to see what money they can make off you. Not much different from any large city anywhere in the world."

"Just like back home," Alan uttered with a smirk.

"Here, in the South Region," Len said, "as well as in major cities like Douala and Yaoundé, government and industry follow a French system of administration. In the Southwest and Northwest Regions, they follow a British system. To a large degree, the English-speaking people don't speak French and the French-speaking people won't speak English. When you speak with a government official in Yaoundé you must use French, so you will need to master that first. At the village level pidgin is the default communication medium." Len poured himself a measure of Grand Marnier, slumped in his chair and took a leisurely sip.

"My French tested at 3.5 on the FSI scale," Alan said. "I know it's got to be better for working with the Cameroonians in Yaoundé, but I'm trying to improve it."

"Are you interested," Len asked waving his glass at Alan, "in some of the pidgin aphorisms handed down from generation to generation? My favorite one goes something like this. Eric, please correct me if I get it wrong. It goes, *Wan an no fit tai bundle.* It means you need teamwork. You cannot tie a bundle with just one hand."

"That's great," Alan laughed while splashing a measure of Cointreau into his glass. "I could have used that phrase with my college study group. Tell me more traditional adages."

Len continued, "It's easy to learn the language if you know a few simple words. Here are some examples: they say *Ah* to mean I and *Yu* for you. They say *I* (pronounced ee) for he, and *Dem* for them. See? It's easy to figure out."

Eric added, "We say *fit* to indicate can do, like *Ah fit go me fo house* to mean 'I can go to my house. Got it?'"

"Got it," said Alan. "What is the past tense of *fit?*"

"Ah. Good question. I think it is *bin,* as in, *Ah bin go fo house,* I went to my house. The language has a nice cadence to it, and it's easy to learn. And fun to speak."

"How would I greet someone on the street? You know, to say, Hi, how are you?"

"That's easy," said Eric. "You say, *Ha na?* Or, *Ha fo yu?* They also say, *ha yu de?* It means how are you? They might ask, *Huskayn nyus?* That means what's new? You should respond, *No bat nyus.* You will hear that every day in my village."

"Great. I want to learn some more of those wise old expressions."

Len smiled. "There's one that the company cook uses whenever he wants someone to hurry up. It goes something like, *Sofly, sofly catch monkey*. I think it suggests that by using stealth you will be successful in getting things done."

Eric nodded his agreement. "*Na so.*" Then he added a few more of his favorite expressions.

Tired heads bobbed and early morning birds chirped. Alan sprang from his chair, "Eric. We have a two-hour drive to get past Douala, and another three or four hours from there to Bamenda. We need to get some sleep." Alan stayed at the nearby guest house, Eric slept in Len's cook's quarters.

Alan slept restlessly. He worried about Mona's safety, but it also concerned him that people were being murdered and kidnapped in Yaoundé by terrorists from Nigeria on the very day he and Mona started their new adventure in Africa.

CHAPTER 7
EDUBAMO

Eight hundred kilometers from Kribi, in remote, tree-covered hills in northeastern Nigeria, a camp of Islamic terrorists began to stir. At the same time that Alan and Eric were eating bagels with Len, the battle-weary cell of insurgents had spent a short respite before again inflicting their scourge of hatred, terror and death on despised infidels.

A light dew settled over the rocks and grass on the foliated hills sheltering the terrorists' remote site. Earthy, medicinal whiffs of moist kikuyu grass drifted in the air. A light breeze carried a hubbub of coughing, hacking and grumbling men.

Commander Yusuf Adaku Edubamo stood by his tent opening, watching lazy smoke curling skyward from yesterday's campfire. He sneered and groused, "Where is my coffee? Mohammed does not forbid me from drinking coffee. Where the hell are my useless compatriots? Six a.m. and the camp is asleep. I will do some serious ass-kicking." *War is hell*, he considered, *even a holy war. My jihad is my path to salvation*. The Muslim jihadist cell leader had already finished his morning prayer.

Edubamo wasn't a commander in an official military sense. He was a cell leader for Nigeria's terrorist organization Boko Haram. His title gave him authority. He wore the same green camouflage uniform as his cell members, but he reported to the somewhat clandestine infrastructure, the shura council, located near the northern Nigerian city of Maiduguri.

His rugged six-four frame, muscular arms and scarred face created a fearsome prominence that few dared to defy. His voice, with its resonating, scratchy bass was recognizable at great distances, and he was well-known for his short fuse and violent temper. His devotion to his religion appeared to be a driving force.

Abnormal for December, the comforting sound of light rain had pattered on his tent during the night, leaving the morning air cool and refreshing. His body ached from yesterday's violent campaign. But he was trained to ignore the discomforts of a military-style existence. Life during this struggle was brutal: sleeping on the cold ground, dealing with every kind of insect, and going without food or water for long periods.

These tribulations were minor compared to the dangers of being hunted and shot at by the Nigerian Army. Edubamo and his men constantly dodged artillery bombardments and air strikes. Their cause was to eliminate non-believers from this world. Hate for the Western world and the lies it taught in schools and churches consumed Edubamo. The commander's mission was to bring his people back to the life and religion of his God. This was a holy war. A jihad.

The goal of Edubamo's Islamic jihad of violence was to institute sharia law, or Islamic law. Boko Haram demanded the total destruction of the Nigerian state and its government. His cell of forty jihadists was a fraction of a much larger terrorist organization. Boko Haram conducted ruthless raids throughout northern Nigeria, decimating villages, and destroying police stations, jails, schools, temples and churches. Boko Haram jihadists despised the education and freedom of women, and the practice of any but the strictest form of sharia law.

Commander Edubamo's childhood had been plagued with family fracture, legal and financial troubles and religious conflict. His Muslim father died at the hands of a cruel Christian jailer when Edubamo was only eight. His mother could not support him, so he stole and killed to survive. In prison he heard hardline religious preaching of fellow Muslims. He soon decided that the only correct way to serve his God was through sharia law. At the age of 32 he attacked a police station, and murdered three Nigerian policemen. That convinced Boko Haram's shura council that he was ready to lead a jihadist unit.

The small group of militants would be idle today. The encampment was well stocked with food and supplies from yesterday's raid on the village of Hafsa, fifteen kilometers west. Thanks to the Hafsa infidels the Boko Haram militants would eat well. Edubamo's jihadists also recovered several barrels of fuel that would keep their vehicles running for weeks.

The Hafsa raid captured several teachers and a dozen girls from a Christian school. The girls, around sixteen or seventeen years old, were subject to conversion to Islam, and may provide reinforcements for revolutionary ranks. They would be given the choice of converting to sharia and serving his men's needs, or being executed.

The main achievement from this campaign would soon be arriving from the Cameroon border. He expected two high-level, Cameroon hostages worth a heavy ransom from Cameroon's president.

The stock of ammunition for the group's assault weapons was running low. Reloads for rocket launchers were hard to secure because of the Nigerian government's rejuvenated anti-terrorism campaign. The Boko Haram leadership wanted Edubamo to strike government targets to acquire weapons and inflict casualties, to attack banks in order to finance operations, to attack villages to spread terror amongst the infidels, and to steal food supplies. Edubamo moved his camp after each major assault. Frequently, they would disperse into local communities between terrorist offensives. This time, however, he needed his men to stay together until a ransom was exacted. Boko Haram wanted the largest enemy body count, with the fewest jihadi casualties. His men were very good at striking terror into the hearts of infidels. They murdered, kidnapped, raped, and burned while spewing hatred for Western teachings. Edubamo's cell must now move as a unit, bringing their prisoners toward Maiduguri in the north. This mission was not complete until Boko Haram collected the ransom money.

Edubamo's Islamic militant organization received support from related cells of Boko Haram in cities like Abuja, Nigeria's capital, Maiduguri in the northeast, and even Lagos in the south. Recruits were brought to training facilities in the northern part of the state and indoctrinated in Islamist ideals. They were taught to use weapons to kill and inflict fear on non-believers. Infidels must convert to sharia law, or die.

*   *   *

Loud shouts and curses from the far end of the encampment captured the commander's attention. Edubamo threw on a sweat-stained camouflage shirt, holstered his Austrian-made 9mm Glock, and stepped out of his tent in his undershorts and socks. Three of his men were forcing a male prisoner from yesterday's raid toward the commander.

"What the fuck is going on?" Edubamo demanded in the local Hausa dialect.

The soldiers wore long, camouflage shirts and loose-fitting green cargo pants tucked into combat boots. Their heads were partially wrapped in *shemaghs*. Two of the young guards tried to talk at the same time.

"Shut up. Both of you," shouted the commander. He pointed to one man. "You." He said, "Tell me what's going on. Who is this man?"

"Sir," the guard said with a strained voice. "This man was trying to escape. He is a teacher we captured from the school yesterday. You said we would use him to…"

"Shut up. I know what I was planning to use him for."

"*Yu.*" he shouted in Pidgin English, pointing to the trembling prisoner, who had blood dripping from his nose and a nasty-looking bruise on the side of his head. "*Husay yu de go? Yu no de lak ma fayne accommodation?*"

When the man did not respond, Edubamo added, "*Na, you be dat focking academic who bin fill wi brothas' and sisters' heads with Western horseshit lies?"*

The teacher quailed, sweating profusely, his eyes lowered.

"Husay yu respect fo yu countrymen? Wha happen yu respect fo Allah?" the commander shouted. *"Yu fit lead young minds away from da trut. You de teach dees young wumans to tink like dey have a higha place in dis world than Allah has given fo dem."*

"Speak." Edubamo screamed at the unfortunate prisoner who had been standing in shock. *"Yu no git mout?"*

The teacher shook with fear. He raised his eyes to meet the insurgent's murderous gaze. Squaring his shoulders, as though to steel himself, the teacher spoke with courage mustered from his convictions. "You are the one who disrespects our countrymen." He stood taller. "You desecrate the minds of Nigeria's children who love this country." The teacher's voice gained strength as he spoke. "You put fear and hate in the lives of your own people. **You** are the…"

The commander raised his Glock and pushed the barrel against the teacher's forehead. The cold steel forced the teacher to take a half-step backwards.

"Go on yu knees." The commander shouted, *"Now. Now. I want hear yu say yu fosakea yu decadent Western idea now now an follow sharia."*

In spite of the cool morning air, sweat mingled with the blood coursed across the teacher's lips and chin. A moment's hesitation measured the last seconds of his life. "I will not be intimidated by you…" the teacher began to shout, but the pistol's bark resounded across the valley. The soldiers flinched and recoiled as fragments of bone, brain and blood erupted from the collapsing remains of their prisoner.

Edubamo holstered his pistol and ordered his men in their language, "Clean up this shit," sorry only that he had not staged this execution in the plain sight of the other prisoners.

Edubamo was both the hunter and the hunted. The Nigerian government sought to eliminate Boko Haram from Nigeria while Edubamo killed men, women and children, destroyed property, and leveled villages to rid the land of Western influence.

Christians and non-Sunni Muslims as well feared Boko Haram.

Educators, police, religious leaders, and government administrators especially feared them. Initially, only people of northern Nigeria were targets, but Boko Haram exported their murderous fanaticism to neighboring countries, such as Cameroon to the east, Benin to the west, and Niger and Chad to the north. Their impact radiated far beyond these countries when the terrorist leaders joined allegiance with other terrorist organizations, such as the Islamic State of Iraq and the Levant or ISIL, or ISIS, and al-Qaeda.

The national government of Nigeria desperately sought to restore the country to a tractable peace, but found the Boko Haram organization to be a stubborn and formidable enemy. Nigeria's government and military harbored individuals with revolutionary ideals. As a result of its attacks on police and military installations, Boko Haram was well-armed and becoming as equipped as Nigeria's national army.

Islamic fanatics like Commander Edubamo despised infidels. To them, Western culture, with its Christian God, its decadent and immoral life style, and immunity to the teachings of his God, were mortal enemies. Women, according to Boko Haram's ideals, were placed on this earth to bear sons and cook food. Women's minds were not equal to the minds of men, who were the true agents of God. By their law, women were not allowed to develop their minds. Anyone who harbored the beliefs pandered by Westerners were the enemies of Allah, and must be destroyed.

Yesterday, Sunday, the commander's militants executed a successful battle plan in two stages. While the bulk of Edubamo's men raided and burned the village of Hafsa, a contingent of twelve armed men crossed Cameroon's border and attacked Yaoundé, a thousand kilometers away, to take two high-level government hostages.

The attack on Hafsa was intended to strike fear into infidels. Boko Haram targeted the schools and churches, where non-believers taught heretical lies to Christians and Muslims. Teachers and religious people, the puppets of Western culture, spread lies to confuse villagers. Those lies had to be stopped, now.

With machine guns mounted on pickup trucks Boko Haram

terrorists stormed into the small, quiet village and indiscriminately killed every man, woman and child in sight. They threw fire bombs on the houses, and shot residents as they fled the fire. Screams from a school building caught their attention, and that is where they found girls and teachers cowering against a far wall.

Edubamo's second stratagem was intended to demonstrate to neighboring countries that the reach of Boko Haram was long and ruthless. A small contingent of militants sped across the Cameroon border while the country was distracted by the news of the sacking of Hafsa and by Cameroon's serious internal disturbances. Boko Haram would capture and demand a large ransom for two minister hostages.

Ransom money funded much of the military might of Boko Haram's guerrilla efforts. Edubamo wanted two high-ranking government ministers of strategic Importance to the government of Cameroon.

By tomorrow, according to his plan, the small excursion force should return with at least two Cameroonian hostages. Edubamo would demand ransom from the Cameroon people for the lives of their ministers. After posting the demand through Boko Haram's surreptitious channels to the international media, he would move his camp and conceal his men and prisoners until his demands were met. Screams from the far end of the camp reminded him that he would have to deal with moving a dozen or so prisoners as well as his troops.

CHAPTER 8
HIGHWAY TO BAMENDA

"**E**xpect to be stopped for security checks," Len warned early Monday morning, "There'll likely be increased police roadblocks because of the Yaoundé incident. Normally, the police or gendarmes will ask for ID, but because of yesterday's murders and kidnapping, they may want to search your car, and sometimes they will ask you to open every bag. Don't panic, and don't pay any bribes to officers. Finally, do not go into Douala. Go straight to Bamenda," Len admonished. Then, making eye contact with the driver, he said, "Eric, you got that?"

Eric, looking very serious, said, "*Yessah.*"

After breakfast, Alan made another unsuccessful attempt to call Mona. His heart sank when he did not even get her voice mail.

Eric filled the Nissan with gas, and before he and Alan left, Len gave them a canvas bag with snacks for the road. They departed Kribi by 9 o'clock.

Alan reminded Eric that he would appreciate lessons in pidgin along the way. Eric, who studiously tried to speak proper English to the Americans and British, agreed to try to speak pidgin whenever he remembered.

Their vehicle was stopped twice before reaching the junction just north of Douala. Local military units looked very serious as they made a show of displaying automatic weapons and handguns. At the first stop a police officer held one hand up as he cradled a semi-automatic weapon under the other arm and shouted, "*Arrêtez.*" The car coasted to a stop two meters from the officer. "*Enregistrement, s'il vous plait.*"

The officer slowly walked to the passenger side, peered at Alan through the windscreen and said "*Qui es-tu?*"

Alan rolled down his window and said, "Excuse me. What did you ask?"

The officer strode to the other side of the car and said to Eric, "*Na, who dis man de fo side?*

Eric explained in pidgin that his passenger was an American diplomat traveling to Bamenda. After showing their documents, they were allowed to proceed. Eric later explained that army, customs and gendarme officers were required by the government to speak both French and English. Most officers would address travelers in French. Some spoke English, but if French and English didn't work they would try pidgin.

Thirty kilometers further along the busy highway, Alan's blood pressure jumped when he saw a Toyota pickup truck blocking all passage. Heavily armed military personnel pointed rifles at his vehicle. When he remembered Len's advice about not panicking, Alan struggled to calm his instincts. The gendarmes seemed menacing with weapons at the ready. Gendarmes wore green camouflage uniforms, and sported either green or red berets. *They seem young. And trigger happy.* Several gendarmes slouched against a rusted-out sedan on the shoulder of the road.

The police officers wore khaki uniforms. They had side arms strapped to their hips but did not carry automatic rifles.

An officer approached the car warily. His eyes washed over Alan's car as he moved with deliberate steps, apparently not missing a feature of the car or its passengers. The officer shouted an order to Eric in textbook French. "*Donnez-moi vos documents.*"

Eric shrugged his shoulders and politely responded, "Sir*, I de speak English. Na whatee yu de ask, please?*"

The officer rolled his eyes skyward, jerked his thumb up, shouting, "Out." The man seemed to know that English word well.

Eric looked at Alan and said with a hint of a smile, *"Na, no fear. This be normal."* He reached for his papers from the sun visor and exited the car. Alan realized that Eric's years of experience on these highways taught him to assume a submissive posture to avoid aggravating the officers.

Two other policemen moved closer as if to back up the first. The first officer, obviously not an English speaker, appeared to choose his pidgin words carefully: *"Na, husay yu de go?"*

Eric responded, *"Ah de go me fo Bamenda side, sah."*

The officer ignored Eric's response and asked, *"Na which man dey fo side?"* The officer seemed more interested in the white man sitting in the passenger seat. Alan assumed the officer must have been trained to suspect everything and everybody. *After all, that white man could be a French arms dealer, or a Belgian mercenary*, he thought, tongue-in-cheek.

Alan watched the officer closely through the windscreen and thought, acerbically, *who knows? This white man could be a terrorist, or a conspirator in some coup plan. Better, maybe he's a frightened foreigner who would pay anything to not be troubled by the police.*

"Na, he be peaceful man. He de wok fo 'merica," Eric said. Alan knew Eric's angle. He had learned earlier that Americans were less hated than some other foreigners.

"Gi paypa, now." demanded the officer.

Eric got back into the car. He told Alan that the officer would search for expiration dates on visas, passports, drivers' licenses and vehicle registration papers. Anything out of place or unusual would give him some reason to detain a wealthy traveler.

The police officer stuck his head inside the driver's side window and asked Alan in an exaggerated friendlier tone, *"Parle' français?"*

Alan's courses in French taught him just enough conversational French to order lunch and ask for a hotel room. *If I let this guy think I am fluent he will have a big advantage. Maybe if I deny that I know any French he will leave me alone.*

"Sorry, officer. Can you please repeat your question?" Alan spoke loudly, as many Americans do, assuming that volume transcends language barriers.

The officer rolled his eyes a second time, and walked around the car. "He could argue with and intimidate you in French," Eric whispered to Alan, "or probably even pidgin, but using his limited English could be exhausting."

The officer returned to the driver's window, pointed to the rear of the SUV, and demanded, "*Ouvrez.*"

Alan got out to observe the officer poking through his belongings. Two policemen gripped their sidearms and moved toward Alan, who bristled. He had never had armed people confront him. He remembered Len's advice and breathed deeply to relax.

Item by item, everything in Alan's bags was handled then set aside. One officer made a pretext of reading documents in Alan's briefcase.

"*Qu'est-ce que c'est.*" One officer demanded to know what a small digital projector was for. The Ah-ha-what-have-we-here tone was clearly evident in his demonstrative gestures. The officer acted as though he had discovered a weapon of mass destruction, certainly an item related to espionage. Even if it was a harmless piece of office equipment, surely he could generate an impression of control that would solicit some remunerative reward.

The policeman's actions required no translation. Coming around the rear of the car, Alan forced a smile and calmly spoke in English, "Please be careful. That's a projector." He applied his best charades techniques, but could not communicate the purpose of a projector. He turned to Eric and said, "Can you describe this projector? It projects images from my computer onto a screen. It cost me a thousand dollars."

The ranking officer held the projector, slowly turning it over. Finally, he grunted something to the second officer, handed the item back to his subordinate, and waved off any interest. The second officer fingered through all of Alan's camera equipment and the rest of his personal belongings, apparently finding nothing interesting.

At that moment, a caravan of three black limos with government license plates pulled off the road behind Alan's SUV. A short, softly spoken conversation between the three officers in a local dialect ended with the lead officer facing Eric and giving a dismissive sweep of his hand. *"Allez,"* he said.

Eric quickly recovered his documents, and climbed into the driver's seat without looking back. Alan got in just as Eric shoved the shift lever into Drive, and they sped off.

After the second check point Alan felt slightly more relaxed. The procedure became routine and Eric seemed to anticipate and easily answer questions from the patrols. At 11:30 they arrived at the junction for their turn north. They had avoided travelling through Douala but were only one hundred kilometers north of where Alan's plane had landed yesterday. The next three or four hours would take them through both French- and English-speaking regions, but Eric, who traveled this road often for his employer, appeared comfortable.

The sun rose high, baking the red soil of the Littoral and South Regions. Alan sensed the heat outside the vehicle, and imagined the leaves on the foliage along the road fade and wrinkle. Ahead of them the mirage of water sent ghostlike waves into the air above the highway. Very few workers tended the scorching hot pineapple fields along the road, but several villagers could be seen resting in the shade of sparsely foliated trees. Alan was thankful for the car's air conditioner, which whirred away on high.

The roar of a crop-spraying airplane caught Alan's notice. The heavily loaded Piper Cub dropped low over a field to his right and emitted a cloud of spray over a distant crop he couldn't see.

Still smarting from the last security stop, Alan asked, sarcastically, "That was very interesting. Were those officers intimating that we should pay a bribe, Eric?"

Eric appeared uncomfortable with the question. His apparent hesitation made Alan realize that the men in question were Eric's countrymen. Although they were very likely from the French-speaking part of Cameroon, they were in effect his brothers. Alan assumed that Eric had been raised to appreciate his African countrymen, to work hard for the better benefit of the community, and to be patriotic. There was no doubt that Eric had to straddle the differences between the Americans he worked for and his own people.

Alan wished he could withdraw the question, remembering from his training that ever since Cameroon first governed itself, there had been occasional political differences within the country. People in the English-speaking regions of Cameroon were in the minority. Their leadership had attempted to insert some political weight into the broader governance of Cameroon, causing a stiff response from the ruling party. Some lingering dislike, bordering on hate, existed between the minority regions and the predominantly French-speaking regions. History showed that in tribal Africa, such imbalances led to mistrust at best, and could be incendiary.

"*Sometimes,* "Eric began, "*men with power use dey office to advantage fraid man. I git no problem with the govment, and dey git no problem fo me. But, I no fit fava get treated badly. I mos never gi dash, what white man ee call bribe. Now, I de tink some police man try profit from scared man. Dey like frighten weak man also, fo tri make yu gi some small dash fo dem.*"

Alan could see that Eric was a good man. He appeared to be honest, and reluctant to criticize his Cameroonian countrymen.

CHAPTER 9
PLEASURES OF THE ROAD

"*Arrêtez.*"

"*Halt.*" Every twenty or thirty kilometers, Alan and Eric encountered additional security checks. Gendarmes, customs officials and police inspected their papers multiple times as the two stood in the glaring sun and answered the same questions. Thankfully, officers did a complete search of the car at only one other stop.

By early afternoon, having already consumed Len Watson's bag of snacks, Alan felt his stomach rumbling. He noticed roadside stands ahead and asked, "Eric, is there a restaurant or coffee shop anywhere nearby?"

Eric laughed. "*Massah, we no go fine sit-down eating place fo here. Only my country-man market.*"

As the car approached a road junction, Alan spotted people milling around fruit and vegetable stands. Several makeshift structures with banana leaf or corrugated tin roofs provided limited relief from the hot sun to sellers and buyers. Several taxis and personal cars were parked on the road shoulders. That morning Len had said, "Travelers can always find fruit stands at major road intersections. Depending on the season and the time of day, you might find mangos, plums, plantains, pineapple, skewered beef strips, roasted corn, dried fish or warm soda. Fresh kill of *bush meat*, or *bif,* such as monkey, *cutting grass*, snakes, deer and more are often displayed by proud hunters. Len had described the cutting grass as a cane rat common in Africa.

Eric slowed the car and took a sideways glance at Alan, shaking his right hand to indicate that the food in the local stands was unsavory. He said, *"Massah, I no de tink you go like my countryman market."*

"Don't be so damn protective Eric." Alan said with a smile, "I'm here to experience Cameroon and taste the food and understand her culture." He nudged Eric and said, *"Na, now we get fo do dis ting."*

Eric laughed, confirming that the man was happy to partake of some local produce. The scorching heat outside shocked Alan, but didn't curb his enthusiasm to check out the market. He headed for the shade of a stand with a banana-leaf awning.

Roasted plums were not so bad. The lady in flip-flops, wearing a grungy, ragged skirt and a faded cotton T-shirt that said *1986 Champions* on the back tended a smoking metal can that looked like a Dutch oven. She rolled the purple plums over and over on a tin plate resting over hot charcoal. When the purple skin darkened and began to blister, the woman handed a roasted plum to Alan, who took a cautious nibble. The skin of the plum had become tender, and the sweet flavor of the meat inside was surprisingly tasty. *With a little time, I could actually get to like roasted plums. If I could only ignore the less-than savory conditions of where they are being prepared.*

Eric asked for six roasted plums. The woman placed them on a half-page of newspaper and handed the paper platter to him. Eric gave her the correct change, then asked, *"Huside my dash de?"* The woman smiled and gave Eric one additional roasted plum. Turning to Alan, Eric said, "In my country, market people like to negotiate. If you don't bargain down the price you can ask for a dash. That just means a little something extra."

Spotting what looked like a healthy looking bunch of ripe yellow bananas, Alan shouted. "Ah, look Eric. Bananas. I want to buy a bunch of those.

"*Na, no be bananas. Dem be plantain. Come, a go show yu.*"

A vendor, nodding to Eric with a conspiring smile, handed him one plantain. Eric partially stripped the peel and gave it to Alan, saying, "*Yu fit try?*"

Alan hungrily bit into the exposed tip of the plantain, expecting the sweet taste of a freshly ripened banana. His eyes widened as he experienced the hard, dry and tasteless meat of the uncooked plantain. He couldn't swallow it, and went to the road to spit it out. "What the hell?"

Eric paid the vendor for the single plantain as both he and the vendor laughed at Alan's surprised expression. "*Na, this plantain ee good'o, but, you must first prepare ee properly.*" The vendor placed the plantain over hot coals for several minutes to bring out the sugars. Eventually, the plantain developed a dry, but pleasing taste.

The mangos were small and juicy, and tasted heavenly. Alan's first attempt at eating a mango produced sticky juice flowing down his arm. He watched Eric peel and consume a mango using only his teeth and the fingertips of his left hand. Biting the tip of the mango, Eric stripped the skin two thirds of the way down while carefully holding the skin at the base. As the golden juices began to flow down the soft flesh he mouthed the mango and sucked it like a Popsicle. When all the flesh was gone from the top end of the mango stone, he stripped off the rest of the skin and devoured the rest of the mango. Alan was amazed to see Eric consume the mango in two minutes without leaving a trace of mango juice on his hands.

A few feet from the mango seller Alan spotted another woman squatting beside a charred coffee can. Nestled at the bottom of the can were three white-hot charcoals. A metal grid on top held an ear of corn. Some of the kernels were turning black. Eric purchased it while it rested over the hot coals. When the vender considered the kernels sufficiently cooked she handed Eric the steaming ear, using a towel to protect her hand from hot kernels. Eric consumed the rows conjuring images of a human typewriter as he clacked away.

Alan spotted a vender skewering beef. Eric explained that it was called *suya*. "It is very nice snack at road food stands and in bars,"

Eric said. "Thin strips of beef are marinated in a red sauce, woven onto wooden skewers and heated over hot coals."

For the equivalent of fifty U.S. cents each, Alan purchased four freshly barbecued skewers of *suya bif* and gave two to Eric. Eric laughed as Alan tried various food items, laughing at his expression of disgust or delight.

They polished off the beef, and washed it down with bottles of warm, locally made soda. Appetites satiated, Alan and Eric returned to the SUV and continued their journey north in air-conditioned comfort. Alan felt good with his belly full and his perspective enriched. He also felt confident that he could handle every roadblock with ease, now knowing how the system worked.

The landscape changed from acres of pineapple fields to huge mango trees and, eventually, to grassy fields and rolling hills. Eric maintained a running monologue as he pointed out the various crops and features.

Alan asked Eric, "Where are your people from? You seem to be comfortable in both the French-speaking and English-speaking parts of Cameroon. Where were you born?

"*Well, sah, my peepo dem comot fo* Nigeria. Ma momma and papa dem *bin* farmers *fo* Cross River, but *life bin tough'o*."

"You are Nigerian?" Alan was surprised, "Why did you leave Cross River?"

Eric switched to English, "I have many brothers and sisters. It was difficult for all of them to make a living on that Cross-River farm, so some moved to Lagos or Abuja, for school or work. As for me I have always been good with wheels. Wheels and motors. I like to drive, and I like to work on motor cars. One day I cross that river, *pass* border to Cameroon. I found I could make a living in this country. So, now I am a Cameroon man. Many Cameroon man *don comot fo* Nigeria."

"So, you were born Nigerian but are now Cameroonian? Where is Cross River?" Alan asked.

"*Na, that riva be important. Ee begin heeya fo Cameroon, and go sout, whea ee become border fo Nigeria*, an continue fo ocean, by Calabar."

Alan watched the countryside slide by. In each village they drove through, they slowed to a crawl as cows, chickens, goats and pedestrians were in no hurry to make way for traffic. Large trucks often blocked the edges of the roadway, causing other vehicles to maneuver around them. Drivers were not afraid to sound their horns, as though blowing the horn long and loud would move other road users out of their way. Eric mentioned visitors say that some Cameroonian drivers negotiate the roads more with their car horns than with their steering wheels.

Approaching one village Alan heard chanting. As the car entered the outskirts of the village, it appeared that the chant, mostly from young children, was directed toward his vehicle. "What are they saying?" Alan asked in a nervous whisper.

"Don't mind them small *pikin*," said Eric. "They say, '*White man. White man.*' not many foreigners travel here. They always do same whenever they see a white man. Maybe it is to alert the adults that an inspector may be coming. Pay no attention."

Several times while traveling north in the right lane, Alan noticed oncoming traffic driving directly at them, and eventually swerving back to their correct lane. Eric told him that the methods for testing before administering driver's licenses was not perfected, and that some of his countrymen's drivers could use training. He also learned that bus and taxi drivers used a system of hand signals to warn drivers going the opposite direction if there was a security check point nearby. Eric confirmed their signal with a shake of his hand outside his window.

Further north Alan spotted a lone figure standing beside the road. The man waved a slow, non-urgent motion with his hand. Alan asked, "Is that man trying to hitch a ride?"

"No. No." Replied Eric. "He is selling *white mimbo*."

Alan hadn't noticed the small gourd sitting at the man's feet until the car was nearly past it. "Okay. Tell me Eric. What's *white mimbo*?"

"*White mimbo* is a local drink, like palm wine. It comes from a small tree called raffia palm. Early in the morning the farmer taps the palm tree. He sells the fermented liquid here on the road. It is customary for village people to drink this *mimbo* when they celebrate weddings or funerals. Some people drink it every day. *Wan day we go try*," he added with a smile. *Dat white mimbo, she be fayne early daytime, when ee fresh.* By late *ee* may become *trong-o. Trong-trong*, as my people would say. By this *time late* that *mimbo* is no longer fresh, but the power is very *'trong*."

Vast plains surrounded by high, rolling hills and grassy valleys formed a scenic backdrop as they neared Bamenda. Alan saw cattle grazing on some of the hillsides in spite of the grass looking a little pale. Eric explained that this was the dry season and that much of this part of the country hadn't had rain since September. Also, the harmattan winds that blow December to February from the northeast bring Sahara Desert dust to coat everything.

Road signs for the large community of Bamenda came into view. Only a few houses scattered on the flat plane, and only one large building, called the Skyline Hotel, were visible.

The hills on the left side of the road seemed to drop away. The SUV had come to the edge of an escarpment. One hundred and fifty meters below sprawled the city of Bamenda. Eric parked the SUV on the shoulder and invited Alan to walk with him to the rim overlooking the chasm. From high above the community of nearly 300,000 inhabitants they could see for miles.

"This escarpment is the edge of a chasm that was caused by the Bamenda volcano hundreds of years ago," Eric said, indicating the sunken valley below them, "Most Bamenda people live there on the slopes of Bamenda Mountain, near the river channels."

"Volcano, huh? Is there still volcanic activity here? Len told me about exploding lakes."

Eric laughed. "Many generations of Bamenda families have lived here safely. I doubt you need be *fraid*. That four-story building with the red sign is the Novotel, where you could stay tonight. In that direction," he said, pointing east, "is Mankon Village, and 10 kilometers more that side is Bambili. That fancy white building near the center of the town is the Union Party Headquarters."

"There, to the northwest," he said pointing across the town, "is the road that could take you to Mamfe. Yesterday I heard Mr. Len tell you about the forests in Mamfe. Beyond Mamfe you will come to Nigeria."

"Nigeria?" Alan suddenly realized that somewhere in that direction his wife should be interviewing subjects for a potential law suit. "How far is it to the Nigerian border?" he asked, suddenly aware how much he wished Mona were by his side to experience the moment. He pushed his glasses up on his nose and looked at his cell phone to see if he had any service. *Hmm, not even one button. This phone's no good here.*

"Maybe just over four hours' drive from Bamenda to Mamfe." Eric removed his hat and scratched his head, deep in thought. "Maybe two more hours from Mamfe to the border. There is a new road on the Cameroon side, but the road used to be very bad, and there were no petrol or food places."

Alan's eyes glazed for several seconds as he considered the significance of Eric's words.

"*We de get airport fo this place,*" Eric said. "It was built in 1986, when Pope John Paul II visited Cameroon and for the Party Conference in Bamenda that same year. People from Israel and Germany helped build the airport. Now it's only used by the Cameroon president and some military people. It sits on what is called the Ring Road which leaves Bamenda there," Eric said, pointing to his right, "makes a big circle past Wum and Nyos Lake, and comes back past the airport, over there," he said, pointing to his left.

The phrase Ring Road struck a resonant chord. Alan blinked when he remembered Len Watson's story about an exploding lake. "Is Nyos the lake that exploded?"

"Yes, *na true*. Lake Nyos is about 50 kilometers from here on that road. Another lake near Bambili," he pointed to the east, "also exploded before. But, don't fear; that has not happened in thirty years."

"Thirty years? Hmm. Maybe it's about time for it to explode again," Alan mumbled with a nervous laugh.

Eric continued pointing to familiar roads and structures visible from the escarpment.

"Great," said Alan impatiently. "I assume the government offices are in that big white building. I may need to visit the Party Headquarters someday. Other than that, that's probably more than

I need to know. If you don't mind, I'd like to get to a reliable telephone so I can get in touch with my office, and hopefully, talk to my wife. She must be worried sick by now." *I sure as hell hope Mona is waiting in Lagos for her escort or arranging a flight to Douala. I must get in touch with her ASAP.*

CHAPTER 10
MONA AND THE LAGOS LAWYER

Mona Burke bounced in the rear seat of a vintage Land Rover, while Joseph, the driver, steered around obstacles on a tortured Lagos boulevard. Detour signs in several languages directed traffic around road construction. Lashed with deep excavations and choked with concrete barriers the route challenged drivers and menaced vehicles. Joseph said that the work had been going on for over a year. With a hint of irony, he said, "Maybe local commercial companies didn't pay enough bribe to the Lagos Planning Department."

Monday afternoon, Mona Burke's second day in Africa. She had spent a fruitless Sunday afternoon in her prosaic hotel room, waiting for a colleague charged to escort her around Lagos. Frustrated with the fleeting time and anxious to complete her assignment, she decided to go alone to visit Mr. Albert Achebe, an attorney recommended by her firm's associate in Paris.

Mona had telephoned Mr. Achebe from her hotel to introduce herself and her mission. Achebe agreed to see her and insisted on sending a car for her. That impressed Mona. She never had it that easy in Washington, D.C. She wore her best traveling business suit. She was a stickler on her clothing choices. She had donned her lucky

59

charm bracelet, placed her favorite gold pen into her briefcase and met Joseph in front of the hotel.

Mona, a paralegal intern, wanted to waste no time in Lagos. She hoped to fly to Cameroon to be with her husband in a day or two. Her employer was a Maryland law firm that investigated product-infringement cases. Several Lagos companies were suspected of pirating American company products. Mona intended to visit those businesses.

Mona, affectionately known as The Bulldog by co-workers, was purposeful to a fault. Sometimes her single-mindedness obscured peripheral information. She could become so engrossed in her objective that she failed to observe caution.

Married to a State Department employee assigned overseas, Mona would eventually have to give up her work. However, at her request, her bosses gave her an opportunity to research her current case that could produce millions of dollars in settlements for her employer.

Mona watched in amazement as the passing landscape changed. She was impressed as they left the hotel and drove past the lush grounds skirting a pastoral golf course along highway A5. They drove through a prosperous-looking steel and glass commercial area. The modern structures soon disappeared, however, as the car approached an area of small, run-down shops and rustic houses. Glancing down unpaved side streets, Mona was surprised to see crowds of people in shabby clothes sitting on the ground in front of tin-roofed shacks with plywood-and-bamboo-matting walls. A vender sat on a stump at the edge of the road selling mangoes and bananas from a cardboard box. Gaunt men and women stood by the roadside with extended palms up asking for food or money.

Less than a quarter mile further, they were in a neighborhood of apparently more expensive homes with high walls that surrounded unseen houses. Stern-looking guards, some with weapons, patrolled in front of metal gates. She puzzled over the contrasts so close to her hotel.

Mona considered the industrial crime that brought her to Nigeria. Dishonest entrepreneurs found it easier and cheaper to steal someone else's ideas than to invent their own products. A few surreptitious businesses took shortcuts to profitability by avoiding much of the cost of research, development and liability. Reverse-engineering of expensive household and electronic products made in Europe or North America was easier.

Those fly-by-night companies took advantage of distance and time to make huge, quick profits. Mona's research uncovered instances of counterfeit high-fidelity sound systems, electronic games, motorized kitchen appliances, shop tools and more. She found that the illegal activity occurred in many countries, but her current case involved products forged in Nigeria. She had also learned that when a legitimate company took legal steps to curtail the manufacture of the illegally copied goods, the offending company often folded their manufacturing plant and moved on to another product, under another name, in a different location. U.S. companies lost billions of dollars in export sales because of this activity. Sometimes they also lost significant money on handling product liability claims.

The Land Rover stopped in front of a gated compound. The number was displayed in four-inch, brass numerals under which were the words, "Law Offices of Albert Achebe." Mona could not see through the eight-foot metal barrier or the tall concrete wall. Broken glass at the top of the wall reflected the sunlight in many colors.

A blast of the Land Rover's horn startled her. Mona assured herself again that she was really going to proceed with her mission. Aware that she had ignored the warnings of her employer in Maryland, those of her husband, and the state department advisor who strongly suggested that someone from Mona's law firm accompany her on any travel in Nigeria, she had nevertheless proceeded alone.

Making a call on her own in Lagos concerned her, but she had little choice. People had told her of the crime and the high prices. Yet, in some ways, the city she saw since her arrival appeared mostly open and progressive, with modern structures, wholesome hotel food, friendly people, and well-lit streets. *Then, you turn a corner and see a darker world, making you wonder about your safety.* So many contradictions. Like the torn-up road in front of this expensive house and the high concrete walls with metal gates separating homes and businesses into isolated islands.

Although proud of the feeling of being her own person Mona felt intimidated. She encouraged herself; *it would be a waste of time to have come this far and not made at least one contact with a local firm.*

A man wearing a white, Islamic kufi hat appeared from a guardhouse, glanced at the car, and disappeared. The metal gate slowly creaked open. The Land Rover inched onto a ten-meter-wide, concrete pad large enough to park four or five cars. Two large vehicles were already in front of a stone, metal and glass structure. One man, assumedly a driver, appeared to be toweling dust off an already gleaming Mercedes. A second person, who had been standing next to a BMW, snuffed out a cigarette in a flower bed.

Mona exited the Land Rover, becoming acutely aware of the warm temperature and a loud mechanical noise. She walked up the drive and passed the two drivers. They nodded and mumbled something Mona assumed was a greeting. Her driver began a discussion with the other two men, his gaze following his charge as she continued to the building entrance. The gateman closed the creaky steel gate. Mona considered for a moment the level of security and recalled the tales of crime in Lagos.

Inside the well-appointed, two-story building, she felt the cool air-conditioning. The noisy throbbing of an exterior diesel generator became muffled as the heavy entrance door closed. Immediately a smart-looking young lady approached. Her British English and pleasant voice were inviting. "Hello. My name is Veronica. You must be Mrs. Burke?"

Hearing her new married name caused Mona to smile. "Yes, Veronica. Please call me Mona. I'm here to see Mr. Albert Achebe. I am with the firm of Adams, Benson & Chang."

"Yes. I know, Mona. My father is expecting you. His earlier meeting is running a bit long. I hope you won't mind waiting a few minutes. I can get you some coffee, or tea if you prefer."

Mona was impressed with Veronica's upbeat and courteous greeting. "Could I get a bottle of chilled water, please?"

It was good, actually, to sit for a moment and relax. Her life had been a whirlwind the past six months since graduation, and her current mission was exciting. The recent meeting she and Alan had with the U.S. ambassador to France was a daunting but exciting experience. She had also enjoyed the dinner with Benoit Laurain, associate director of her law firm in Paris. The short stay in Paris with Alan was like a honeymoon.

Mona had listened as the ambassador to France talked about the intimate relationship between France and Cameroon and advised Alan on the importance France placed on maintaining positive relations with an important trading partner. Cameroon produced oil, timber and agricultural products that the French people relied on. Cameroon imported cars, parts, electronics, alcoholic beverages and numerous other products from France.

That evening, the gregarious Benoit had treated Mona and Alan to dinner. Benoit had already researched Mona's mission and had provided contact names. "In Lagos," he had advised, "you should meet a Nigerian attorney who worked with me for the plaintiffs on a case involving theft of commercial secrets."

"Please tell me about him," Mona had said.

"My observation is that Albert Achebe is a very intelligent attorney," Benoit began, "I don't know a lot about his character and qualifications other than what I witnessed while working with him. Achebe grew up in Nigeria, but he studied four years at UCLA. He graduated with honors and went on to study law in England. After passing the Nigerian bar he set up practice in Lagos along with two partners."

Mona was pleased and felt more comfortable knowing that the attorney Benoit was recommending had studied in the U.S. and England.

"Four years ago," Benoit continued, "he had a disagreement with his partners and left that firm to set up his own. I met him shortly after, when he came to Paris to represent a major electronics company on a patent infringement case not unlike the one you are working on. Our paths crossed again in Nairobi at a conference on African issues. To the best of my knowledge, he is a reputable man. A word of advice, however: We can all put on a good face when we need to. Some people also have invisible priorities, and in a tribal country, I suggest you be careful who you trust completely."

That was just two days ago. Today Mona sat in Mr. Achebe's office. Had Benoit told her not to fully trust her primary Nigerian contact? Being alone and far from home was disconcerting. She felt vulnerable and resolved to reserve her trust for Mr. Achebe until she had certain proof of his character. And the same for everyone she met in Africa.

Just then a door opened and two men wearing suits and ties entered the lobby, engaged in loud, animated conversation. They opened the main door and the diesel generator smothered the sound of their voices.

Veronica came through a side door. "Mrs. Burke, that is, Mona, my father is available to see you now. Please follow me."

Veronica's father posed an impressive sight with the stature of a lineman for an NFL football team. A robust Nigerian, probably six foot, six inches tall and at least 275 pounds, Mr. Achebe's large, penetrating eyes seemed to pierce Mona's mind and read her thoughts. His smile projected a comfortable self-assurance, and his first words were disarming. "Mrs. Burke, I have been so looking forward to meeting you. I am sorry for keeping you waiting. Those gentlemen took up much more than their allotted time." As he clasped her proffered hand he added, "Your firm has said many wonderful things about you. I am very pleased to have the honor. Please, sit there," he said, pointing to a comfortable-looking visitor's chair.

Mona felt awed by the size and presence of this huge black man, with his shrewd, piercing eyes and deep, resonant voice. Only his friendly smile and kind words brought her thoughts back to her present task.

Mona cleared her throat. "Mr. Achebe, as we discussed on the phone this morning, I am here to interview the principals of several companies that my law firm suspects of certain unfair business practices, such as misleading consumers into buying illegally produced goods. I have the names of several companies presumably located in Lagos. Are you able to give me some guidance on how to approach setting up a meeting with them?"

Mona soon realized that Albert Achebe was conversant with the nature of her cases. Naming the first company on her list, US-Toys, she stated that she had a particular interest in them. Achebe said he knew the name and had represented a wholesaler who charged that company with copyright infringement.

"US-Toys could be a tough nut to crack," said Achebe. "They are very aggressive, and very resourceful. They produce a wide range of products from different, small locations, and they relocate often. In fact, they no longer have offices in Lagos. I heard that they moved north, somewhere north of the capital, Abuja. They have their own in-house legal team. They fight hard and can hold you up in court for years. They seldom lose these battles. Before that happens, they rename their product, or move."

Achebe leaned forward and peered into Mona's eyes. "Mrs. Burke," he said in a serious tone, "local sources suggest that US-Toys does much more than make toys. These fellows are involved in something more clandestine, possibly weapons trafficking, or worse."

Alarmed by Achebe's warning, and disappointed that her target company was no longer in Lagos meant either giving up the chase or taking the risks of tracking them to another city. Nailing an adversary in the United States, Canada or Europe was challenging, but in Nigeria it was bound to be nearly impossible. Language was a barrier. She didn't know enough about Nigeria's culture, and her lack of knowledge about the geography, customs and people were sure to be impediments. The biggest obstacle, however, could be the fact that she was a female in a male-dominated society.

"You said you personally had experience in court with US-Toys?" she asked.

Achebe hesitated. His hand under his chin, eyes directed toward the slowly turning ceiling fan, he appeared to be searching for words. Finally he cleared his throat and began. "I am never beaten before the courts. Twenty-five years of experience have been very good to me. I must say, that the biggest battle I ever encountered in court was fighting against that company which called itself Nintendo at that time. My partners and I lost in the preliminary round, but won on retrial. It's a long story, but that battle caused the breakup of our partnership."

"I'm sorry to hear that. Do you mind talking about it?"

"I'd rather not go into the gritty detail if you don't mind. It is a long story. Suffice it to say that my former partners had opinions about ethics that differed from mine. I feel much better about myself when I deal with clients according to my judgment of what is right and wrong."

Mona heard only the soft whoosh of the ceiling fan as she considered Achebe's response. *Whose ethics were more professionally correct, Albert Achebe's or his former partners?* "Are your former partners still practicing law?" She asked.

"I have not been in contact with either of these attorneys since 2012 when we did a final allocation of assets. But, Mrs. Burke, we digress. To sum up what I know about US-Toys, I heard through an informant that they now have a manufacturing plant in Kaduna District. Kaduna is north of Abuja Capital Territory. They produce metal, wood, and electronic children's toys. They market them through the internet. God knows what else they do. Much more than that I cannot tell you. Except, of course, that I would advise you to stay far away from that company and that district."

It was Mona's turn to stare at the ceiling. "How far is Kaduna from Lagos? Is there an airport there?"

"Madam Burke, I wouldn't recommend just dropping in on these people. That is, not without a small contingent of professionals to assist you. That place is at least 650 kilometers, or 400 miles from Lagos. Kaduna does not have an airport. One would have to fly into Abuja and rent a car. It is a two-and-one-half-hour drive from Abuja to Kaduna." Mona noticed Achebe's concerned stare, but ignored it by continuing to take notes. Achebe added, "Again, madam, I strongly advise you not to go there on your own. If you need to correspond with them I can get you their contact information."

Mona heard Achebe's warning clearly. Everyone was making a fuss over her safety. Nigeria had a dark side, but were men like Achebe being overly protective because she is a woman? So far, people here seemed to be very friendly and helpful. Nevertheless, she made a mental note to call her employer as soon as she returned to the hotel to demand that Ben Warner gets her escort here soon.

"My firm is sending someone to assist me. He was supposed to be here yesterday but had some visa problem. I hope they resolve that soon. In the meantime, can you give me their address so I can correspond with them?"

Mona's mind was made up. Her employer directed her to contact US-Toys, and by god, that is what she would do. *I just have to find a way to do it safely.* Mona's bulldog instincts intensified when someone suggested that a task was too much for her. *Humpf. Need a small contingent of professionals, indeed. I just need a couple minutes with the principals of US-Toys and I am out of there.*

Mona thanked the lawyer for the US-Toys contact information, and Achebe's driver brought her back to her hotel.

At four p.m. Lagos time Mona placed a collect call to her office in Maryland from her room. The phone on Ben Warner's desk rang at ten am Monday morning. The senior partner heard the operator say, "I have a collect call from Mrs. Mona Burke from Lagos, Nigeria. Will you accept the international charges?"

"Of course," Ben responded, "please, put her on."

Mona heard Ben say hello, but it sounded like he was standing in the middle of a busy freeway. "Hello?" she shouted through the static. "Mr. Warner, it's Mona Morgan, err, Burke, Mona Burke. Can you hear me?"

The line noise cleared somewhat, "Yes. Hello, Mona. It's good to hear your voice. Where are you? You sound like you are in a storm."

Shouting into the hotel-room telephone Mona said, "Pardon me, sir. I'm calling from Nigeria. Lagos, Nigeria. I'm sorry for calling so late. I just want to let you know my status."

"Mona, it's not late, it's ten a.m. here. How are you? Tell me what's going on."

"US-Toys is no longer in Lagos. The attorney, Achebe, said that they moved to a city called Kaduna, about 400 miles north of Lagos. I can't go there without some support."

Mona related her discussion with Achebe and her intention to locate US-Toys. "I need your authorization to fly to Abuja and to rent a car to drive to Kaduna." Ben asked her about safety, she sensed hesitation. *He's reluctant to authorize the trip?* "Well, I am doing fine in Lagos. Mr. Achebe was very helpful, and so far, I have had no problems, but I'm not sure how safe it is to travel outside of Lagos. Air and road travel to Abuja and Kaduna and back would probably be a day trip, or two days at the most."

Finally, Ben said, "I don't want you to travel outside Lagos alone. We will have someone there to accompany you in two days."

"Two days? Why is it taking so long, Ben? Where is this person coming from, and what kind of visa problem is he having?"

"He's an attorney from another law firm. He's a U.S. citizen but was born in Nigeria. His firm has an assignment for him in Lagos, and we thought he would be a very knowledgeable person to assist you. The Nigerian Embassy apparently needed to do some background checking on him but said they would have it resolved in two days."

"What? This guy was born here, but now he can't get a visa to return? I don't get it. Is he some kind of a security risk? And if he knows this country why didn't you just hire him to interview these Nigerian companies instead of me?"

"Mona, listen. I know I can trust you. You've been working on these cases for a long time and you know the right questions to ask. Pail Okeke, the person we are sending, submitted his travel request last week. He is being held up for some unknown reason. He hasn't given me all the details."

This was confusing. *Why would I be safer with some guy who can't even get his visa prepared correctly?* "Ben, I'm fine. I can't wait two days. If I can't get a flight to Abuja I will drop this assignment and fly to Cameroon to be with Alan. It's just that I'm here now and we should take this opportunity. If this doesn't work, you'll just have to spend the money to send someone else later. It's costing you five hundred dollars a day while I wait here doing nothing."

Ben sounded annoyed with Mona's abrupt change in attitude. "Mona, your safety is more important than the cost. I suggest you wait in Lagos. If we can't get my guy there by the day after tomorrow, you should just catch a flight to Cameroon, and I'll work this out later."

"Okay, Ben. Call me when this guy Okeke is on his way. Bye."

Cradling the hotel phone, Mona glanced at her cell phone and saw a voice message from Alan supposedly received the previous evening. *Funny. Why am I only seeing this now?* Then it occurred to her that cellular service for her carrier was not consistent throughout the city. She listened to the message.

"Hi, honey. It's Alan. I'm calling from a place called Kribi, on the southern coast of Cameroon. Just want to say hi, and that I hope you are doing well and finding your way around Lagos safely. I'll call again in half an hour, but if I don't reach you then, I'll be on the road to Bamenda tomorrow and may not be able to get in touch with you until late. If you get a chance to call back in the next thirty minutes call this number." Alan gave her Len's land line number. "Love you. Bye."

Mona quickly called Alan's cell phone, in spite of the fact that Alan might be traveling to Bamenda. The call failed. *Maybe there was no cellular service where Alan is at.* She punched the land line number from which Alan had called. After several rings on a phone in a Massy Construction, Inc. cubicle in Kribi, the call went to voice message. An unfamiliar male voice told her in workman's French, to leave a message "...*après le bip.*" Mona knew she would have to await Alan's call on Tuesday. *Why was he in Kribi, and why is he going to Bamenda? We were supposed to meet in a few days in Douala.*

Frustrated with the delays and the ineffectual telephone connections, Mona paced her hotel room. Spotting the room's television, she found an English-language news channel. Television cameras focused on police and soldiers in animated discussions. Her attention riveted on the screen when she heard the word "Yaoundé." A reporter summarized a story of an attack on the capital of Cameroon on Sunday forenoon. "Wow." she said out loud. *This is unbelievable. In one more day Alan would have been in Yaoundé. That must be why he's going to Bamenda.*

She dug out her laptop, entered the hotel's Wi-Fi code, and searched for more information on the raid. Reporters had not yet suggested that the attack had anything to do with Nigeria, however, both the Douala and Yaoundé airports had been temporarily shut down. Seeing this as a Cameroonian issue, Mona felt safer staying in Lagos for the time being.

Since Alan would not be in Yaoundé for another two days, she had to rethink her plans. With a day to waste, she should be resourceful and productive. She googled Kaduna, Nigeria, to get some idea of the size and layout of the city. On impulse, she decided to check on flights to Abuja. To her surprise, seats were available on Nigerian Air for a 10:45 a.m. flight from Lagos the next day, Tuesday. There were no seats available for the following day. *What the heck. Beats wasting time doing nothing here.* Then, for the umpteenth time, she searched for more information on US-Toys and several other companies on her list.

Mona woke up very early Tuesday morning. Her first thought was to talk to Alan. She needed to hear his voice, and she wanted his advice on her plan to fly to Abuja. She tried his cell phone again but could not get a connection. She lingered over a cup of coffee after finishing her room-service breakfast. In spite of a premonition that travel to Kaduna was ill-advised, she was perplexed that Alan would not be in Douala to meet her if she traveled there today, even if the airport was re-opened.

She was effectively trapped in Lagos until the airports were re-opened and she contacted Alan. After pondering her predicament and considering the advice of Alan and her boss, Mona allowed her emotions to make a critical decision. She took a taxi to the Lagos airport at 9 a.m., and found her 10:45 flight. Shortly after noon she was on Abuja's Nnamdi Azikiwe International Airport tarmac with her briefcase in hand and a change of clothes in her shoulder bag. Mona asked the airport information attendant for directions to a car rental agency.

The information desk attendant, a smartly dressed middle-age woman wearing a colorful traditional wrapper and matching head piece, said, "Madam, there are seven auto leasing companies here but no cars are available at this time. You must go into the city to find a car. You may take the bus shuttle, which is located on the first floor at the far end of this terminal building."

"Shoot. Are you absolutely sure? I need to get to Kaduna today."

Mona heard a smooth male voice behind her state in English, "Madam. You want transport? *Ah fit* help? My name be Yabani. I am auto owner, get permit to drive passengers. You want go Kaduna?"

Mona briefly glanced at Yabani, a short man of about thirty wearing traditional loose-fitting pants and white pullover shirt that hung to his knees. She nervously focused high over Yabani's *taqiyya*, the traditional Muslim skullcap, hoping she could find a better alternative.

Men stood nearby unburdened with luggage, apparently not travelers. A number of them would glance in her direction from time to time. She became annoyed with the attention. *Are these men waiting to offer services like carrying luggage, or taxi services?* She leveled her gaze at Yabani and looked into his wandering eyes.

Mona felt confused and now questioned her decision to travel to this unfamiliar place. The thought of walking to the shuttle, riding into town, and searching alone in this heat for a car rental company was out of the question. She considered the man's offer, and cautiously stated, "I want to go to Kaduna, today. I am looking for a car that I can rent for two days."

"Madam," Yabani responded with a slight bow, *"Ah git moto. Please, you like, Ah fit drive yu Kaduna. Ee far'o, but ma moto ee fayne. Yu fit relax, enjoy ride, na so? Yu de git* baggage?"

Before she could respond, several other men moved closer offering driving services. Mona wished she had made car arrangements before leaving Lagos. She did not want to be the center of any competition between these drivers, and she had no basis for choosing one over the other. *I will just get back on the plane and return to Lagos.* She closed her hand tightly around her briefcase and shoulder bag and pushed through the gathering crowd searching for an airport arrival/departure monitor. A small cluster of men followed her. To her disappointment, the 2:00 p.m. flight to Lagos had been canceled. The next flight was 11:45 the next morning. *Crap, I'm stuck here until tomorrow. Now what do I do?* Perspiration dotted her forehead.

In desperation, she turned to the first driver and asked, "What do you charge for two days?" The man stated a price of 60,000 naira per day, plus petrol, which cost 3000 naira per gallon. Mona made a quick mental calculation: *One U.S. Dollar equals about 300 Nigerian naira, 60,000 naira must be about $200 U.S. That's not all that bad, since this comes with a driver.*

A loud shout startled Mona. "Meessus Burke. Meessus Mona Burke."

A man with a pronounced limp hobbled toward her. He waved a sign with large, black lettering. She could make out "MRS. MONA BURKE." He elbowed his way through the throng and came to a stop facing Mona. "*Yu be Missus* Burke?" he gasped.

Mona was dumbfounded. How could someone here, at the Abuja Airport, know her name? She studied the man in disbelief. Although it comforted her to think that someone was looking after her convenience, the coincidence aroused her suspicion. *Did Ben arrange this?* She watched as two arguing drivers shrugged their shoulders, grumbled, and melted into the crowd. Before admitting that she was Mona Burke, she looked the puffing newcomer in the eye and briskly demanded, "Who are you?"

He struggled for oxygen as he introduced himself in a mix of pidgin and English. "My name eess Bennett Ngu. *Ah de wok fo courier, dey fo Abuja.* Boss man tell Mr. Albert Achebe, Lagos attorney, ask that driver meet you at airport. *Ah very sorry Ah late to meet yu plane. Yu are travel Kaduna, na so? Boss man say I drive you there, and safely back to airport.*"

This was too much to believe. Mona thought, *if Achebe was planning to have someone meet me at the airport why didn't he tell me? This sudden change doesn't make sense. Achebe didn't even want me to travel.* Her inner logic alerted her to some imbalance in happenstance that just didn't seem to add up. Her desire to get to Kaduna loomed heavily, and the milling crowd was daunting. She should call Achebe to confirm this arrangement, but her immediate thought was to get far away from this place. "Who is your boss?" she demanded.

"The owner of courier company. Please, follow," Mr. Ngu said as he reached for Mona's shoulder bag. "We *fit* reach Kaduna today."

Mona hesitated. She desperately wished that Alan or someone from the law firm was here. The arrangement with Mr. Ngu just didn't seem right. *I should call someone to confirm that they sent a driver, but who? Achebe? Ben?*

She saw Mr. Ngu look at his watch and state excitedly, "Come, we go now. I park nearby. Must move car now."

Pressured, Mona looked up at a nearby flight status board and saw that today's last flight to Lagos was still marked canceled. She would have to wait twenty hours in this airport. Looking around, she noted the lack of shops, restaurants and seating areas. *What the heck, if the meeting with US-Toys goes smoothly, I could be back here for that 11:30 flight tomorrow morning if I leave for Kaduna now.*

"Please, madam, we should leave. Mr. Achebe said it is important that I get you safely to Kaduna."

"Where is your car?"

"Just close by," he said, and reached again for her shoulder bag.

"I can manage," she said, sharply pulling her shoulder bag back. "Just show me your car."

CHAPTER 11
NIGERIAN HINTERLAND

Bennett Ngu limped as he strained to maintain a fast pace out of the terminal. He led Mona towards a parking area marked "RESTRICTED PARKING—SECURITY ONLY."

Interesting, thought Mona, *is this guy connected with security?* She followed Ngu's shuffling pace and reflected on his statement about instructions to meet her at the airport. That coincidence caused her consternation.

Ngu ignored Mona's questions, chattering incessantly, stating useless observations, and asking too many questions of his own. Ngu's attempts at conversation seemed strained and unnatural, as though he wanted to distract her. *This guy isn't answering my questions.*

"Ignore those noisy airport rascals who want drive yu," Ngu said pointing at a white van. "They fight over all patron 'cause they know there *no be* rental cars. They fight over passengers like monkeys fighting over banana. *No be so?*"

Ngu hopped into the driver's seat, leaving Mona to pull open the passenger door herself. Heat blasted out of the hot interior. Ngu cranked the engine to life, and turned on the AC. eventually Mona felt a waft of cool air.

Before entering the van, she scanned the parking area, taking mental pictures of her surroundings. Her instincts suggested that she needed to be alert. She noted that the back of the van was empty. *No one lurking.*

Ngu drove out of the airport and headed east, past a sign marked "University of Abuja." At the junction of Highway A2 he said, "This *be* road to Kaduna. We arrive in two hour. Where in Kaduna you want go?"

Mona asked some questions to sooth her anxiety before giving away more information, a habit she had learned while working with attorneys. "I'm sorry, sir, what did you say your name is?"

"I am Bennett Ngu." He responded. "Bennett, with double n and double t. You *fit* call me Bennett. I *comot fo* northern Nigeria, but I *wok fo* Abuja. I *don* take two, three day leave *fo get yu* to Kaduna and back to Abuja."

She continued, "Okay, Bennett. Who told you to meet me at the airport? I was not expecting anyone to meet me."

"Madam, it was Lagos attorney man who contact my company, as I say before. I am told to meet *yu* at airport and take *yu fo* Kaduna."

Mona continued, "What is the name of your company?"

Bennett hesitated. "Oh, Madam," he said, "*ees* small company. *Yu* will not have the name. We are like courier service for companies. We move information and goods between various business throughout Nigeria. Headquarter is in Abuja, capital city."

Mona noticed the hesitation in Bennett's response. Her anxiety spiked again, as it seemed he had to think hard to improvise an answer. "How long have you been working for them? Do you have a business card?"

"No, Madam. *Ah no fit* carry card. They are in printing. I am new to job." He drove on, pointing out various roads and buildings. His forced attempt to maintain a conversation was distracting. *Was he trying to avoid my questions with his tour guide comments?* Silence persisted for several minutes before he again pursued his queries. "Do you want stay in hotel in Kaduna? *Dey* only *git* four-star hotel *fo* Kaduna, but very nice. Tell me where in city you want stay and I *fit fayne* nice hotel."

Mona thought for a long time before she responded. During that delay Bennett glanced in her direction several times, as if to confirm that she had heard his question. She was not sure how much she could trust this man. She just wanted this Kaduna trip to end so she could complete her assignment and be with Alan. Finally, she asked, "Do you know of a company called US-Toys?" She watched closely for any sign of recognition from the driver.

Mona saw no change in Bennett's face. He said, "*Ah tink sey that be* manufacturing company on industrial side. I seen *dey* sign when I make deliveries close by. It is best to go directly there? We *fit* arrive before closing time."

Mona looked at her watch and agreed that it was better to not spend any more time before contacting the company. *A surprise visit may generate more and better information.* "Yes, let's go directly." For the fifth time since leaving the airport she checked for reception on her cell phone. Not even one service indicator button showed. It had been two days since speaking with Alan, and she desperately wanted to talk with him. *I need to let Alan know where I am. He must be very worried about me.*

About ten miles further, Bennett said, "They get petrol bank some two kilometers in front. We fit make small stop to fill tank. You *fit* use W.C. They get small place to buy small foods. *Ah no be long time.*"

During the stop, Mona noticed that it only took two minutes to fill the tank before Bennett went into the small shack, presumably to pay. She used the rest room, which was marked with the British styled "W.C." for water closet. The door pictured a black figure of a woman covered in a burka, reminding Mona that she was in a Muslin country. Mona returned to the van from which she saw Bennett standing on the far side of the structure talking on his cell phone. *I wonder if he is asking for directions.* He glanced toward the van, and abruptly turned away when they made eye contact. He quickly ended his call.

"Do you have cellular service?" she asked, checking her own cell phone again. "What carrier are you using?"

"Service very poor, madam. *Ah no* reach *ma patron.*"

Forty-five minutes later, before they crossed a wide bridge, Mona noted a sign that read, "River Kaduna."

"We are in Kaduna," advised Bennett, pointing. "That be industrial area on right. See the sign for Peugeot Automobile Company? The place you want is ten minutes."

"I noticed the name of the river we just crossed is the same as the name of the city. What is the significance?" asked Mona.

Bennett chuckled and said, "Madam, the name Kaduna means crocodile in my native Hausa. That *riva ee very long'o*. She cross all Nigeria and go to mighty Niger in southwest. One time they *git* many crocodiles *fo* that *riva*, but many *don kilt fo dey* skin. *Dey* still crocs, but not so many. It is normal that the city has same name as *riva*, because this be where most croc hunting happen 'til government outlaw it."

The van exited the highway and entered an area of aging steel and concrete buildings, most of them roofed with corrugated metal and surrounded by high walls. Barred gates kept casual drivers from entering. Bennett eased the van through the narrow spaces left by trucks that loaded or unloaded goods in the roadway. He drove nearly a kilometer on the congested street. Mona looked for names and numbers on the buildings along the way, but there were very few markers to guide them.

Ngu made an abrupt turn into a narrower street and parked in a shadowed alley. Mona craned her neck to search for street signs or company names. None of the few signs indicated US-Toys. There was nothing to indicate company names on the buildings on either side of the parked van. "Where are we?"

Bennett pointed to the building to the left of the van and noted, "This one on left must be US-Toys. I make deliveries to company across that main road. Come, we go in now."

Mona hesitated before slowly stepping out of the van. She searched again for names or addresses. Above the door of one brick building was a hand-painted number that was barely readable. It was not the street address Mr. Achebe had given her. Below the number was the name, "Associated Industries." Mona took a step backward, her eyes scanning for some indication that she was in the right place. She demanded of Bennett, "How do you know this is the right place?

The name on the door says Associated Industries, and the number I see is different from the address I was given."

Bennett, in a controlled and soothing voice said, "Madam, is *fayne*. That company *yu* want is part with Associated Industries. They are located just here. Come now, enter. *Yu fit* see."

Mona's heart beat faster, as she wondered how her driver knew all this. Her instincts sensed something clandestine, she turned to get back in the car. She would demand to be driven back to Abuja. Something was definitely not right here. She stood still before the door and fought to end this quest right now and return to Lagos.

"Madam. Please come. *Yu* people are just inside, I swear. *Yu* come long way. Better *yu* finish *yu* mission."

"Just wait." Mona said, as she reached into her shoulder bag and removed a scarf. "I must cover my head." She also grabbed her briefcase and her shoulder bag.

Ngu walked up to the building, turned the door knob and pushed the door open. In a soft, encouraging voice he said to her, "Its *fayne* madam, they are expect *yu*."

She stopped and stared at the driver. *What did he mean by that? How could they be expecting me? I never called, or told anyone I would be here.* She turned back toward the van.

"Madam, where *yu* go? These *peopo fit* close soon. *Yu comot fo merica* and are close to finish. Please, finish *yu wok* now."

She turned to face Bennett, walked toward him and waited for an instant to let him precede her. Inside, a sliver of sunlight from a high window illuminated dust in the air of the cool room. Mona spotted a crudely painted yellow door to her left. Two decrepit folding chairs rested sadly on her right. On the floor were several shipping crates, each about four feet long and stamped with Associated Industries' name and the word PHARMACEUTICALS. *Hmm, that box is about the size for rifles. Achebe said he wouldn't be surprised if this company dealt in weapons.*

She heard people talking and machines humming beyond the yellow door.

Bennett pointed to a chair, suggesting that Mona sit. He went to the yellow door and found that it was locked. He reached for something near the door jamb, then he placed his hands in his pockets sighing heavily. After a full minute the machine noise quieted somewhat. Someone threw a lock and the door creaked open. A tall, mustached man peeked into the room, studied the two occupants, and stepped back to allow a white-haired, bearded man in wrinkled pantaloons and a long shirt enter the room. Before the door closed behind him, Mona glanced into the large room full of machines. Men in work clothes and burka-covered women toiled over the equipment and moved boxes on dollies.

The white-haired man's eyes shifted back and forth between Mona and Bennett. He finally spoke in a local dialect. Mona cocked her head. The bearded man spoke louder, "Welcome. How I *fit* help you?"

Mona nervously cleared her throat while holding up one hand toward Bennett to indicate that she would speak, and began in slow, loud English, "Hello. My name is Mona Burke." She offered her hand to the white-haired man to shake, but he did not take it. "I am here in connection with a letter my employer, Mr. Benjamin Warner, sent to the president of US-Toys." She looked for any apparent recognition of the company name and saw none. Your company produced and sold items that may be in violation of international patent agreements. I wish to speak to the president of US-Toys Company. Are you an officer of that company?"

The man stared at Mona briefly before turning toward Bennett, and said something Mona didn't understand. Through his body language and tone of voice, Mona guessed he said something like, "What is this lady talking about?" Bennett and the bearded man conversed in another language. Bennett then turned to Mona and said, "Madam, this mon *ee* name be Abdul. *Ee* go talk with you. *Ah fit* wait in moto." He turned, opened the exterior door, and departed. Mona drew a breath of apprehension.

Abdul faced Mona. His face reflected little emotion, except a measure of contempt for a woman with the audacity to ask him questions.

Ngu was definitely not her protector, nevertheless, he was her main hope to getting back to Abuja. Mona had an uneasy suspicion that Bennett was not waiting in the van. The introduction had been mysteriously eerie.

"I am Abdul," the white-haired man said, "Manager of Associated Industries of Kaduna. How I fit help you?"

"Mr. Abdul, can you speak for the company known as US-TOYS, or is there someone else I can speak with?"

Abdul placed his hand on his beard and started to turn away. Mona considered that either he did not understand her question or was considering a response. His silence made her more nervous. She said, "Sir, may I have your business card?"

Abdul turned back to Mona. "No madam, *Ah no de git card just now.*" He stood straight and tall, non-committal in word or act, eyeing Mona with a look of mistrust.

The silence was awkward. To break the ice, she smiled, extended her business card and began again. "Mr. Abdul, I am happy you are able to meet with me. My company, Adams, Benson & Chang, is a United States law firm. I am interested in interviewing you about your company. Removing a small audio recorder from her briefcase, she switched it on. Do you mind if I record our discussion?"

"*Madam, Ah much pleased fo meet yu, but very busy. Ah no get time from wok. Yu come betta tyme.*" He turned toward the yellow door.

"Mr. Abdul," Mona leaned forward, "is this company US-Toys? Please, what is the relationship between Associated Industries, and US-Toys?" Again, no visible reaction from this man to show if the name registered recognition.

"Madam, *Ah fraid the name you speak does not exist. My company git no relation.*"

"Well, sir. May I speak to your company president?"

"Madam*, ee no dey fo hiya. Ah be only person in charge.*"

"How about your company attorney? I will only take five minutes. I came all the way from the United States to meet someone from US-Toys and…"

"Please, Madam. *A no fit gee yu* information about US-Toys. What is purpose? Why *yu* talk a name that no longer exists?"

"So, Mr. Abdul, was there ever a company called US-Toys?"

"Madam. *Please wait this place. A fit fayne mon who help.*" Abdul rapped his knuckles on the yellow door, which opened immediately. He left without saying another word.

When Abdul had not yet returned after ten minutes Mona's tension increased. With a feeling of foreboding, she opened the exterior door to check on Bennett. To her horror there was no Bennett and no van. Biting her lip in fear and indecision, she scanned up and down the alley. She ran to the main road and looked in both directions. No van. Her anxiety level jumped another notch. *What the hell is going on? Where did that bastard go? Why did he leave me stranded in this god-forsaken place?* She screamed, "Bennett. Where the hell are you?"

She felt overwhelmed and ran back to the building she had just left. Tears filled her eyes. Inside she went directly to the yellow door. It was locked. She wrapped twice. *Where is that damn button that Bennett had pushed to get Abdul?* Mona's hand trembled as she ran it up and down the door jam. Eventually, she noticed a slight indentation about one foot from the door's edge. *That had to be it, but how did Bennett find it so quickly?*

The cruel realization hit her. Bennett had deceived her from the very beginning. He never intended to get her safely back to Abuja. *How could I have been so foolish? Why didn't I follow my instincts?* Her earlier suspicions were confirmed. *If only I had been more observant. What the hell have I gotten myself into? Why didn't I listen to Alan? Why didn't I listen to Ben? I never should have come here. Did Achebe set me up? What about that attorney who was supposed to escort me? Had he been a no-show for a reason?*

She pushed the button. Nothing else mattered anymore. She was stranded. In the middle of Nigeria, she was alone and, now, very afraid. *This has got to be a bad dream.*

She repeatedly pressed her finger on the button and pounded on the door. When there was no response, she started pushing the button every five seconds. She put her ear against the door and heard machines, scuffling feet and voices. She shouted. Frustrated, she turned to the entrance door with a new idea. She would just leave the building and hail a taxi to get back to a commercial area, where there were more people. She grabbed her briefcase and shoulder bag and started for the exit door.

Before her hand touched the handle, the door flew open. Startled, she instinctively stepped back to avoid colliding with it. Two men with covered faces rushed in, grabbed her arms and threw a black hood over her head. She frantically fought back, swinging her shoulder bag like a club. The sudden appearance of these two aggressors so surprised her that she couldn't catch her breath. In her violent struggle the hood over her head slipped partially off. her right arm reached for the shemagh covering her nearest attacker. She pulled with all her strength.

She screamed as she saw the face of her driver, Bennett Ngu. "You!" Before she could catch her breath, a fist smashed against her chest pushing her violently backward. She stumbled over a chair and fell awkwardly to the floor. Half rising, she collided with another hard fist as it hit the side of her head. She tasted the dust on the floor.

Mona faded in and out of consciousness. Her arms failed her attempts to strike back. Her legs felt useless. She was scooped up by the two aggressors and roughly thrown over someone's shoulder. She was too weak to protest when bands were placed around her wrists and ankles. She moaned as she felt herself carried outside and dumped on a hard surface. Then rolling motion told her she was in a vehicle.

Even as she hit the floor of what seemed like the inside of a van, her mind raced. The bindings on her hands and legs compressed her flesh and the hood over her head made her nauseous. Her will to live awakened every sense. Though she was hobbled and bruised, the fight in her was strong. She would find a way to break free.

CHAPTER 12
NORTHWEST VENTURE

Weary from his long road trip and feeling grubby Alan was happy to check into the Mawa Terrace Hotel. His lodging, an inviting modern four-story building, was near the center of Bamenda. He arranged to meet Eric there for breakfast the following morning. They exchanged phone numbers, and Eric left to visit his Bamenda family.

Before washing the road dust out of his hair and changing clothes, Alan tried again to call Mona.

"*Puis-je vous aider, Monsieur?*" The hotel desk clerk asked. When Alan hesitated, the clerk said, "Can I help you, sir?"

"I need to make an urgent call. May I use your telephone?" He followed the clerk's hand motion toward a nearby booth. Alan struggled with the numbers before he remembered to use the international codes. Finally dialing correctly, he heard the ring but got no answer. "Where the hell is she?" he shouted in frustration. "Why can't I reach her?"

It was 6:05 p.m. in Cameroon, about lunchtime in Maryland, so he called the 800 number for Mona's employer, Ben Warner, at Adams, Benson & Chang.

Alan identified himself and reminded the receptionist that he was calling from Cameroon. He asked for Benjamin Warner. "I'm so sorry Mr. Burke, but Mr. Warner is attending Senate hearings in D.C., and will not be available until late this afternoon. Mona's supervisor is in a meeting at the moment."

"Look, my wife, Mona, is doing research in Nigeria, on contract with your firm. I work for the U.S. State Department, and I've been trying to reach her for two days. I need to know if anyone from your firm has had recent contact with her."

In a friendlier voice, the secretary reported, "Yes, Mr. Burke, I'm aware of your wife's assignment for Mr. Silverton and Mr. Warner. I can tell you that yesterday Ben Warner received a call from Mona." Alan breathed a sigh of relief when he heard that Mona had at least made contact. The secretary continued, "Mr. Warner said that Mona called from Lagos, Nigeria. He told me that your wife had met with an attorney in Lagos and wanted authorization to travel to somewhere north of the Nigerian capital today. As far as I know, we haven't received word from her since. However, Mr. Warner mentioned that he advised her not to travel in Nigeria, but to wait two days for the escort he is sending.

"Did Ben authorize any travel?"

"He said he didn't want her to travel outside Lagos without an escort, so no, I don't believe he authorized it."

"What's the status on the escort who was supposed to meet Mona at the airport?"

"Mr. Warner will have to address that question. Give me your telephone number and I will ask him to call you. I can send him a text message as soon as we hang up. I'm sure your wife is fine, I understand that sometimes telephone communication is difficult in foreign countries."

Alan, slightly relieved, still felt anxious about being cut off from his wife. If she was north of the Nigerian capital, she could be somewhere west of him right now. "Please," he said, "have someone call me. It doesn't matter what time of day, I want to know as soon as you get word from Mona."

Momentarily satisfied to know that Mona was fine as of yesterday,

Alan decided to call his Bamenda contact, Marcel Ndobe. Marcel, a Cameroonian who worked for the USAID office in Yaoundé, was stationed in Bamenda. He supervised a number of projects located in the Northwest and Southwest Regions. Through a forestry project located in Kumba, Marcel had come to know Dr. Len Watson, Alan's first contact in Cameroon.

Marcel answered on the third ring. Over Marcel's pleasant greeting, Alan could hear a crying baby and spoke louder than normal to be heard over the baby. "Good evening, Mr. N dobe, this is Alan Burke." Alan was not accustomed to Cameroon names that began with double consonants. Before Alan could continue, Marcel broke in.

"Yes. Mr. Burke. Welcome to my country. Len Watson called me this morning and said I would be hearing from you. Where are you now? Please forgive this noisy baby. He is crying for his mother who is busy preparing dinner. Will you be able to join us tonight?"

Alan was relieved to hear a cheery voice, and the baby's cry made him feel nostalgic. Engaging voices and crying babies signaled a young family and a happy home. "Thank you so much for your offer, but it's late. I was just hoping to get an update on the status of the incident in Yaoundé. Have you heard any recent news?"

"Mr. Burke. I will be happy to fill you in on all the news, but I must inform you, it is my people's custom to treat new arrivals as special guests. My wife has been preparing food all afternoon with the expectation that you will join us. She and I will be very disappointed if you cannot come. We want to give you a traditional Cameroonian welcome."

They met in the hotel at seven-thirty. Feeling much better after a shower and a change of clothes Alan was anxious to learn news about the murder and kidnapping in Yaoundé. They climbed into Marcel's Chevrolet Tahoe with the USAID emblem on the door. Marcel's low-keyed approach appealed to Alan, as they engaged in friendly conversation on the drive to Marcel's house. *I think I could like working with this guy.*

Ten minutes of negotiating narrow streets gave Alan a hint of village life. The Tahoe's headlights lit the way as there were no street lights. A kerosene lamp in a roadside cigarette stand came into view as villagers scurried in front of the vehicle. A mother carrying a child slung on her back held a burlap bag in each hand. She stumbled on the uneven shoulder and stepped into the dark roadway, the Tahoe's headlights accented extreme fear in the woman's eyes. The car skidded on loose dirt. The woman screamed, scrambled off the road, and turned toward the car's open driver's side window, eyes wide. Marcel stopped and politely said *"Ashya,"* to the woman as she motioned for Marcel to pass. Marcel turned to Alan and said, *"Ashya* means 'sorry for your troubles.' It can also mean, 'excuse me.' She seemed very fearful. People are nervous here because not only are Boko Haram zealots not far away, but there is some political turmoil in Bamenda as well."

Marcel slowed in front of a modern, cement-block house that flooded light from every window. The gravel drive was lined with banana trees with nearly ripe fruit hanging from each plant. A late-model Peugeot was already parked on the drive. It looked as though Marcel's family was doing quite well.

Marcel's wife, Taniya, greeted them at the front door. She spoke the English of a school teacher and had gracious manners. Alan guessed that she and Marcel had not spent their entire lives in Bamenda. Either they came from a larger city, or they were educated in Europe or the U.S.

Two young children, about two and four, clung to Taniya's long, colorful Cameroonian wrapper. Marcel turned to Alan and, with a proud smile on his face, said in pidgin, *"Na, ma pikin dem."*

Taniya admonished her husband and said, "Silly." And, to Alan she said, "He means that these are his children. And there's a baby sleeping in the next room." She added with a proud smile.

Alan remembered the word *'pikin'* and said, "Your husband sounds like he is very proud of his family."

A word from Marcel and two *pikin* scurried off to another room. Taniya reminded Marcel and Alan to not wake the baby. Turning towards Alan she said, smiling broadly, "I hope you are hungry. I prepared a special bush meat dinner to introduce you to my country style." Pointing toward a large, open room she added, "Please, have a seat in the sitting room while I finish the salad. We can eat in about ten minutes." She turned on the heel of her flip-flop and headed for the kitchen.

"I am sorry for imposing on you so late in the day," Alan called after her, "but I really appreciate your hospitality."

Marcel steered Alan toward a comfortable-looking chair. "Please, sit."

"Marcel, thank you so much for having me over. It's great to feel like a guest in someone's home." Sitting, he added, "Now, can you tell me about the incident that occurred in Yaoundé yesterday?"

Marcel nodded as he sat across from Alan. "Of course. We will get to that. But first I want you to relax and enjoy a Cameroonian dinner. There is nothing I will tell you that will change what you have to do immediately."

Weary from a long trip, the tense security checkpoints, the inability to contact his wife, and just being in an African environment for the first time, Alan inhaled deeply to control his anxiety. He closed his eyes until he could feel his heart rate approach normal. Looking up he saw Marcel staring at him with concern. Alan blurted out the first thing on his mind, "What bush meat?"

Marcel smiled, and chuckled. "Of course. I think my wife was playing with you just a bit. She has a great sense of humor, which I think she got from her paternal grandfather, who loved to play jokes. We Cameroonians call any wild game as bush meat. For this special occasion, Taniya has chosen to cook a rabbit curry. I hope you are not a vegetarian."

"No. No. And even if I were, I would not refuse your wife's preparation. Not after she has been working at it all afternoon." They laughed together.

After enjoying glasses of pinot noir and a scrumptious dinner, Marcel invited Alan back to the sitting room where, in the typical local custom, he offered Alan an after-dinner liqueur before getting down to business.

Marcel explained that the president had declared tomorrow, Tuesday, to be a day of mourning. Cameroonians were to pay respect to the minister of the interior and the other people killed or wounded in the terrorist attack, and for the minister who was kidnapped. All government offices would be closed. People are advised to stay in their homes.

"The government military tracked the offenders north, toward Garoua," Marcel said, "and are searching for them. We closed the border with Nigeria, but it may have been too late. There has been no official claim of responsibility for the attack, however, it is believed to have been staged by Boko Haram. Also, there have so far been no ransom requests for the return of the Honorable Minister Stany Ngey."

Alan leaned forward and closed his eyes, deep in thought. He ran his fingers through his unruly brown hair. Suddenly, he sat upright. "Marcel, I don't understand. You said the kidnappers fled north, toward Garoua, and that they have not been apprehended. How far is Garoua from Yaoundé, by car?"

Marcel screwed up his forehead, and said, "I don't know exactly. Maybe close to a thousand kilometers. Say, around 600 miles. But you can fly between Yaoundé and Garoua in less than two hours."

Alan continued, "I just traveled maybe four or five hundred kilometers from Kribi to Bamenda. We were stopped at least six times by heavily-armed patrols of police, army and gendarme soldiers. How is it that these bad guys can make a clean get-away on the highway and not be stopped? Assuming that these kidnappers are Boko Haram terrorists, can we assume that they are headed back to Nigeria?"

"Yes. I cannot explain why the security forces have not encountered the attackers, but I suppose that your assumptions are good."

"Then, unless they had a helicopter or airplane to fly, how did they manage to get past all the security? As tight as security is between here and Douala, I just can't believe they could get away. The Cameroon military must have some idea where these terrorists are."

Alan continued, "You know, Marcel, I should be in Yaoundé right now. I need to be there to support the ambassador's team. I'm in a very strange position. I'm part of a U.S. State Department team that I haven't even met, and I'm not involved in the response to this crisis. I've got to get in touch with the ambassador."

"I understand," Marcel said calmly. "I cannot help you get in touch with the ambassador, since he is still in Washington, D.C., but I can get you in touch with his office in Yaoundé. At the request of your Yaoundé office, I reserved a flight for you for tomorrow afternoon at one-thirty. The Bamenda Airport will not have a flight tomorrow, but Camair-Co has one from Bafoussam. The airport is about an hour's drive from Bamenda." Withdrawing a small note pad from a nearby lamp table, Marcel scribbled something and handed Alan a page. "Here is the number for the in-charge officer at the U.S. Embassy. His name is David Steinhouse. You can call the embassy tonight to get additional instructions."

"That's fine," said Alan. "I'll have my driver get me to Bafoussam." Then he quickly added, "Ah, Marcel. I don't know if you can help me, but I have another concern. My wife is doing some investigative work for an American law firm. She is somewhere in Nigeria as we speak. I've been trying for two days to contact her but have been unsuccessful. I found out this evening that she might be travelling somewhere in northern Nigeria." Marcel's eyes widened, but Alan continued, "Do you think she is safe travelling by herself, north of Abuja?"

"I would be careful sending a woman alone in most parts of the world, but I would not advise anyone to travel alone in that part of Nigeria at this time. I am sorry to worry you, Alan, but if I were you I would advise her to travel with an escort."

Alan returned to his hotel with a heavy heart, thinking about Marcel's warning. He tried again to call Mona's cell phone. It rang but went immediately to voice mail. *Why didn't she answer it?* He did not sleep well again.

Alan's cell phone came alive at one a.m. with a burst of music and a blindingly bright screen. He lunged for it, shaking the sleep out of his eyes, donned his glasses and was disappointed to see that the number was Mona's law firm, not his wife's cell. "Hello?"

"Mr. Burke, this is Ben Warner. I'm calling from my office in Maryland. I apologize for calling so late but I just returned from hearings, in Washington." Warner detailed the telephone conversation he had with Mona and stated that he had not heard from Mona since. "I'm sorry that you're not able to get in touch with her, but she sounded fine when we talked. I'm sure she's all right."

Alan slapped his own face to help him focus. "Ben, thanks for calling. I am beside myself trying to figure out where Mona is and why she hasn't answered her phone." He thought for a moment, then asked, "Can you give me names of any of her contacts in Lagos and Abuja? I'm worried for her safety. There's a terrorist group in Northern Nigeria that is raising hell, burning villages, killing people and kidnapping children. People here think that the murders and kidnapping in Yaoundé were carried out by Boko Haram.

"Yes, we hear similar news here. I'm very sorry you haven't been able to reach Mona. You know your wife is very resourceful and extraordinarily intelligent. I hope she has not gotten into trouble. Please let me know as soon as you find out where she is and how she's getting along. In the meantime, I will get you the names of her Nigeria contacts."

Looking at his wristwatch, Alan replied, "You have my number, but I will leave Bamenda in about 10 hours, to fly to Yaoundé. I may not have cellular reception for a while. Once I arrive in Yaoundé I will give you better contact information."

The next afternoon, as Eric dropped Alan off at the Bafoussam Airport, Alan's small reserve of optimism took another blow. Standing on a narrow, dirt landing strip was an ancient Fokker twin-propeller aircraft that maybe should have been in the Smithsonian Air and Space Museum. Eric laughed and said, "Mr. Alan, I drive to Yaoundé tomorrow. Maybe you best come with me then."

"Thanks, Eric, but I can't waste another day. I'll take my chances with that flying antique."

The airport terminal building was a small, one-room shack with seven folding chairs for waiting passengers. The chairs were filled with travelers clutching briefcases and handbags. The ticket master stood behind a makeshift wooden counter, a clipboard in one hand and a pencil tucked behind his ear. "You be Mr. Aran?" he asked.

Alan nodded nervously, and made his way to the counter to sign in.

Thirty-five minutes later, an explosion just outside the building startled everyone. The loud noise was followed by a scratchy-squeaky sound like metal scraping on metal. Heads turned toward the window, as the plane, sitting next to the building came to life with a deafening roar. Puffs of blue-gray smoke erupted from the starboard engine. The propeller spun in a jerky attempt to rotate as the engine coughed and sputtered. Another explosion, more smoke, and the engine caught. The blades whirled faster and the engine growled louder. Just as Alan adjusted to the engine noise, the left engine came to life with an ear-splitting racket. He scanned the room to see if the other passengers looked terrified. No one appeared to be backing out of their reservations. Alan searched his soul for whatever confidence he could muster. One elderly passenger looked at him and tendered a devilish smile.

With both engines screaming loud, metallic noises the passengers were led out of the make-shift terminal, prompted to climb steps and locate open seats. Alan was sure he could taste the airplane fuel. Only the apparent resolve of the other passengers gave him courage to buckle his seat belt.

The Fokker's engines revved to a high pitch just as the terminal clerk and a young helper pulled the chock blocks from the plane's tires and dove away from the blue exhaust. Slowly at first, the tires crunched across the gravel runway and the plane lumbered forward. As it picked up speed the passenger cabin began to vibrate wildly, and a piece of plastic from a luggage rack fell to the aisle. Everyone seemed to ignore the fallen debris, but their fingers dug into the upholstered arm rests, and the blood drained from their knuckles.

The plane rumbled along the dirt runway, faster and faster, and eventually picked up enough speed to get airborne. The engine roar became a reassuring background noise as the engines hummed more smoothly. Alan resolved that he would drive if ever he had to travel from Bamenda to Yaoundé again.

His thoughts focused on Mona, praying that she would stay close to Lagos and out of harm's way.

Less than an hour later, the outskirts of Yaounde came into view. The pilot, who Alan could see through an open passageway, spoke

English as he contacted the control tower in Yaoundé. Alan couldn't recall seeing a control tower in Bafoussam. Relieved when the hard thump of the wheels contacted the Yaoundé tarmac, Alan was happy to be in the hands of a qualified pilot. As soon as the plane stopped at the terminal he rose on wobbly legs and clambered down the stairway.

CHAPTER 13
MINISTER'S ARRIVAL

Commander Yusuf Adako Edubamo shouted toward the sky in his native Hausa, as though mere humans were incapable of assuaging his frustrations. "Why haven't those bastards called in? Where the hell are my hostages?"

The commander gulped the last of his flask of *white mimbo* and released a loud belch. Several jihadists sitting nearby on rocks and tree stumps chuckled softly. Loud enough to reassure their superior that they prize his manly outburst, but subdued so as not to be the target of his demeaning and sarcastic criticisms.

"Sir," cautiously advocated one of his squad leaders, "they've only been gone three days. We heard on the radio that they succeeded in their mission, and I'm sure the Cameroon military is making it difficult. It could take several days. We already sent the trucks to meet them at the Nigerian border. We have to wait."

"To hell with Cameroon military," said Edubamo. "Those imbeciles couldn't track down a bunny rabbit. They are cowards, and they will not stand up to our militia." The commander spat a mouthful of sour *mimbo* that raised a puff of dust. "The ransom for one government minister would buy fuel and supplies for a year. That is what you lost when you killed one. We could have bought two years of support. Now we might get but one."

The ground shook ever so slightly, and the militants heard the tinny clatter of a four-cylinder engine. A plume of dust headed in their direction. A white pickup truck approached from the direction of the town of Michika. Several men shouldered their weapons until, at 200 meters, they identified the driver as their associate, Abraham.

Abraham Abuzo braked his Toyota pickup ten meters from the knot of armed fighters. A thick cloud of dust wafted over the truck, engulfing vehicle, driver and passengers. Camouflage-clothed militants, now at rest, appeared from the shadow of tall foliage and looked on curiously. Abraham was a scout for Edubamo's terrorist cell.

Yusuf Edubamo watched as Abraham ejected himself from the dust-covered vehicle and brushed off his shirt. Smacking his hat against his leg he approached the cluster of armed men and made a respectful half-bow to the commander.

"Sir," Abraham said, speaking in a mixture of Yoruba and Hausa, "our spotter in Michika received information from Kaduna that they captured an American spy interrogating our people."

"Well, that is just wonderful, Abraham," said Edubamo with a hint of sarcasm. "So, what are they going to do with him?"

The driver shook his head, "No sir. It is a she, not a him."

Edubamo rolled his eyes and scoffed, "What the hell are the Americans doing sending a woman to do man's work? Do they think we cannot see through their stupid Western tricks? I hope the people in Kaduna shot the infidel whore on the spot."

Abraham hesitated, but finally said, "Sir, the woman is being transported to Michika now. I think our friends in Kaduna want us to dispose of her, or use her for other purposes."

The first thought that came to Edubamo's mind brought a slight sparkle to his eyes. *We'll find ways to use her all right.* Then, as he considered his resources and his plans, he remembered that his men murdered one of the intended Cameroon hostages, thus leaving him with less bargaining power. *This woman is American, and those people would pay a good price to get one of their spies back, even a despicable women spy.*

I wonder how much they will be willing to pay. Americans have money. Maybe this will work out fine, inshallah. "Yes. God willing," he said out loud. He turned to Abraham and commanded, "See that no harm comes to this woman spy. Tell the Kaduna people to send her here. I'll demand ten million American dollars from the infidels. Go. Now."

The commander's mind worked quickly. He needed to assemble his officers to begin planning how to convey ransom demands to the two targets: the presidents of Cameroon and the United States. He would need his radio technician to communicate with the shura council leaders and to construct channels that could deliver his ransom demands without surrendering his identity or location. He would need a way to demonstrate convincing evidence that he actually held the hostages. He turned to the small circle of troops who had gathered near his tent, and pointing to various men, shouted, "You, and you. Go get Hosni, Hassan and Ahmad. I want them here in two minutes. And you," he shouted, pointing to a third jihadist, "get us a table, our maps, and a large pot of coffee. Make it fresh. Now go."

The camp stirred with activity. The insurgents sensed danger and excitement and another opportunity to demonstrate their strong faith and commitment to their holy war.

Many of the militants were underprivileged young men whom Boko Haram strong-men and clerics recruited from schools and trained in the desert in northern Nigeria. Their first lesson was understanding that Allah was the only motivation for their lives and that their mission was to serve God well so they could enjoy eternal peace after this life. Their indoctrination insisted that life on Earth was nothing but a test. You pass, you enjoy everlasting peace and contentment in the next life. Failure means your life has been useless.

All other beliefs were heresy. Western culture, with its twisted educational principles, its Christian religions, its worship of wealth and its loose morals was sinful and directly opposed to the teachings of Muhammad. Those who do not follow the laws of God are considered infidels and must be converted or killed. To that end, all remaining lessons dealt with the use of weapons and military strategy. Like a sports team hyping up to play a game, these soldiers were emboldened to kill non-believers. Likewise, they were ready to offer their lives as weapons to eliminate infidels.

Two hours later, Commander Edubamo and three subordinate officers emerged from their strategy session with a plan to extort large sums of money from two governments. Through their headquarters in Maiduguri they would send messages to the presidents of both Cameroon and the United States, and they would demand large ransoms for Cameroon's minister of the treasury and for the American woman spy. They would send video tapes to both countries to prove that the prisoners were in jeopardy of being beheaded on international television. Ransom money they hoped to receive would be deposited in a Boko Haram foreign bank account.

The commander used a military satellite radio to contact Boko Haram leadership in Maiduguri to arrange for the receipt of ransom monies. He did not request permission, rather he informed them. Edubamo was impatient with those who questioned his movements or implied that he needed to be a better team player. He understood, however, that he needed the support of his sura council superiors. They would be the ones to face down the president of the United States. Edubamo only had to wait for the two hostages to arrive at his camp.

Late that Tuesday afternoon whoops and cheers greeted two gray vans and two military personnel carriers escorted into the encampment. Excited militants who were exhausted and dirty were happy to report that their prisoner survived the torturous cross-country journey.

The militants jumped out of their vehicles and forced their prisoner to face the commander. Edubamo scrutinized the weary men and the lone prisoner as a militant pushed the hooded figure toward him. Flinging off the prisoner's hood and giving her a gentle push forward the terrorist said, "Commander, we captured the Cameroonian minister of the treasury. She is an important member of the Cameroon People's Democratic Movement. Her name is Madame Stany Ngey."

Stany Ngey stumbled forward on unstable legs, which Edubamo assumed was due to cramping from the personnel carrier. Her eyes widened with fear as she glanced at the rough-looking fighters surrounding her. Her clothes were covered with dust, her headpiece had dropped to her shoulders and her hair had tangled about her face in disarray.

"Why?" shouted Edubamo in Hausa, "Why did you bring back only one hostage? And why, why in the name of Allah, did you bring back a woman? Do you think the Cameroon president will pay money for the return of an ugly woman?"

The excursion leader tried to explain, "Sir, we were under fire from the presidential guard. We had Cameroon's minister of the interior in our grasp, but he resisted strongly. He managed to grab the weapon from one of my men and was about to shoot. I had to kill him."

"You are foolish. Your dangerous mission ended as a useless trek across the desert. How many casualties did you have?"

"Sir, we were blessed. *Mashalla.* God has willed, only a few injuries. We had to kill security guards at the Cameroon-Nigerian border, and a few people in Yaoundé, but we lost no men and no equipment, thanks to the surprise attack and your good planning."

Edubamo considered the mission marginally successful but was relieved that none of his men were killed or seriously injured. He resolved to move forward with his plan to demand ransom money for the single hostage. To one of his fighters he said, "Put her head cover back on, bind her hands and put her in a place separate from the Hafsa prisoners. We will video her statement later." He scoffed as the captive was hustled away. He smiled when she roughly shrugged her guard's hand from her shoulder and spat out something in Bantu dialect. *This wuman seems to be a fighter. A bit fat, but stubborn.*

The commander would never know his prisoner well, and he didn't care. After all, she was a woman. Her political position, however, represented a currency: her life for a ransom large enough to sustain his fight.

CHAPTER 14
YAOUNDÉ

At half past two Tuesday afternoon Alan Burke stepped onto *terra firma* relieved to exit the Fokker. David Steinhouse, Deputy Chief of Mission for the U.S. Embassy in Yaoundé, greeted him on the tarmac. Alan recognized David from photos and knew that he was temporarily in charge of the embassy while Ambassador Tyler Morrison was out-of-station. Over the loud ticking of the cooling aircraft engines they shouted greetings and ambled to a waiting embassy car.

Alan felt a weakness in David's handshake and noticed the way he grasped his one hand in the other. *Is he holding his left hand to keep it from shaking? Does he have Parkinson's?* Alan scrutinized David who looked to be in his sixties with brown age spots on his cheeks.

During the drive to the embassy, David spoke, "Look, Alan, I know you've been bounced around since you arrived in Cameroon. That's unfortunate, however, we need your help right away in responding to critical situations here in Yaoundé. The entire country is in political and economic turmoil. There is civil unrest in two regions and this terrorist thing has got everyone on edge. Things haven't been this disrupted since the 1983 coup attempt. People are scared as hell over this terrorist attack, and the government has been slow to take resolute action."

"Are the U.S. citizens living in Cameroon at risk?" Alan asked. "Is there something we need to be doing to either protect them or assist their evacuation?"

"Not yet. We already contacted and advised all registered U.S. citizens," David said.

Alan politely nodded his understanding, but anxiously looked for an opportunity to inform David of Mona's situation. He needed to see how David's message would affect his first day on the job, and he wanted to make a favorable impression on his superior.

"Ambassador Morrison is cutting his vacation short," David continued, "but he won't be here for three more days. He's in Washington. The president and Secretary of State Townshend are briefing him. We spoke this morning. He wants you to call him as soon as we reach the embassy. U.S. intelligence thinks the attack was staged by a Boko Haram cell. State is working with the governments of Cameroon, Nigeria, and France but needs Cameroon to take first action."

"That's fine, David," Alan said, "I look forward to talking to the ambassador and getting involved with the situations here, but there's something you need to know. My wife is somewhere in Nigeria, and I can't reach her. I'm very concerned because she may be traveling to northern Nigeria. Locating her and making sure she is safe is my first priority."

David grimaced. "Shit, Alan. What the hell is she doing in northern Nigeria? I'm sorry to hear that. We have enough problems without that. You've got reason for concern. Is she traveling with a group?"

"She's doing some research for a law firm. She was supposed to have an escort, but the person had visa problems and didn't show. I don't know if she tried to travel without an escort or if she's still in Lagos. I just can't reach her, and I'm worried."

"Well, Alan, in this part of the world communication problems happen. It may just be a telephone utility issue. The coverage is not all that reliable. Embassy staff will do everything they can to locate her and make sure she's okay. In the meantime, your first priority is to respond to the problem of Sunday's terrorist attack. The safety of U.S. citizens in Cameroon is our priority, but we also have to be of assistance to the local government. The Cameroon President asked for assistance from the French to help track down the terrorists. The French, in turn, asked the U.S. to intervene by contacting the government of Nigeria. The Cameroon Army has not been able locate the attackers."

Alan was annoyed that Deputy Chief of Mission so quickly brushed aside his concern about finding Mona. *After all Mona is a U.S. citizen whose safety needs to be assured.*

Steinhouse's cell phone buzzed. "Yes?" David said. "I'm with Alan now. On our way to the embassy." David glanced up at Alan, eyes wide and hand shaking. David seemed to grit his teeth and his cheekbones bulged. Pebbles of sweat appeared on his brow. He said, "Can you repeat that last bit?"

Is this conversation about Mona? Has something else happened? Alan reached for his own cell phone to see if he had service. His phone showed two reception bars, but, before he could dial, David grabbed Alan's arm to stop him.

Closing his phone and tucking it away David said, "Alan, remember that your phone is not secure. I'll take care of that as soon as we get to the embassy."

Alan reluctantly complied.

Putting his own phone away, David said, "That was embassy staff. The latest word is that the French are not sending military or advisory support. They refuse involvement in a conflict with Nigeria, and are deferring to the British and the Americans. We need to contact the Cameroon authorities to find out what we can do to help them and decide if we can assist their efforts to stop the terrorists."

In spite of his growing concern for Mona's safety, Alan now had to focus on David's urgent demands. "What's the State Department's stance?" Alan asked.

"We need to contact Ambassador Morrison as soon as we get to the embassy."

Remembering something from his preparation at the State Department in Washington, Alan said, "I understand that the U.S. has a small military contingent in northern Cameroon for the very purpose of deterring Islamic terrorists. Can't they help with air surveillance to find the attackers?"

"That's true, Alan. We have several hundred U.S. Army personnel in Garoua. Cameroon officials requested U.S. assistance last year, but that unit is still being staffed-up. We already asked Secretary Townshend to request that unit's help. She reminded me that we need the local government's approval."

Alan's head whirred with the avalanche of activity. Still trying to get his feet on the ground, he was suddenly dealing with people he did not know. He had risked his life and health on Cameroon's highways with guns pointed at his head. He rode in a shaky, antique airplane, and was thrown into a terrorist situation before he even saw his new office. Above all that was his concern for his wife who seemed to have vanished.

On arrival at the embassy Alan received a brief reception from senior staff. Before he could begin to memorize half the names of his associates, he was rushed into a wood-paneled conference room to be briefed on the current kidnapping situation. Whisked out of that meeting into the office of the mission's Security Officer, Alan was assigned a secure cellular phone and instructed on its use. "Don't worry, calls to your old number will automatically transfer to the new number."

Amidst Alan's attempt to phone Mona, a knock on the door broke off the instruction and Steinhouse whisked Alan away to another room. Several high-ranking embassy staff gathered in a secure room to make a telephone call to the Cameroon Presidential Palace to offer the embassy's support to the Cameroon government.

Steinhouse spoke with the prime minister's secretary. In spite of the government closure for the official day of mourning he was able to arrange a meeting with Cameroon's president and prime minister regarding Sunday's attack in Yaoundé. The meeting was scheduled for eight that evening.

Alan then joined the deputy chief of mission and other embassy officials in a planning session for the evening meeting with Cameroon's president.

A staff member knocked on the door and poked her head into the room. She announced, "David, Ambassador Tyler Morrison is on the secure line."

"Come with me, Alan," directed the in-charge officer, as he dashed toward the door.

Pointing to a chair in his office, Steinhouse said, "Make yourself comfortable, Alan. I think he wants to talk to you, too." Assuring himself that his office door was closed, he lifted the receiver and punched a button on the console.

Steinhouse, serious all afternoon, now seemed grave as the color drained from his face. With the phone tight against his ear David listened for a long time, seemingly avoiding eye contact with Alan. Finally, he said, "Yes. He's right here in my office. I'll put him on."

Alan had met the ambassador six months before when he interviewed at the State Department. Tyler Morrison had made the final selection from a short list of candidates, and he personally offered Alan the position of Assistant Program Officer for the U.S. Embassy in Yaoundé. Morrison had welcomed Alan to the department as they enjoyed an expensive lunch. When Alan took the telephone from David he felt confident that he was talking to a friend. "Good afternoon, Ambassador Morrison, this is Alan Burke."

"Alan. First of all, I want to say that I'm sorry your arrival in Cameroon has been so chaotic."

"Well, sir..." Alan started.

The ambassador cut Alan off. "It's unfortunate, but that's the way international statesmanship goes. I wish I had been there to welcome you, but we have to adjust to events as they occur. I will be there by Saturday. In the meantime, I need you to help David set up a protocol with the Cameroon government. Secretary of State Lisa Townshend informs me that the attack in Yaoundé was terrorist-motivated. She also tells me that the government of Cameroon has been unable to confront the terrorists."

Alan glared at the phone in his hand. *Crap. This job is serious business. I'm trying to find my wife and these guys want me to solve an international crisis?*

"We can offer the Cameroon government some assistance with satellite surveillance," continued the ambassador, "provided they are willing to use it. As you recall, Cameroon recently asked the U.S. to install a small U.S. Army base in the north for this very purpose. We need the Cameroonian government to let us help them. You need to get the president and his cabinet to agree to our assistance."

Alan felt an immense burden falling onto his shoulders. *Who am I to convince a country president and prime minister of anything? Hey. I'm the new guy here.*

Morrison continued. "David will take the lead in tonight's meeting with the president and prime minister. I want you to be there and to support him. Keep in mind that Cameroon has strong ties with France. Not always on the best of terms, but politically and economically important. The president of France has asked us to assist but has no authority or diplomatic ties with Cameroon's neighbor, Nigeria. It gets complicated, but we will need total cooperation among the governments of five countries if we are going to be of any assistance. You may have to move quickly but make sure that you have solid agreement among all the parties. We don't want to risk any lives or invade sovereign territories. Can you handle that?"

Alan felt overwhelmed, and suddenly very tired. Too much responsibility too soon. Never one to back down, he had always felt in control. But how could he ignore the fact that his wife was unaccounted for and concentrate on his job? Exhaustion and concern for Mona created mounting tension. He dug deep for the courage and confidence that had always been his strengths. Finding a trace of resolve, he replied, "Yes sir. I will do my best."

When the ambassador didn't immediately respond, Alan continued, "Sir, I want you to be aware of a personal problem that is becoming more urgent. This past Sunday my wife traveled to Lagos on an assignment for her law firm. She is supposed to be here in Yaoundé in a couple of days. For three days I've tried repeatedly to contact her without success. I'm extremely worried for her safety." He briefly outlined the frequent attempts to contact Mona, and her employer's concern that she may have traveled alone to Abuja.

Much like David Steinhouse's earlier reply, the ambassador briefly commiserated with Alan then reminded him of his official assignment. Passing the telephone back to David, Alan felt depressed. His dread of something terrible happening to Mona grew to near panic. He felt trapped. No one seemed interested in helping. Gloomy images of highway accidents, murders, and hostage-taking haunted him. He felt powerless to do anything about it.

CHAPTER 15
THE INTERROGATION

M ona was jolted when the cargo van hit a deep pothole, shaking her back to the present. She had lapsed into semi-unconsciousness. It was dark inside the hood, but she sensed the presence of her captors who crouched several feet away, saying little but reacting to the rough ride with grunts.

Sobbing and near despair Mona was confused and afraid. Her confidence had been shattered, and her hope for rescue had dissipated. Her self-assurance melted into self-pity. She was exhausted and in pain. Her head hurt where Bennett Ngu had struck her. Her arms and legs ached from the bindings and the rough sides of the vehicle. Terror and fear for her life surpassed the aches and pains. Her youthful innocence and love for life suffered as she experienced the heartless brutality of her captors. Her trust in human kindness had dissolved the instant she had been betrayed in Kaduna.

Why do these people hate me? What do they want from me? Maybe US-Toys had bigger secrets than simply re-engineered toys.

She bounced around on the floor of the van, a smelly, moth-eaten blanket her only insulation from the metal floor. The plastic bindings created sores on her wrists and ankles. Her hood had come loose several times, only to be roughly replaced by her guards. Her dress slacks, blouse and light jacket were mostly intact, so at least some of her dignity remained.

Mona knew none of the many languages spoken in Nigeria. Occasional words spoken by her guards in pidgin or ambiguous English revealed little about these angry, obsessed men. She had no idea where they were taking her, or why they had not already killed her. She hoped she wouldn't at some point wish they had. She prayed that they had some good purpose for keeping her alive.

Stories of ruthless extremists who hated Western culture, and especially Americans, haunted her. Though she was beginning to suspect that these people might be members of a terrorist group, she hoped there was another explanation. She recalled that strict sharia law forbade the education of women, and essentially left them with no rights. Some extremists despised the loose morals of Westerners. Mona remembered news stories about a group that had raided villages in northern Nigeria and kidnapped hundreds of young girls. At the time, she felt badly for those girls, suspecting that they were raped, induced into marrying members of Boko Haram, murdered or sold as slaves. She felt the debilitating terror that must have consumed those captured girls.

Mona sensed that the vehicle was slowing down. The swaying motion indicated several right and left turns. Finally, smooth pavement was replaced with the rumble of rubber tires on gravel. The motion stopped. *Oh, good. A pee break.* Thirty seconds passed, as intense voices floated around the exterior of the van. She heard the door open. Rough hands grabbed and yanked her from the van.

The distant sounds of car horns and street traffic suggested they were near a large community. Her hood dislodged partially when her head brushed against the open door of the van. Blinding sunlight stung her eyes, but just before someone roughly shoved the hood back over her head, she saw she was standing on the shoulder of a road near an open field. Tall grass partially obscured distant multi-storied buildings. A road sign in both Arabic and English characters stood five meters away. The English clearly read "Michika." *Is that the name of this town?*

Someone started to lift her off the ground, but she shouted, "Wait. Wait. I need a bathroom." She sensed a stir of confusion. Several male voices seemed to suggest they either didn't know what she said or didn't quite know how to deal with her request.

Finally, someone who spoke a few words of pidgin asked, *"Na whattee? Wetin dey happen?"*

"I need to pee."

"Yu…pissing?"

"Yes. I need to piss."

The man hesitated. Finally, *"Go fo side."*

Mona was relieved that she might get some relief but wondered how this would work. She heard more discussion amongst male voices. Finally, a firm grip on her arm guided her away from the sounds of traffic, until she nearly stumbled in knee-high vegetation. She felt someone grab her wrists and cut her binding. A gruff voice said, "Go now."

Rubbing her sore wrists, she waited for the sounds of steps going away from her before proceeding. When the voices seemed distant enough to allow some privacy, she chanced a peek through the bottom of the hood. In that small moment she saw a van, a pickup truck and three or four men, some of whom carried weapons. She hid her inhibitions and swallowed her pride. Some things were just too important to let modesty get in the way. When she stood up again she sensed heavy steps coming toward her. She considered the experience a small, but important, victory.

The men re-tied her hands, and dumped her, *sans* ceremony, onto what felt like the bed of a pickup truck. Two guards climbed in, dragged her to the front of the truck bed and forced her to sit on a pile of smelly burlap bags. She felt the truck pull onto a tarred road and accelerate. To Mona that meant: she was leaving Michika, the men guarding her were not policemen or soldiers, and someone was expecting her to be some place, soon.

The next segment of her journey took almost as long as the first. After what seemed to be about thirty minutes she sensed the vehicle turn off the paved road and again travel on coarse gravel. Mona's knees and shoulders took a severe beating as she bounced into the sides of the truck travelling at high speed.

The suffocating road dust that covered her hooded head made her feel nauseous. When the pickup finally came to a stop, Mona's lungs felt congested. Her head throbbed. She feared for her life, but had little remaining strength to fight. *God, please help me. Alan, where are you?*

She could hear men shouting as she was grabbed by the arms and roughly pulled from the truck bed, her captors taking a few liberties. Her strength dissolved, but she still struggled to fight free. Her courageous efforts only precipitated more abuse, until she was smacked across the side of her hooded head with an open hand, making her left ear ring. Firm grips on both arms kept her from falling to the ground. A raspy voice shouted instructions in an unfamiliar language. Then, in English, "Take spy *wuman* to my tent. Take hood! Mohammad! Bring water and hot tea!"

Mona dug deep for courage. When someone pulled the hood off her head she shuddered at the sight. The sun had moved low in the west, but in the waning light she saw at least a dozen armed men whose menacing stares terrified her. They wore ankle-high combat boots and olive-drab shirts that hung long and loose. Some had towels or scarves hiding portions of their faces. Beyond the frightening men she saw numerous tents and armored vehicles, a military camp.

She didn't know who these people were, or what they wanted. *Is there a connection to US-Toys? Why are they so angry? I only wanted to investigate some illegal activity. Did I ask the wrong questions in Kaduna? Maybe I should have worn a burka. Where is Ben Warren's protective escort? Jeez, I wish Alan were here now.* She swallowed hard, *I may never see Alan again. What have I done?* Her head drooped, and the tears flowed.

A soldier gripped her arm firmly and nudged her toward a canvas tent. He shoved her inside. She wondered what would happen to her if she bolted and made a run for the trees surrounding the camp. She quickly scuttled that idea. Men and weapons were everywhere. *There must be a hundred soldiers in this camp.*

Inside the tent she faced the leering eyes of the man with the raspy voice. Commander Edubamo introduced himself in marginally understandable English. On his instructions a man removed the binding from her wrists. The commander then directed her to sit on a canvas folding chair, and another man gave her a towel to wipe dust and sweat off her face and arms. Blood smudges appeared on the towel.

Edubamo's initial questions were simple and had nothing to do with US-Toys. Mona saw through his phony cooperative demeanor, assuming that he was playing the good cop role now, but may try to extract information from her in a more forceful manner. She shivered with fear as she imagined his possible methods. She didn't think she could withstand any torture.

"Yu name? *Whatee yu* name? Why *yu* spy in Kaduna?"

Mona refused to respond at first, her mind racing. She desperately tried to understand where this interrogation was headed. She understood that the camouflaged men with guns were not the Nigerian Army but some band of guerilla fighters. *ISIL? Taliban? Boko Haram?* She was curious that the commander didn't mention US-Toys.

Her eyes desperately searched her surroundings for anything to restore hope or comfort. Instead, she spotted a black flag partially unfurled near the tent flap. Her heart sank. She had seen that flag several times on television. It was the flag of a jihadist terrorist group. Images of angry, face-covered terrorists threatening to slit the throats of prisoners flashed to mind. She trembled convulsively. She felt faint. Bile acid crept up her throat. She nearly gave up hope at the sight of the Islamic terrorists' flag.

Mona soon realized that Edubamo's questions were simply to establish her identity. He apparently assumed she was sent to Nigeria to spy. He demanded to know her name, who she was associated with and what she was doing in Kaduna. It became clear to her that he needed to get enough information to identify her to a third party.

Her interrogator shouted an order in a local dialect to someone outside the tent, and soon a man in street clothes stepped in carrying a camera. The man took multiple photographs. He seemed to focus on her bruised and bloodied head. She was too exhausted to protest.

Another man entered and handed her a cup of hot tea. After a few sips, some of her spirit returned. Still afraid for her life, she decided to explain her presence in Nigeria, hoping that once it was clear that she was not a spy, she would be released.

She gave her name, and someone handed her a notepad and pencil. Edubamo, indicated that she should write her name. *Was she being held as a hostage to elicit ransom money from someone: her employer? Her parents? The U.S. Government? Oh, god. What is happening to me? Please, please make this nightmare end.* She began to wonder if she was a victim of a major conspiracy. Was this some sort of political revenge plot? For all she knew, her abduction may be related in some way to Alan's work. *Could Alan also have been abducted?*

Eventually, Commander Edubamo grunted and scribbled a few notes on a pad. *Was he finally satisfied that he had elicited enough information?* She had given her name and the fact that she was an American citizen. Against her better judgement, she had also written the fact that her husband worked for the U.S. Government and was in Cameroon. That seemed to pique the commander's interest.

Just as Mona sensed that the interrogation was about to conclude, a shout went up outside the tent. She heard the sounds of vehicles approaching. Edubamo barked orders and left the tent. Mona was lifted off her chair while someone tied her hands in front of her, and placed the repulsive dust and sweat-covered hood over her head. A gruff militant unceremoniously pushed her out of the tent and led her away. She tried to turn toward the noisy commotion, but the guard roughly brushed up against her and pushed her with his chest in the opposite direction.

Mona stumbled, but her escort caught her arm and pulled her upright, his other hand sliding into the space where her shirt had lifted. Anger fired in her veins as the guard's hand touched her bare skin. Mona jerked away, and swung her bound hands at the guard's head. She missed, and again received a hard slap on her head. She heard a raspy shout from some distance away.

Is this where they shoot me? Dazed and confused she heard laughter from other male voices as she was pushed forward.

Mona sensed the fading light through her hood, as the evening sun inched below the trees to the west. A militant pulled the hood off, and she studied her surroundings in dismay. She was led to a rugged enclosure framed with thorn branches that formed a corral on three sides with a natural rock wall on the fourth. The prison was partially hidden by low trees and shrubs. She saw several armed men in camouflage uniforms, with heads wrapped in *shemaghs* guarding the makeshift prison. Many pairs of eyes looked up from inside the thorny corral as one guard undid a rope latch and opened an improvised gate. Several African women and young school-age girls rose to their feet, and stared at Mona. Two young men sat on the ground in a far corner of the prison, their heads remained down as a militant pushed Mona into the rickety stockade.

Turning around to face one of the soldiers, Mona asked, "Where am I? What are you doing with me?" It earned her a backhand slap across her cheek that made her weakened legs fold and sent her tumbling to the dirt. A woman nearby reached out to support Mona's head and kept it from hitting the compacted red soil. The woman, wearing a bright orange and blue dress and blouse, immediately put one finger to her lips to signal Mona to remain silent. The man who struck her laughed. He closed the thatch gate and re-tied the latch. The other guards chuckled in amusement.

After several seconds Mona sat up. She felt the hard ground and wept. A drop of red landed on her lap and she realized that the guard's slap had drawn blood. Her body shook as she again considered the hopelessness of her situation. *I have no idea where I am. I don't know what or who those men represent or why I am imprisoned like a convict. I am tired. I am hungry. My body hurts everywhere, and I sit on the dirt with people who don't speak English. I can't believe there is no one to help me. Alan has no idea where I am.* She realized that even if Alan was there, he would need an army to fight off all these soldiers with guns. She felt herself slip closer toward desperation. She inhaled the cool evening air, straightened her back, and vowed to not give in to depression.

The woman who helped break Mona's fall squeezed her shoulders and softly rubbed some of the dirt off Mona's arms. Then, to Mona's surprise, she whispered in a soft, soothing tone, *"Amerika, yu?"*

Mona instantly ceased her crying and sobbed a whispered "Yes."

With teary eyes Mona turned to face the dark-skinned prisoner. Before she could clear her throat and gain enough composure to speak, the woman again placed one finger on Mona's lips and said in a conspiratorial whisper, *"Quiet, Ah beg. Dem pipo go beat all if dem see any one talk."* The woman continued in a hesitating manner while looking from side to side. *"Ah be teacha* for Hafsa school, near from here. Young girls," she said, gesturing to other prisoners with her chin, *"be ma pupil dem."* The Nigerian woman looked toward the guards and again pointed in the direction of the far corner of the enclosure with her chin. *"Tu man pikin dey fo corna also be teacha man dem. Bad man what put you here maybe be Boko Haram. Dem don burn ma village near riva tu-day past. Dem killt many pipo and burnt down dey house. Dey 'ttack ma school where I bin teach. Some dem were make prisona and bring fo dis bad, bad place."*

Mona struggled to understand the woman's pidgin, but was able to decipher enough to know that a school nearby had been attacked by the Boko Haram, and that the people around her were students and teachers.

The woman continued, *"Dei don take head man of that ma school. But yestaday dem come and took heem. Dei neva bring ee back. We don heaa gun shooting. Ah tink sey dey try make ee give up ee Christian religion and join sharia."*

Mona softly cleared her dry throat and whispered, "What are they going to do with us?"

The woman looked at Mona with sad eyes and said, *"Wit you, Ah no no. Wit us, de be small-small hope."*

CHAPTER 16
THE PRIME MINISTER

Alan sighed in disgust when Cameroon's prime minister announced that his president would not attend the eight-p.m. Tuesday meeting. The young diplomat was not averse to demonstrating his impatience. Two high-ranking U.S. Embassy officers accompanied David Steinhouse and Alan to the venue. On the other side of the table, two Cameroonian army generals joined the prime minister, posing stern and business-like.

Alan whispered to David as they entered the room, "Something about those stiff expressions doesn't bode well." David waved Alan off with a frown.

David introduced his staff and shook hands with the Cameroonians. He then sat at the conference table and began by announcing that the U.S. ambassador was on his way to Cameroon, and that the U.S. president sent his condolences for the loss of life in the Sunday raid in Yaoundé. He said, "We are here on behalf of the president and the secretary of state to offer assistance from the United States.

The military generals appeared to understand David's English. They stated that the president and prime minister had already taken steps to track down the people who committed the atrocity, and that Cameroon would take full control of the situation. The prime minister stated that the government of France would assist Cameroon.

"I'm sure you are aware," David interjected, "that France's president notified the U.S. president that they are expecting the U.S. to initiate action."

The P.M. did not smile. "As you know," David continued, "our countries recently agreed on installing a small detachment of U.S. troops in Garoua, in northern Cameroon. That unit is staffed and operational. With your president's permission we could assist with satellite surveillance to track the terrorists."

With a wave of his hand the P.M. dismissed that idea. His translator informed the Americans that Sunday's incident in Yaoundé was this countries concern, and the government of Cameroon could handle the situation.

During the drive back to the embassy Alan was furious. "I can't believe those people! They wrote us off without even trying to work together."

David held up a calming hand and said, "Most countries guard their national sovereignty. Pressuring the Cameroonians to allow the Americans to intervene is a sensitive matter. It's better to back off for now."

It was about three in the afternoon in D.C. when David initiated a call to the secretary of state. Lisa Townshend answered immediately, and was not surprised to learn that Cameroon's officials were ambivalent. There was not much the U.S. could do without the consent of the host country.

Alan was given temporary quarters in a room at the embassy. He walked with David to the Steinhouse residence where he nibbled at a barbequed-steak dinner with the Steinhouse family. His attempts at friendly conversation were distracted by thoughts of Mona. He politely thanked his host and hostess and excused himself. He returned to his quarters to get badly needed sleep. He hoped to receive word from Mona, but her number was now silent. He dropped into a fitful slumber close to midnight. At half past one in the morning, he leapt for his buzzing phone.

"Good afternoon, Alan, Ben Warner here. I apologize for calling at this hour, but I have some information you asked for." Ben gave Alan the names and other information of Mona's intended contacts in Lagos. He also stated that his office in Paris had already contacted Mr. Albert Achebe, the attorney in Lagos. "Mona was investigating a company called US-Toys. When she called Monday, she asked me for authorization to travel on Tuesday to the city of Kaduna. I called Achebe today, but he had not heard from Mona since their meeting on Monday."

Damn, thought Alan, *I should have insisted that I be the one to call the contacts.* "Where is Kaduna? Did you authorize that travel?"

"Kaduna is north of Abuja, the capitol," Ben replied. "Several hours' drive from Abuja."

"Oh, my God." exclaimed Alan. "Why the hell was she going there? She was doing your work. What the hell, Ben? Why did you allow her to travel to Kaduna? Sending her there was negligent on your part." Alan's temperature rose, his anger flared. He instinctively knew that Mona was in some kind of trouble. Sweat soaked his under shirt as his voice pitched in panic. He felt helpless.

"Alan," Ben said. "Yes, she was attempting to investigate a company that is a subject of our firm's product-infringement case. We thought the company was in Lagos, but, according to Mona, they moved to Kaduna to avoid prosecution. We knew US-Toys was suspected of violating international law but we have no reason to believe they were capable of violence or terrorist acts."

Alan wasn't convinced. He suspected that directly or indirectly Ben's firm had encouraged Mona to pursue her target beyond Lagos.

"I understand your concern," Ben said, "and you have good reason to be upset, but know that we instructed Mona to remain in Lagos until her escort arrived. That was supposed to be today. You have to assume that Mona is okay. Maybe the hotel she is staying in doesn't have good telephone service."

"Bull shit." Spat Alan. "You know how resourceful Mona is. She would find a way to communicate. I just know something is wrong.

Hell, Ben. Put two and two together," he shouted into the phone. "She is a woman, traveling in a violent country. She is not answering her cell phone. No one has heard from her in three days. Look, Ben, I've got to find a way to do something to locate her. I'm hanging up now, but please, when you hear any news, call me. I don't care what time of day it is. Just keep me informed." He cradled the phone slowly as he slumped into a bedside chair and placed his face into his clammy hands.

Alan jerked upright as the house phone nearby sounded a shrill jangle. His hand jabbed toward the phone, but stopped. *Could this be more bad news?* Alan's weary mind confused him. The house phone rang again. He strained to focus blurry eyes on his wristwatch. It was two a.m. Wednesday morning. With a shaky hand, he picked up the phone. David Steinhouse's urgent voice instructed Alan to meet him in thirty minutes in the embassy conference room for a call from Washington. David hung up before Alan could ask why. *What now?* His mind shifted back to the embassy's attempt to help his host country. *Does the prime minister now want our help?*

He put on the same rumpled shirt he wore yesterday, slipped on his pants and shoes and stumbled down to the conference room. David was waiting alone in the cold, wood-paneled room. A Keurig coffee maker spat out the last of a brew into a clean porcelain cup.

"How about a cup of hot coffee?" David asked with a concerned smile.

"No. Just tell me what's going on." Alan was not up for formalities at two-thirty in the morning. He was so weary that his stomach revolted at the thought of consuming anything.

Not convinced that Alan's head was clear enough for what was to come next, David said, "Secretary Townshend will call in ten minutes. She wants both of us to be present. Are you sure you don't want some coffee to wake you up at this wee hour?"

The phone buzzed. A male voice asked who was present in the room. David identified himself and Alan, and stated that no one else was present in the secure room. The voice announced the secretary of state.

David led off, "Good morning, Madam Secretary. There is a six-hour time difference, so I guess it is a late Tuesday evening for you. What can we do for you?"

"Please. Call me Lisa. And, by the way, I think the hour is more inconvenient for you. It's just a little after eight-thirty Wednesday evening here in D.C.

"Listen, I am calling because we just received information from a reliable source that will impact you both. I wish I could be with you at this moment as I'm afraid the news is not good.

"First of all, the news wires received word that the terrorist group that attacked Yaoundé on Sunday is definitely Boko Haram. We found this out in the last ninety minutes. Boko Haram claims to have two hostages. One of the hostages is the Cameroonian Treasury Minister Stany Ngey, who was abducted from the Cameroon assembly hall on Sunday. Boko Haram is demanding ransom from the government of Cameroon.

"Now, Alan, I wish I were there to tell you this in person. Please forgive me, but the second hostage is your wife, Mona."

Alan groaned and grabbed the sides of his head.

Lisa paused to give Alan a chance to digest the painful news. Then she added, "I'm terribly sorry to tell you this, Alan, and my heart goes out to both you and your wife. The terrorists gave a deadline of midnight Sunday, Nigerian time. They demand a ransom for Mrs. Burke of twenty million U.S. dollars."

Alan's jaw dropped. He felt the room sway in a nauseating motion. He grabbed the edge of the conference table and slowly lowered himself into a chair. The room felt stiflingly hot. He struggled to breathe. He sat holding his head between his hands, trying to get his breath back. His greatest fear over the last several days was realized. Since Sunday, Alan had run a thousand scenarios through his mind. He understood the dangers Mona must have faced when she traveled alone to Nigeria. *I should have known she wasn't prepared for an assignment like hers in Africa.* She spoke none of the Nigerian languages. She had to rely on the goodness of people to give her directions, and she had no idea what people would do when they followed a fanatic cause. He slumped forward in his chair and lowered his head to the hard table.

He heard the secretary of state's voice. "I am so sorry Alan. Please be assured that we will do everything we can to make sure your wife's safe return is the president's highest priority. We want to get her back home safe and sound, and we will do everything we can to try to keep her from harm. I know this is devastating news, and everyone in the State Department feels the burden of your agony. I want you to take some time off, Alan. David can deal with the embassy affairs, and Ambassador Morrison will arrive there soon."

Alan let out a soft groan. Slowly he extricated himself from his chair and, moving like a senescent man, he stood before the speaker phone. In a subdued voice he began, "Madam Secretary, Lisa, I appreciate your situation. I can't think now. I am numb. I just want to know: Cameroon is taking no action; France is waiting for the U.S. to do something; and the Cameroonians won't allow the U.S. to act. How are you going to get Mona back home safe and sound?"

For security reasons international transmissions had to be kept short. The secretary of state gave a few final instructions to David, but just before ending the call, she listed several things her office would do, including making sense of the ransom call. Alan barely heard the secretary's last words, although, his ears did pick up something about a critical mistake the kidnappers made when they sent their video transmission. It didn't register with him until later.

David and Alan sat together in the silent conference room for nearly ten minutes. Finally, David rose. strode to the Keurig, and removed the cup of tepid coffee. He placed another thimble of coffee in the machine, placed a clean cup on the stand and pressed the red button. Arabica coffee aroma drifted across the room. David turned toward Alan, who looked up with red and swollen eyes. Alan nodded and David extracted the steaming cup of brew and carried it to the conference table.

Staring at the iroko-wood-paneled walls, the two men agonized over the shocking news and discussed their options. They sipped hot coffee. They stared at maps on the wall. They fiddled with the electric motor-powered screen, and they sat and stared at their coffee cups.

Eventually, Alan stood up, and walked across the room, and back. Several times he circled the room. Finally, he stopped in front of

David's chair and said. "David. I've got to do something. I can't imagine what my wife is going through, and it's killing me. I've got to find a way to help her. We only have a few short days, and no one is giving us any help."

"Alan, I can't imagine what she is experiencing either, and what's more, I can't begin to imagine what you must be feeling. Remember what Lisa said. They will do everything in their power to get your wife back safely."

"Fuck that shit." Alan blurted. "You know there is nothing they can do without getting authority from the president of Cameroon. You know France says their hands are tied. And, you also know that even if the U.S. were to pay ransom to the Boko Haram, those fucking terrorists will still kill their hostages."

"Please calm down, Alan. There is something we can do. We can work with the Cameroon government to help them utilize available resources. We can also work with the Nigerian government through our embassy there. The Nigerian army has confronted the terrorist group in the past. I can talk to our ambassador there and ask for help."

"I'm… I'm sorry, David. It's just that everything seems so hopeless." Alan paced up and down, deep in frustrated concentration. "Those terrorists are ruthless. When government soldiers approach them they simply kill their hostages and run. People like that have absolutely no consideration for human life."

"No one could possibly understand your anguish, Alan, but it is better that we concentrate on the things we can do. At least the activity will keep our minds busy."

Alan's thoughts drifted elsewhere. He had already concluded that none of the countries relating to this hostage situation were going to take any action. He knew time was slipping away, and he imagined his terrified wife being abused by terrorists.

Suddenly, it hit him. *What was it? Yes, the secretary said the terrorists made a mistake. What was it?* "David, what mistake did Townshend say the terrorists made?"

David contorted his face in thought. Finally, his eyes lit up. "Oh, yes. Lisa said that they gave away some coordinates when they transmitted the ransom message. She didn't go into detail but suggested that the information would be helpful when we negotiate with the prime minister."

"Did she give you the coordinates? We need to know where those bastards are hiding."

"The secretary said they may have heard or seen something in the ransom transmission. She didn't give me the details. What would you do with that information? We cannot take any action without state's approval," he warned.

"I know. I know," Alan said while wiping beads of perspiration from his forehead, "but maybe we can use the information to get the local government to get off their asses and go look for them. It's all we have."

"Okay, maybe you have a point. Thing is, we have to be careful with that information, and we have to work through diplomatic channels. You know that, Alan, right?"

"Of course." Alan agreed. "Maybe we can ask the PM's office for another meeting. How do we get the location information for the Cameroonians? Can we call the secretary back? Wouldn't that be the diplomatic thing to do?"

Alan didn't mind pushing David beyond his comfort zone. Alan knew he was right, and he also knew that David should have asked for that information while the secretary was on the line. Alan stared at the wall for a long time, thinking, rationalizing a balance between his personal discomfort and his diplomatic responsibilities. Then he turned to David, wondering why he hadn't yet acted.

Alan watched the changing expressions on David's face as they both struggled with the recent facts and the limited options. Yet, the germ of an idea was forming in Alan's brain, driven by his love for his wife who was now in the hands of violent men. *What will happen if the Cameroonian or Nigerian armies took some initiative to free the hostages? How will the terrorists react? What will happen to the hostages? For that matter, what will happen to the hostages if ransoms are paid? The United States has a policy of never paying ransom money. What happens when the U.S. refuses? Can I personally pay a ransom? Even if I could round up enough money to pay a ransom, would the terrorists release Mona?*

Answers to his questions were negative and offered no vestige of hope. Alan would rather die trying to help his wife than sit in Yaoundé doing nothing. He watched as David turned toward him, a decision at hand. Alan picked up the secure phone and handed the receiver to his boss.

Lisa Townshend answered almost immediately in a clear and alert voice. "Hello again. I was beginning to think you two were not going to call back. What can I do for you?"

"Madam Secretary," David said, "you stated earlier that the terrorists may have inadvertently given away the location coordinates for the Boko Haram terrorists. That information may be helpful in our discussions with the Cameroon president."

"I quite agree. My advisors are here and will provide the information you need. I remind you, however, the Cameroonians need to be very careful how they use that information. The U.S. agreed to assist the government of Cameroon on antiterrorism, but that agreement does not extend to Nigeria. We can only provide limited information to them at this time."

Alan noted Lisa's reference to Nigeria. *Looks to me like she already knows the terrorists are somewhere in Nigeria.*

"Boko Haram will move their hostages to new and well-protected locations," Lisa continued. "They may already have moved. The good news is that we now have a fix on that spot and may be able to track future movements through satellite tracking. That assumes the governments of Cameroon and Nigeria agree, and it doesn't violate any nation's territorial rights."

"Satellite tracking's good," Alan added.

"You know that the United States does not pay ransom money, period. I'm sorry to remind you, Alan. Our efforts will be primarily diplomatic. We are working with the U.S. ambassador to Nigeria and Nigeria's presidential staff to open up discussions to persuade the terrorists to free all their hostages."

CHAPTER 17
MONA'S RANSOM MESSAGE

Shortly after 6:30 p.m. on Tuesday, December 5, a message went out to CNN and BBC network contacts in Cameroon and the United States. Bad news travels fast, and before midnight in Nigeria, much of the world learned that Boko Haram terrorists had captured and were threatening to behead two women hostages. The response was an immediate international expression of protest and outrage.

Mona tossed about on the cold ground. The chilly wind and the hard, stony earth made restful sleep impossible. The only warmth came from the fidgety bodies around her. Pitiful whimpering of the young hostages induced haunted images of a frightening, uncertain future. She squinted through the dim light and spotted the woman who had helped her. The Nigerian woman was stirring, apparently also affected by the cold. Her colorful dress appeared too thin to provide warmth, and the matching headpiece did not serve well as a blanket.

A commotion attracted Mona's attention. In the dark she saw the silhouette of a girl being forcefully removed from the enclosure. Muffled cries suspended at the sound of a slap. The guards shouted something to the remaining prisoners who cowered away.

Mona observed that the younger girls were only fifteen or sixteen years old and huddled in sympathy. She turned slowly toward the woman who had earlier spoken pidgin and whispered, "What is your name?"

"*A beg, yu fit call me* Oneka, *though is not ma true name.*"

"Oneka, that is a beautiful name. What's going on? What happened to that young girl?"

"Shhhh," admonished a nearby prisoner. Then a whispered, "*Soldier man dem watch yu.*"

After a minute of silence, Oneka responded in a whisper. "*We no know, but we fear fo girls dat bin taken. No wun come back. We wa twelve, plus three man, when dem brought we here. Now we be ten and two.*"

Mona wrung her hands thinking about the terrified girls in this makeshift prison. The cold penetrated deeper, and she began to shiver. Until that moment she had only felt concern for her own situation. Now it became clear that others suffered far greater misfortunes. Mona laid her head on the arm of Oneka and sobbed. She felt Oneka put one hand on her head to comfort her.

As light began filtering through the nearby trees on Wednesday morning, Mona's exhaustion finally brought restless sleep. But, oblivion was short. Bodies around her began to move. Through bleary eyes she saw that food was being disbursed by guards. It was only bread, but it was edible. She scrambled to her feet and urged her sore muscles to propel her toward the handouts.

With the stale bread clutched in her bound hands, she surveyed the enclosure, and noted that it was formed partially by steep, natural rock. Felled trees crisscrossed with thorny shrub branches and men with dangerous-looking weapons kept the prisoners corralled.

Counting heads, Mona noted ten girls and women, and two men. That meant that the young girl taken last night had not returned.

Mona bit off pieces of stale bread but found it difficult to swallow without water.

What is that strange odor? It reminds me of a wet puppy. Searching for the source she finally concluded that it was coming from her—and from the other prisoners. Every one of them had endured heat and dust. They slept on the bare ground, where the morning dew combined with earthly organics and sweat, concocted an irritating odor. Adding to the malodor was an area on the far side of the stockade used as a latrine.

Mona spotted Oneka huddled with two of her students. The girls wore expressions of horror. They knew that the girl taken away had not returned. Mona assumed that the girls not only feared for their virginity but for their lives. Oneka had revealed to Mona the shock the previous morning when the prisoners witnessed shouts and commotion. One of the male teachers was dragged away. That disturbance ended twenty minutes later with a gunshot.

Mona was profoundly miserable as she maneuvered to a sunny spot in the enclosure. She forced herself to permit only positive thoughts. Her sunny nature resisted the depression that threatened her. Thoughts about her family only brought tears to her eyes, and she again asked herself: *How did I get into this situation? Why was I so naïve to disregard everyone's advice?*

Just then, a guard shouted, and pointed in her direction. Oneka moved to Mona's side and said, *"They are call fo yu. You fit go. A beg, be careful what yu tak. We pray yu return safe."*

Fear froze Mona. Her spine tingled while sweat matted her clothes. Her legs refused to move. One guard opened the rickety gate and stepped inside the compound, motioning to her with agitated arm thrusts. Another guard impatiently pushed prisoners out of his way, stomped over to Mona, roughly seized her arm and half-dragged her out of the compound.

Mona wanted to fight back. Her mind told her to run. Run anywhere. It is better to be shot trying to save yourself than to be tortured, raped and summarily murdered. But her body didn't have the strength to run. She stumbled, but strong hands held her upright and forced her to walk. A hundred meters away they stopped near a cluster of canvas tents. Her interrogator from the previous evening, Commander Edubamo, was dressed in camouflage leggings and a long, olive-green shirt. Mona smelled Edubamo's sour breath as he grunted an order and pointed toward a tent. "Madam. *Yu fit get photograph. Go, clean face, now, now."*

"What?" Mona stammered in bewilderment. "You want me to do what?

"Please. Yu wash face and brush hairs. Yu de get wata dey fo inside tent. Girl dey fo inside go helup yu. Go." Then, impatiently, he shouted, *"Go. Now."*

She reluctantly stumbled toward the tent and reached for the flap, not sure what to expect. Inside, she saw a small table. A porcelain basin rested on it. On the floor, nearby was her shoulder bag, which she hadn't seen since Kaduna.

Standing at the rear of the tent was a girl who Mona considered to be about sixteen or seventeen. The girl's eyes looked down. Her bare knees trembled. The girl wore a wrinkled dress, likely a school uniform. Slowly she lifted her eyes, and she and Mona gazed at each other for a long moment, with unspoken questions.

Finally, Mona stepped toward the girl. "Do you speak English?"

The girl shied away, then slowly nodded, and finally said, "Small, small."

A purple bruise on the girl's temple suggested a recent beating. "Are you the one who was taken from the enclosure last night?"

Tears streamed down the girl's cheeks. She nodded again, hesitating, as though not sure of the white woman's intentions. She picked up a wash cloth, held it out, and pointed to the water in the basin. *"Ah beg. Yu wash now."*

Mona considered the dried sweat on her arms, back and legs. She shook her head in wonder at the anomalous thought of this traumatized child assigned to help her clean up. *Oh, for a hot steamy bath, a change of underwear and some clean clothes.* She struggled with the strangeness of her situation, but was too tired and exhausted to think, or argue. She accepted the proffered wash cloth, and carefully sponged the dried blood off her face and arms. Water stung when it touched the abrasion on her cheek.

She rummaged through her carry-on, noting that some personal things, including her fresh underwear, were missing. "Shoot, where are my panties? Damn. I need clean underwear." Remaining were the extra pair of slacks and the shirt she had recently purchased in D.C., a hair brush, and her makeup kit. Checking the tent flap for privacy, she washed herself as thoroughly as she could, changed clothes and brushed grass and dirt from her hair. Feeling slightly better, she turned toward the girl.

Mona pointed to herself and spoke slowly, "Mona. My name is Mona." Stressing her words clearly and pointing to the girl she asked, "What is your name?"

The girl looked fearfully toward the tent flap. She seemed to understand the question, but hesitated. After a moment, she softly uttered, "Chioma."

Mona smiled. She desperately wanted to communicate. She now knew two people in the camp: Oneka and Chioma.

The voice of Commander Edubamo jolted her when he shouted from outside. "Come yu, now. Quick. *Camera mon ee ready'o.*"

Mona reached for Chioma's hand. Suddenly, the girl lunged toward Mona and gave her a strong hug, sobbing. Mona thought that Chioma sensed that her own fate was sealed, and that Mona, an American, may be her last friendly human contact.

Chioma's tears and sobs were muffled against Mona's shirt. She pulled back slowly and stammered, "*A, Ah beg, tak fo miz Oneka that Ah be fayne.*"

Then, to Mona's surprise, Chioma spoke in a mixture of French and Pidgin English to state that during the previous night she saw another female prisoner. "*Dem army mon don take some madame minster fo Cameroon. A bin hear dem make her sit fo tent, close dat ma own. Una tak small French when guards no look'a. Dem don kill peepo for Yaounde, and dey don beat madame minister, bad.*" Then, the young girl pleaded, "Yu *fit go now.*"

"Wait," Mona pleaded, as her eyes moistened. She feared what might happen to Chioma, and sensed that her own chance of survival was better than this young girl's. She hugged the girl tightly. Then she gripped Chioma's shoulders and said, "Chioma. Please have faith. You must believe that you will survive this." Their eyes met in hopeful gazes. "Thank you for being my friend." The girl pulled away slowly and nodded. Mona tried to make sense of Chioma's story as she turned to leave the tent. *Who is this Cameroon hostage? What kind of minister is she?*

It all came together before Mona reached the tent entrance. The television news reports she had seen in Lagos spoke of two terrorist attacks. One was about the destruction of a village. *That must have been Hafsa, which Oneka spoke of.* The second was the raid in Yaounde where a woman minister was abducted. *That must be the minister Chioma refers to.*

Edubamo was pacing outside the tent when Mona emerged. His wry grin indicated approval of Mona's appearance. He grabbed her arm and nudged her toward another tent. Inside she was forced to kneel. The commander propped three flags behind Mona and positioned a lantern to shed soft light on her face. Mona nervously glanced at the flags near her and shuddered. She recalled several CNN videos of al-Qaeda terrorists where they threatened American and British prisoners. Those prisoners lost their heads.

At the commander's order, the cameraman shot still pictures of Mona with the flags of ISIL, al-Qaeda and Boko Haram propped to demonstrate that she was indeed captive of a feared Islamic terrorist organization.

After a dozen photos, the commander thrust a sheet of paper at her and said, "*Read loud, fo camera. Yu fit read words one time before. Then, we make fine video.*"

Mona struggled to read the scrawled text. The words identified her as an American spy and a prisoner of Boko Haram. It stated that she was being treated fairly, but that her life was in danger and subject to a price. The script demanded that the United States pay twenty million U.S. dollars for her release.

After grasping the gist of the text, Mona glared at Edubamo, controlling the true feelings of hate that welled. *So, this is why I was abducted and brought here. This is why I washed my face. This is why they took photographs.* She realized that announcement of her abduction may already have been sent to the U.S. *For all I know the world already knows I was abducted. Maybe even Alan knows. He must be wondering where I am. I wish I were with him in Cameroon.* She grabbed a handful of her long, dark hair and sobbed in self-pity.

Remembering the girls in the pen, she knew that she was not the only victim. *What about Oneka, and those poor school girls? Are their lives*

not worth a ransom? How can I help them? How can I send a message to Alan?
Hell, suppose I refuse to read this stupid message?

The commander exclaimed, *"Time don pass. Sit fo chair. Read fo camera*
now."

Looking up, Mona saw that the video camera was aimed at her
and was already recording. She looked again at the wrinkled paper,
noting that her captors did not understand English well. She thought,
maybe they don't know French. Suddenly, it occurred to her what she had
to do. She squinted at the paper and shook her head, pretending it
was difficult to read. She constructed several French sentences in her
mind, but began in English, adding some text of her own.

"My name is Mona Morgan Burke. I am a citizen of the United
States. I am a prisoner of Boko Haram. Mister Yusuf Edubamo, near
Hafsa, claims that I ama spy for the United States."

When Mona named the village of Hafsa, the commander looked
alarmed. He stretched forward, out of camera range, as if to inspect
the script. Mona shrugged her shoulders and gave a befuddled look,
to suggest that she was reading the script as best as she could.
Edubamo's suspicious frown suggested that he thought she might be
improvising. He glared, maybe resenting the title of mister instead of
commander.

"I am being treated well. You must pay twenty million U.S. dollars
to Boko Haram or they will cut off my head."

Mona inhaled deeply as she visualized her head falling on the tent
floor, then, in her best French, said,

"Je vous conseille de ne pas les payer." (I advise you not to pay them).

"Stop." Shouted Edubamo, pointing to the cameraman. The red
light went out. Turning in fury toward Mona he said, *"What kayn tak*
you de tak? Ee no be English."

"Sir," Mona said in a reproachful voice, "The Cameroon minister
and her people speak French. I am trying to help her people also
understand."

"How you know? How you know about minister?"

"Sir, it doesn't matter. I know."

The commander rubbed his thoroughly confused-looking face.
His eyes indicated mistrust. Mona studied the commander intently.

Finally, he shrugged his shoulders and indicated to her and to the cameraman to continue.

Mona, pretending to translate from the paper, said,

"*Douze prisonniers de Hafsa sont ici.*" (Twelve Hafsa prisoners are here). "Boko Haram *a également un ministre Camerounais*" (Boko Haram also holds a Cameroon minister.) "*Nous sommes près de Hafsa et six heures de Michika.*" (We are close to Hafsa and six hours from Michika.)

Switching back to English she concluded, "The Boko Haram demands twenty million U.S. dollars in four days."

The commander angrily shouted, "Stop."

In his dialect, he loudly summoned someone from outside the tent. A tall, bulky figure dressed in black burst in. Shrouded in a black hood with cutouts for eyes and nose, he looked like the grim reaper. His hands were gloved in black leather, and one hand held an ominous-looking ten-inch, shimmering steel blade.

Mona's breathing stopped, startled by this huge figure. She sensed that something dreadful was about to happen. She started to rise from her chair when a gloved hand grabbed her by the nape of her neck and forced her to her knees. Gravel beneath the canvas floor sent shock waves up her spine. When the hooded figure grabbed a handful of her hair, she was nearly overcome by the body odor coming from the sweaty, frightening creature. She felt the urge to vomit.

Mona saw the red light on the video camera go on as her head was being forced to one side to give the long knife a better angle. She was startled to hear a heavy male voice speak English. Mona lost her will to fight. She screamed. She began to sob as her remaining courage dissipated.

The executioner addressed the camera. "America. Look. See this wretched woman whore. She is an infidel spy. And, she has committed a grave sin against Allah. She defiles herself by shamefully moving in public with no head cover. Her name is Mona Burke. Her life is in the hands of your people. I, the avenger of sins against Allah and my people, will take her life as you watch. With this weapon, I will remove her spying head from her worthless body. I will deliver her head to your president and I will burn her body in the fires. I give you four days, ninety-six hours, to decide if her life is worth my demand. You will give twenty million dollars by midnight Lagos time. I repeat, Boko Haram demands twenty million United States dollars by Sunday midnight, Lagos time."

The executioner gave contact information and shouted, "Allahu Akbar."

With those words, he pushed Mona's head so hard that she sprawled to the canvas floor. There she sobbed in a pathetic heap. The commander shouted to several men who picked Mona off the floor and half carried her to the stockade.

CHAPTER 18
DIPLOMATS IN DISARRAY

Alan scoffed at the suggestion that diplomacy could convince a terrorist to hand over its hostages. "Play nice" doesn't enter into a fanatic's lexicon. He watched as David Steinhouse recorded the coordinates and other information provided by the staff. Alan committed to memory everything David jotted down. Alan could read coordinates and was impatient to act on what diplomacy couldn't.

Later that Wednesday morning, Cameroon's prime minister confirmed a meeting for three p.m. It was after four before the appropriate government and military staff were assembled. The PM arrived, listened to David, and adjourned the meeting with a perfunctory dismissal of the new information. He said that the president was unable to send his army on a premature chase across the countryside, and that he had no authority to cross the borders of Cameroon's neighbors. His generals explicitly rejected U.S. soldiers or drones crossing into Nigeria on Cameroon's behalf.

Alan, disgusted with diplomatic delay, groaned dramatically, with little attempt to conceal his disappointment. David placed a firm hand on Alan's arm to keep him from displaying more emotion. Such outbursts could be considered rude and undiplomatic. In spite of

David's warning, Alan rose from his seat, glared at the Cameroonians, and stomped out of the meeting. He bolted past the security guards, out the front entrance and climbed into the embassy car.

The embassy driver commented, "*Yu no look happy. Yu no like parle' wit* PM? *Dem govment pipo vex yu so?*

The words were barely out of the driver's mouth when an idea occurred to Alan. Looking out the limo window he saw that his group were still chatting near the building entrance. He leaned toward the front seat and asked, "Do you know a driver by the name of Eric Mbando?"

"*Eric? Yes sah. Eric, na he ma frien, dat. He be first-class driver-cum-mechanic. Everybody know he. He no be for dis place, but he de come here many time. Yestaday I si heem in Mfoundi Market. Yu want I should fine heem?*"

Relieved to learn that Eric was still in Yaoundé Alan said, "Can you locate Eric? I would appreciate if you could give him a message. Here is my card. I, ah, I left something in his car. I need to get it back." Alan considered Eric to be mature, honest and trustworthy, and he knew his way around Cameroon. Eric was the only person Alan knew who might help him.

"*Yessah. I go find heem, now, now. When I get fo finish wok-o.*"

Just then the limo door opened. David Steinhouse sat next to Alan. "Hey, Alan, I know we didn't get very far in there with the PM, but you have to think positive. One other thing, as your officer-in-charge I have to say, please don't ever show that kind of disrespect for the local government officials. I understand that you're going through a lot of stress, but your actions in there may have set our relations with the Cameroon government back several years. We are trying to build a positive foundation for future cooperation. Your show of discontent was noted by everyone in the room. I stayed back to explain to the PM's chief of staff about your wife's abduction. I hope that smooths things over for now."

Alan pushed his glasses up on his nose and snapped, "Dammit David. These people are driving me nuts. I've had it with their pussyfooting around. For Christ's sake. My wife's life is at stake."

David drew back, eyes wide.

Alan quickly stated, "I'm sorry for jumping on you, but I'm frustrated. I know I was rude in there, but those jerks aren't doing anything to find their own minister."

A pall clouded the occupants during the drive back to the embassy.

Alan went straight to his office, closed the door, and sat with his head in his hands. He wept with frustration.

A knock on his door twenty minutes later startled him. He dried his eyes, cleared his throat, and said in a shaky voice, "Yes. Come in."

David looked serious. *Was there more bad news?*

"Alan, you okay?" When Alan nodded, David sat down, hesitated, and finally continued.

"Alan, I'm truly sorry for what has happened here, and the predicament your wife is in. Still I need to tell you something. We just received a transmission from D.C. The news is not good."

Suspecting the worst, Alan sat up straight and stared at David. "What? What is it?"

David stared at the ceiling searching for the right words, then said, "The BBC and CNN ran stories. There are two videos. Boko Haram stated that they are holding two hostages. One is Cameroon's minister of the treasury. The other is your wife."

Alan jumped up. "Have you seen them? Is Mona shown in them? Has she been harmed? I need to see the report and the videos."

"Okay, okay. I assumed you would, so I asked Steve to download them. At this point, your wife is a hostage but is alive. Boko Haram demands $20,000,000 for her safe release. They are also asking a huge sum for the Cameroonian hostage. Frankly, the local government hasn't committed to paying any ransom and you know the U.S. doesn't negotiate with terrorists."

Alan's eyes grew wide with anger and pain. "Is there any more information on where the kidnappers are located?" He paced the room wringing his hands. "Did they say they would return my wife safely if the ransom is paid? What if I paid the ransom?" He plunked into a chair. "Oh God. How did she get into this situation?"

"I don't know. Even if you had access to that much money," David said, "the terrorists might not honor their agreement, even for an innocent woman." David's cell phone buzzed. "Yes, Steve." He turned to Alan and said, "The download is ready. Let's go."

Alan watched the CNN reporter announce, "Breaking news from Nigeria, Africa." Alan stood and nervously moved toward the large screen, a chilling thought made him shiver. When the video flickered on the screen his legs nearly gave way. The image was dark and poorly focused, but he saw a hooded man holding a long knife above a kneeling figure. The man's left hand roughly grasped the woman's hair, forcing her head down. For a moment Alan wasn't certain that the person was Mona. He hoped it was someone else.

Then the man spoke in a rough, muffled voice and jerked the head up, displaying the fear-stricken face. Alan gasped. There was no longer any doubt. The victim was Mona. She looked terrified. Alan collapsed into a chair.

The visible bruises on Mona's face and the scrapes on her arms caused Alan to wince in sympathetic pain. The stress lines on Mona's features burned a terrifying image. He knew Mona as a gentle and kind person, intelligent and creative, with a pleasant and loving nature. To see her treated in this barbaric manner tore at his heart. His thoughts erupted in a vow for vengeance.

The CNN newscaster introduced a second video. Alan winced when he heard Mona's voice. She spoke in English as she read from a crumpled paper in her hand. She abruptly switched to French. *What did she say? She wasn't looking at the paper.* The video ended. Alan shouted, "What did she say in French? Please re-run that second video." The CNN report ignored most of the French dialogue, but focused on the fact that the victim was a United States citizen, was a woman, and that Boko Haram demanded twenty million dollars.

The technician ran the video multiple times. Alan strained to glean everything he could from every pixel, every syllable, and every change in body language. *Why didn't I spend more time learning French? Why did she change to French?* He asked David if someone could translate.

"Of course," David said, "we work in a French-speaking country."

Staff conferred, translated Mona's French, and presented the result. Alan pored over every word, surprised to learn that there were a dozen other hostages. Then his eyes lit on *Hafsa. Of course. Hafsa is the Nigerian village that was attacked last Sunday.* "This says that the terrorists are camped near *Hafsa*. Do we have a map of Nigeria?" He used the internet to get longitude and latitude readings for Hafsa. He compared those with the coordinates David received earlier from the State Department, and found that they were very close.

Embassy staff helped Alan locate the village on a map. "What do you know about the Cameroon and Nigerian border area?" Alan asked, anxiously, thinking about what Eric told him about the proximity of Bamenda to the Nigerian border. Field staff were well-versed in diplomatic relations between the two countries, but none of them knew much about the actual border security. Alan made mental notes of everything he saw and heard. He reviewed the two videos several more times. He noted the times they were filmed and found that Mona's statement was recorded before the video with the potential executioner. Though relieved to see Mona alive, he was deeply alarmed to see how cruelly she was being treated.

David sternly motioned Alan away from the video room. In a private office, he closed the door and said, "Alan, you are becoming too concerned about details. I'm not sure what you are thinking, but we should leave the liberation efforts to the authorities." Eyeing Alan he added, "I'm placing you on administrative leave." After a moment he added, "I will make sure you are kept informed of every development."

Right, and what authorities would that be who will liberate my wife? Alan reluctantly left the room and returned to his office to study maps. It was late in the day and most of the embassy staff were leaving for the day. His cell phone rang thirty minutes later. David invited him to his residence for dinner. "I think it would be good for you to get away from the embassy for an hour or two, have a healthy meal and relax, maybe with a glass of wine."

Alan politely refused, saying he was too exhausted to be good company. He would just catch up on personal emails then try to get a good night's sleep. "Have a nice evening."

In the building's eerie quiet, Alan tried to wrap his head around the visuals he had just seen and the ransom message he heard. *According to these maps, Mona could be just three hundred miles from me. She is being treated badly, and her life is in serious danger. The U.S. doesn't pay ransom, so her life is definitely at risk. The Cameroon government leaders and military haven't been able to help their minister. I'm not sure how dedicated they are to taking action or whether their forces would be sophisticated enough to be of much help even if they knew what to do.* His thoughts were interrupted by his cell phone.

It was the USAID driver.

Eric apologized for calling so late, and asked, *"Yu leff something dey fo car? Ah no fit see anything dey fo moto."*

"Thanks for calling back, Eric. Actually, I didn't leave anything in your car. Listen, is there some place we can meet? I'm thinking of going on a mission, and I need your advice." They agreed to meet one block from the embassy gate in half an hour. Eric sounded concerned but intrigued with Alan's mysterious request.

When Eric approached from a side street, Alan recognized his short, well-filled-out frame and perfectly round head before recognizing Eric's face. They greeted and walked toward a small, nearby park. When they sat side-by-side on a bench the dramatic contrast between Alan's six-foot-two and Eric's five-foot-six nearly disappeared. Their skin colors, however, made an interesting contrast.

"I was afraid you had already left Yaoundé. Thanks for agreeing to meet me."

Eric replied, "That is not a problem, sir. I was delayed in Yaoundé because of a *krai dai*. I have taken leave. I return to Douala in two days."

Alan's face contorted into a wrinkled frown and he asked, "I'm sorry, did you say *cry die?*

"Oh, sorry sir, but here in Cameroon it is my people's words for a death celebration."

"I'm sorry to know you lost a loved one."

"Thank you, sir, but the celebration brought many family and friends together for good memories."

Alan shook his head and smiled. He cleared his throat, adjusted his glasses and began, "Eric, in the car on the trip to Bamenda, you told me that you grew up in Nigeria? You said that you crossed the border between Cameroon and Nigeria. I want you to tell me what you know about a place called Hafsa."

Eric's eyes focused on Alan, as though he had already guessed what was going on. Alan was relieved to see that Eric didn't frown. While driving from Douala to Bamenda, Alan had told Eric about his wife traveling in Nigeria. Eric witnessed the numerous attempts Alan made to call Mona, so it was probably easy to assume that the questions had something to do with her.

Alan explained everything he had learned that afternoon about Mona's capture by the Islamic terrorists and their demand for a large ransom. Life on the African continent had challenged its inhabitants too many times to cause surprise over one more hostile act. Thus, Eric looked concerned, but not overly surprised.

Alan felt comfortable sharing the details about Mona's abduction with Eric. He couldn't say why, but he felt more relaxed speaking with Eric than with embassy staff. Eric, at least, appeared to pay attention, and he made sounds and gestures that Alan took as concern and understanding.

Alan and Eric talked late into the evening. Alan asked dozens of questions about the border between Cameroon and Nigeria. He wanted to know about road conditions and bridges, distances and travel times. He asked about the towns in Eastern Nigeria. He asked about border patrols and customs checkpoints. Alan even asked about the general attitude of the villagers along the Cameroon border. Eric was able to identify the areas in Nigeria where Boko Haram activity was greatest.

Eric's eyes seemed to sparkle with interest as he listened to Alan's developing plan. It was as though he sensed an adventure in the making. Alan was encouraged by Eric's rapt attention. The man had been a good choice to work with. He seemed resourceful, and made good suggestions, being quick to point out weaknesses in the plan and equally quick to suggest alternatives.

Fear of Boko Haram alarmed all Cameroonians, some to the point of paranoia. Eric insisted that it was his duty to protect his family and friends from the savage cruelty of the terrorists. Alan was surprised when Eric waved off his promise of a considerable sum for driving him to the Nigerian border. He only asked that Alan cover all the vehicle expenses.

They shook hands when they parted in agreement on a plan for the next two days.

CHAPTER 19
BURNING HAFSA

The U.S. Embassy in Yaoundé stirred with action on Thursday morning. Steinhouse sent a car to Douala to meet Ambassador Morrison. As soon as the driver left for the four-hour drive, Alan used his cell phone to call David's office number.

"Hey, David, I'm going nuts worried about Mona. I'm taking your advice and staying out of the office. I'll check in for any updates. I feel totally helpless, not much good to you. Call me the minute you get any news."

"Sure, Alan. Good idea. It's in the hands of capable people. Maybe you could be checking out the housing situation. Try not to worry."

Alan clicked off. "Try not to worry. Humph," he said to the muted instrument. "You try not to worry with your wife a captive of bloody terrorists."

He grabbed his jacket and set off, ostensibly to look for breakfast. The morning was already warm and the streets were full of women carrying baskets on their heads, progressing toward the market place. Girlish laughter made him wonder how they could laugh today. But, of course, they don't know.

Alan was determined to act. If governments couldn't save his wife, he would at least try, even if he had to break a few rules. He had a plan, and now he had time and resources to carry it out.

He met Eric in a commercial area a half-mile from the embassy. The two spent most of Thursday shopping. Eric suggested several stores that sold camping and hiking gear. Alan picked out a good pair of hiking boots, a long length of climbing rope, a compass, some waterproof containers, maps, a camping shovel and a folding knife. At a grocery store he stocked up on two dozen bottles of water, beef jerky and other packaged snacks.

They loaded provisions into an older Peugeot 404 wagon Eric had managed to borrow. Alan insisted on having the car checked out by a good mechanic. Eric reminded Alan that he was a good mechanic and had already satisfied himself that the car was in reasonably good condition. *"Cept, say, that rubber ee be a bit smooth'o."*

Alan kicked several tires, grunted his disappointment and told Eric to get new rubber. It was late afternoon before a local garage found and mounted four new mud and snow tires and serviced the spare. Alan and Eric ate dinner at a chicken house, and they each retired early.

Before six Friday morning the two conspirators navigated the road leading out of Yaoundé toward Bafoussam. From there they turned north and followed the same tarred highway they had recently traveled to Bamenda. Highway security was vigilant, but the experienced travelers were able to get through the checkpoints with little inconvenience.

They stopped for fuel and food in Bamenda. Around one in the afternoon they started toward the Ring Road, but soon turned west and south through a small town named Bali. A security check there delayed them for twenty minutes, while gendarmes insisted on explanations for the unusual assortment of food and sports paraphernalia in the car. Since the Nigerian terrorists may have passed this way on Sunday, Alan asked an English-speaking officer about unusual traffic, but the man simply shrugged his shoulders and waved them through.

The recently-built road to the city of Mamfe moved traffic swiftly through the tall trees that blocked the late afternoon sun. Toward evening they arrived at the Cross River, about seventy-five kilometers from the Nigerian border. The dense, humid air was stifling. Valuable timber had been hauled from these forests by the Germans many years ago. Alan recalled his discussions with Len Watson when he spotted a red stinkwood tree, surrounded by a tall, protective fence to keep poachers out. They stopped briefly for food and fuel then moved on. Numerous buses and heavily loaded trucks passed in both directions, carrying people and commerce across the Cameroon-Nigeria border.

"We are lucky it is not the rainy season," Eric said. "The new road ends soon, and sometimes the road between here and Nigeria can be troublesome." The car bounced in and around deep depressions in the dirt road, as he observed, "We are also lucky that it is peaceful today. There have been serious riots recently, with many people killed."

"Are you referring to the riots by people of the Anglophone regions against the treatment from the national government? I'm sorry that people are being killed over a language dispute."

"Yes sir. Soldiers killed many people from the Northwest and Southwest Regions. Some have fled in fear to the forests in Nigeria. Thousands of people are unhappy. The government says we must teach our children in French language, and the courts will only accept arguments in French. Some people here want their own independent state. They already call it Ambazonia."

"Shoot, Eric. I knew there was disagreement, but I didn't realize how serious it has become. I saw some burned villages earlier, but I assumed they were torched by the terrorists."

"No," Eric said, "the fighting within Cameroon has become very serious."

"Eric. Stop the car before we get near the border," Alan said. "I don't have a visa for Nigeria, and I don't want to hassle with border patrol agents." He explained that he planned to walk across the border at some remote spot far from the checkpoints.

When Eric pulled the car onto the shoulder a while later, Alan got out and began stuffing gear into a backpack. Eric stopped him. "Sir. Leave your things. I will drive you."

"No way, Eric. You've completed your part of the bargain. I will go alone from here. There are taxis and cars to rent in Nigeria. Here is the money I promised you. Thank you so much for your help. I hope to see you back in Cameroon when this is over."

Eric protested, "Sir, I cannot let you go alone into Nigeria. It is dangerous for a lone traveler. We will soon be in heavy jungle. You do not know the roads, or the language. There are rivers to cross. I will take you to a place near to your destination. You cannot carry all this many gear to a town to find transport. There are no taxis, and we are still far from Hafsa. Also, no driver would pick you and not report you, maybe to the terrorists themselves. Those people burned villages, robbed and murdered my people. I want to help you get back your wife. I need to get my revenge."

Surprised at Eric's firm reaction, Alan looked at the dark, forbidding forest guarding the roadway. an unseen creature jostled the foliage not far off the road. The muggy air combined with eerie noises made him shiver and reconsider.

Eric had only agreed to get Alan close to the Nigerian border. It was comforting to think that he could also get him into Nigeria, but Alan could not let him risk getting hurt. Alan had assumed that he could pay someone to keep him from having to carry his climbing and camping gear a hundred and fifty kilometers. He knew, however, that Eric was correct about running into the wrong people. "Eric," he said, "what I am planning to do is dangerous. You have family in Bamenda. You cannot risk your life or safety for my problem. My wife is my only family, and her life is in serious danger, so I've got to do something, I can't have you risk your life as well. You already lived up to your part. Now, I must do the rest."

"No sir." Eric insisted. "This is also about my life and my people. My mother *born* her children in Nigeria, and they have given that country their *lifes*. I no want terrorists spoil my parents' memory. I have to fight for my people. I *fit* bring you to Hafsa."

The two men studied each other for several moments. Alan wavered between sending Eric home, and accepting his offer of help. Eric solved the stalemate with his resolute response, in pidgin. "*Na, ma pipo don say, 'Wan an no fit tai bundle.'* (One hand cannot tie a bundle) We need help in this world to get the work done. I am here to be your second hand. *Na, we fit go fo befo.*" Alan remembered the phrase, and with those words, Eric shifted the Peugeot into gear and Alan hopped back in.

It was dark when they arrived at the border station. The headlights of the car eventually picked up a sign that indicated they were leaving Cameroon. To Alan's surprise, there was nothing but the burnt-out remains of two guardhouses and some strewn rubble and garbage to indicate that there had ever been a border check point. A whiff of smoke from smoldering timbers suggested that the fire was not that old. Alan looked at Eric and saw shock and fear in his eyes.

Most vehicles only slowed as they approached the checkpoint. Seeing that the gate lay broken on the side of the road they picked up speed and continued down the road. A few drivers had stopped and shook their heads as they stared at the devastating scene.

Alan gasped when he realized that this was where the terrorists had crossed with their kidnapped Cameroonian minister. He got out of the car to see if there was any evidence of life. Amid the charred remains of the guardhouse, illuminated by the Peugeot's headlights, there were no bodies, but there were signs of a struggle and traces of dried blood. Remains of charred tires on a blackened motorcycle sent wisps of putrid smoke slowly drifting skyward. Alan guessed that the Nigerian and Cameroonian authorities had removed the bodies, but had not yet replaced the guard patrol. *If they removed the bodies, the Cameroon authorities in Yaoundé must have known the terrorists passed this way. Why didn't the prime minister's staff inform us?*

If the United States' drone surveillance in northern Cameroon had been doing its job, it would have detected this tragedy and reported it. Why didn't my own government disclose this?

Alan began to understand the extreme treachery of the terrorists. The scene was horribly unreal. *Something I have never seen or hope to see again. Imagine that less than a week ago innocent people brutally lost their lives here.*

Eric slowly drove past the ruins and across the border. Alan urged Eric to pick up speed, and they drove off through the dark forest of Cross River National Park. Eric turned north at Ikom and made good time on a paved highway. Taking turns at the wheel, they drove another ten hours before they stopped for rest. The few villagers moving about eyed Alan and Eric suspiciously and spoke in whispers. "These villages appear nervous," Alan said. "I'm not surprised, seeming that outsiders must appear as threats, considering that terrorists destroyed villages and murdered people not far from here."

Eric spotted a self-service petrol pump and filled the car's tank, while Alan found tea and biscuits at a nearby stand. The attendant accepted Cameroon's CFA currency, and became more sociable once he saw that the travelers did not carry weapons or appear aggressive. Alan had learned that the CFA is a currency used in several west and central African countries but not Nigeria. The CFA is guaranteed by the French treasury. After a short rest, Alan and Eric continued their journey toward Hafsa.

As the sun broke above the eastern horizon on Saturday morning, they saw a road sign that indicated the village of Hafsa was fifteen kilometers away. They began to see more traffic. A cluster of white tents bearing bright red crescents caught their attention. Eric explained that the Red Crescent and Red Cross were related organizations, both provided humanitarian aid.

Beyond the tents and trucks, they saw military vehicles and personnel. Further on was the burnt-out village of Hafsa, where building after building was marred with black smoke stains above the windows and doorways. In other places they saw rings of charred debris where once stood grass homes.

Grieving villagers lined up near two white and red trucks. Alan spotted uniformed soldiers milling around two gray personnel carriers and a Red Crescent panel truck.

Hafsa had been leveled. Piles of rubble were scattered on the ground. Several survivors lingered outside a shattered mud-brick building that may have once housed a school. They moaned and held each other. In the distance, under the embrace of a large, leafless tree, was a huge stack of wooden coffins. An unseen human wailed a long, sorrowful cry of despair. Several soldiers moved about, apparently attempting to restore some order for the community. Workmen constructed temporary housing for the homeless villagers.

Eric stopped the car twenty meters from a group of soldiers. The Nigerians had been squatting next to a military vehicle, but grasped their weapons and stood facing the approaching car as if to determine if it contained a threat. Eric said, "*I go parle'* with the soldier man. *Yu fit wait fo moto.*"

From the car's windows Alan nervously scanned the horizon. Every nerve in his body was on full alert. He realized that he could be near the Boko Haram encampment where Mona was being held. He was sure that she had called out to him through the CNN video. That was just three days ago. *Could the terrorists still be nearby?* Terrorists would not stay in one place more than a couple of days. Boko Haram was being hunted by the Nigerian army and would surely move camp. Army officers must have made the same connection he did when they heard the French portion of Mona's ransom statement.

Would U.S. satellites have picked up the camp's location and tracked its movements? He wished he had a satellite communication radio so that he could know what was happening. Suppose the U.S. agreed to pay a ransom and Mona was already free? It would be tragic if he were killed trying to save her if she was out of danger. However, he could never turn back until he knew for certain that she was safe.

Eric returned. The soldiers were here to protect the surviving villagers from further attacks and to help them restore temporary housing. The soldiers are in contact with their headquarters in the town of Jos, some 300 kilometers from Hafsa. According to them, it was suspected that the Boko Haram unit had already moved camp further north. The Nigerian army was in pursuit. This worried Alan. He was afraid that if the terrorists felt they were being cornered they would simply kill their prisoners and run. The only consolation was that, alive, Mona was worth ransom money to the terrorists.

"I want to find Boko Haram's last encampment," Alan said with conviction.

"Sir," Eric said, "that would be a waste of time. The terrorists have already moved to a new camp. We must wait for word of their next camp."

"No. We've got to move now. I need to see that camp. Ask the soldiers what road to take to find that camp."

Eric seemed reluctant to face the soldiers a second time, but he finally went. Alan watched from the car and witnessed a loud, animated exchange, with Eric apparently on the defensive. The soldiers shouted and jabbed fingers at Eric. An argument festered. Alan quickly exited the car and approached the group. Eric scratched his head and grimaced as though he had failed his mission.

"What's going on, Eric? What's the problem?"

"Sir. These fellows say it is not our business. That the Nigerian Army is hunting for terrorists and they no want civilians involved."

Alan asked the officer who had shouted at Eric, "Do you speak English?"

An officer focused on Alan. Nodding, he said, "Who *yu*? What business *yu get fo* here?"

"Sir, I am Alan Burke. I am here to find my wife who was abducted by Boko Haram."

The officer looked up sharply. "*Ah, na,* she that white wuman? That American who speaking French?"

"Yes sir. She is new to Africa. She is terrified. I must find her."

"How *yu* get here? *Yu de comot* from which side? Why *yu woman not with*? *Ah beg*, explain why she is prisoner of Boko Haram and you be free. Show *yu* paper, now."

Alan sighed audibly. The last thing he wanted was to be delayed for an unrelated technicality. Reluctantly, he bit his tongue and fumbled in his shirt pocket for his passport.

The officer fanned the many blank pages, frowning. Finally, he turned to Eric and said something in Hausa. When Eric shrugged his shoulders, the officer turned back to Alan. "Passport say *yu don* enter Cameroon one week past. *Yu* get valid Cameroon visa. But, I *no see* visa for Nigeria. Explain please."

Shit. How the hell am I going to get out of this one? He adjusted his glasses in distraction, and said, "Sir, I am the assistant program officer in the U.S. Embassy in Yaoundé. However, I am in Nigeria on unofficial business." Alan emphasized the unofficial. "When I heard that my wife was captured by Boko Haram I took leave and came here to find her. Can you help me?"

The officer studied the ground for a moment, then held up one hand, "Wait." He left to confer with an officer who appeared to be a superior.

Waiting in the warm Nigerian sun, Alan's attention drifted toward activity in the village. A soft breeze carried small particles of ash and dust that stung his eyes and smudged his glasses. He became aware of crying children and some solemn movement. He heard muffled sobbing, apparently from several women accompanied by a Red Crescent worker. From somewhere a sorrowful wail again penetrated the quiet. Two children, heads down, each with an arm around the other's shoulders, trailed two workers in white gowns. The workers carried a stretcher bearing a still figure.

Upset by the depressing sight, Alan turned toward the car when an officer beckoned him. This officer handed Alan his passport, and said, "Mister Alan, I am Second Commander Obwale Ebi, of the Nigerian Army. My officer discussed your situation with me, and I have several questions. First of all, can you prove that you are the spouse of this American hostage?"

"What? For god's sake, I'm not carrying my wedding license." Then he remembered the picture of Mona in his wallet. The picture did not convince the soldier.

Eric quickly spoke up, using a local dialect. Alan caught names of cities and guessed that Eric was explaining why Mona was in Nigeria while Alan had gone to Cameroon.

Hearing Eric's use of the local vernacular, the two officers exchanged surprised looks. They summoned a young soldier working on a personnel carrier some thirty meters away. That soldier spoke briefly with the two officers, then with Eric. Suddenly the young soldier let out a shout and rushed to embrace Eric. They laughed and spoke excitedly, like old friends meeting after many years. After much happy greeting, Eric turned to Alan and said, *This mon na ee be ma cousin. I watched ee and ee brotha when they be small pikins."

"That's great," said Alan. "I'm happy for you both. Now, can we get on with our mission?"

"Don't be too hasty," cut in Second Commander Ebi. "Mr. Alan, why do you think you can track down Boko Haram and rescue your woman? The British, the French, the Americans, and the

Cameroonians have had little success stopping those terrorists. How do you hope to find them, save your woman, and survive?"

"Second Commander Ebi, the woman they are holding hostage is the most precious thing in my life. She is the only family I have left in this world, and I will do anything to find and help her. If I die trying, at least I will have done my best." Then in a voice one octave higher, as a horrifying thought made his eyes water, Alan said, "Today is Saturday. If we do nothing she will die at midnight tomorrow. Please help me, sir. The terrorists' message said Sunday, midnight. She may be dead in a few hours."

The army officer opened his mouth to speak, but Alan cut him off. "Sir, the second part of my answer is that, as a young man I spent many days in rough country, camping, climbing, and living off the land. I learned survival skills, and I know how to negotiate with people." He paused, then added, "It has been said that a desperate man is a good colleague. With your help I can find those bastards. Please, I ask you again, will you help me?"

Ebi's gaze drifted toward the distant hills. Alan thought he saw the man's eyes water but assumed that the tears were caused by the fire ash whirling in the wind. The officer cleared his throat as he turned away, but called back, "Mister Alan, come."

Ten meters from Eric and the others, Ebi turned to face Alan. His eyes were moist, and his voice cracked. "Mister Alan. You must excuse, but I find this, ah…, what you say, emotional time. I suffer for your woman, and I like to help. Six months ago, these same Boko Haram terrorists attacked my home village. They savagely killed my mother, my sister and my young brother. They burned every house to the ground. Even they took away my sister's young daughters who were studying in school. We have not heard from those girls since that day."

Alan's hopes soared with Ebi's apparent empathy.

"What I am about to do," Ebi continued, "could end my military career. You are in Nigeria illegally. I am obliged to arrest you. You could pay heavy fines for entering this country without a visa. Yet I find that my people have not been able to stop those animals. I also understand you owe your woman a chance to find her whether she is alive or not."

Alan took a step back, appreciating that Ebi was not an antagonist.

"So, Mister Alan, it will be as though I did not meet you. Your driver is my countryman. He understands, and will help you find your woman. My men will not stop you. Know that other Nigerians you encounter may treat you as enemy intruders."

Alan was astounded. He was free to go. However, any future encounters with Nigerian authority could end his mission.

"Sir, I appreciate that very much," Alan said. "You give me hope. Can you help me with information about my wife? I need the location of the terrorist cell. Do you have satellite tracking?"

Ebi signaled Alan to wait and went to confer with his signal operator. On his return he reported, "The latest intel shows that the Boko Haram unit that was camped fifteen kilometers from here has moved north, but that is not confirmed. I have asked my officer to search further for guidance from the army. The commanding officer in charge, General Rasaki, may enlist the help of your government."

Alan remembered having read that name in the newspaper on the plane and assumed General Rasaki was searching for the terrorists. "And my wife? Do you have any information about her, or the ransom threats?"

"Yes, some better news. The U.S. president has asked the Boko Haram terrorists for more time. Our information indicates that no ransom has been paid, but that the hostages are still alive."

Alan grasped the thin whisper of hope and exhaled his relief.

The officer then unstrapped a heavy object from his waist. He handed it to Alan and said, "This is my field radio. It can get satellite signals up to 400 kilometers. My men will relay any new information they get to you." In ten minutes of instruction Alan was comfortable with the radio's features

Ebi pointed to the road that led toward the hills where the Boko Haram had last been detected. He suggested that in twelve to fourteen kilometers they would see a crossroad, and to be careful.

The terrorists would very likely set traps to keep anyone from approaching or following.

Alan knew that time was running out. As he and Eric reentered the car, the danger of their undertaking weighed heavily on them. How could they, of little experience, find a lethal enemy in unfamiliar country when the armies of four nations were unable to subdue the terrorists? Even if they were fortunate enough to find them, how could they fight them?

Alan leaned back and closed his eyes. His thoughts quickly drifted to happier moments. He visualized the smile on Mona's face as she walked up the aisle on her father's arm. He could almost feel the warmth of her body against his as they spent their first night together. He remembered their graduation day; what a beautiful time. Thoughts of that daring moment when he impulsively made a reservation to be with her in Iowa at Thanksgiving caused a smile to cross his lips. The sound of jangling car keys jolted him back to the present.

Before Eric could turn the ignition, Alan said, "Eric. This is very serious. We could both be dead within an hour. The people we are looking for are not local-variety bad guys. They are killers. Killers who use every kind of lethal weapon and have no love for or patience with people like you and me. I cannot lead you into danger like this. As I said before, you have young children who are counting on you to come home. I want you to take this car and return to Cameroon. I will proceed alone."

Eric tapped his pudgy fingers on the steering wheel. "Sir. *I tink sey you de get open eye. Na, fo my countryman that mean sey you* bossy." Eric chuckled. "No offense, Mister Alan, but we are already here, in Hafsa. We have a mission. I know about Boko Haram; my people live in fear of them every day. I cannot go back to my children and leave you. *Na,* what kind of father would I be if I left my *tight frien* to fight the enemy by *hisself? Na I de tink sey dem fit disown me.* No sir, I have come this far, *Ah no fit go back without yu.*" He smiled and said, "Also, you have my gas money."

Alan smiled relief, and said, "Okay then *ma tight frien, let's go fo befo.*"

CHAPTER 20
FIRST TERRORIST CAMP

A lan and Eric approached a small village ten kilometers from Hafsa and stopped. Eerie silence replaced the car engine noise. No human was visible, and the thatched huts appeared to be abandoned. No chickens scratched the dirt nor goat munched on roadside greens. The nearby fields looked weedy. Idle implements were scattered near unattended crops. A half dozen broken clay pots lay strewn on the ground. It appeared the inhabitants had left in a hurry. Eric shook his head, muttered a prayer and drove on.

Driving further they came to a crossroad. "Ah. That road must be the road north that the Second Commander Ebi referred to." Eric began to turn right. "No." Shouted Alan. "I want to see the terrorists' old camp. Keep straight. But stop in two klicks."

Eric slowed the car further up the road and parked deep within some tall elephant grass. Except for the hunting knife Alan bought in Yaoundé, they were unarmed. Alan hoped that they would spot the militants before being discovered by them.

Eric asked, "Sir, why stop here? I think the camp is empty."

"I don't know, Eric. I just want to approach quietly on foot. I need to see where Mona was held." Alan couldn't verbalize his emotion, but he wanted to confirm that he wouldn't find Mona's remains in that camp. "If some terrorists are still there I don't want to drive into a trap."

The two men crept with the stealth of hunters, paralleling the road for a kilometer, using brush and tall grass for cover. They bristled at every sound or movement. Eventually, they spotted a smaller dirt road on the right, partially hidden in the shadow of tall trees. The narrow road angled sharply uphill toward dense foliage. They followed tire markings in the dirt, and, just two hundred meters up the hill, Alan caught a whiff of burnt wood. Crouching and peering through the trees, he spotted a slow swirl of smoke curling from the smoldering coals of an abandoned campfire. Further, he noticed signs of discarded water bottles and food packaging.

A mournful wail broke the silence. Alan froze at the distant sound. It was eerie, like a human voice calling him. He rose slowly to peer through the tall, dry grass, fearful of a bullet to his head. *This must be the Boko Haram camp.* Deep tire tracks in soft soil attested to recent movement of heavy equipment. *It looks like we missed whoever was here.*

The two continued their slow, crouching pace. A fetid odor tickled Alan's nose. He tried to decipher whether the offensive smell was rotting garbage, or worse.

The ghostly moans of a human in agony again cut through the warm breeze. That woeful lament made the hair on Alan's arms rise. *"Not Mona. Please, not Mona."* Alan stood upright and ran toward the sound.

Eric bolted forward, keeping pace with Alan, as they drew closer to unmistakable cries of pain. They soon found themselves in what had been a large encampment.

Alan was well aware that he could be standing on the spot where his wife had been held hostage hours ago. His knees faltered as emotion swelled over him. He sank to the ground, feeling drained of energy. His head jerked up abruptly when Eric shouted. "Look. Over there. Someone there."

The stockade was crude, made of woven thorn branches. A makeshift gate lay twisted on its thong hinges. An anguished moan came from inside the enclosure. On the ground, leaning against the thorny inside of the enclosure was an African woman, holding her side in pain. Dried blood caked on her face, one arm hung limply at her side and her clothes were in disarray. The startled woman looked up as the two men approached.

It's not Mona. Thank God. Alan's emotions went hot and cold. Disappointed that he had not found his wife, he was relieved that she was not the person covered in blood. Yet his heart wept for the woman who now gazed up at Eric.

Eric rushed to her side as she rolled forward into his arms. He crouched low beside her, and she mumbled something indecipherable. Eric talked in a low, soothing voice, first in Hausa, then pidgin. She became agitated, and her eyes widened. Her mouth quivered when she attempted to speak, but her injuries made her gag and cough. Her lips were dry and cracked. Her cupped hand indicated that she wanted to drink. Eric turned to Alan, "She wants water. *Ah beg,* you find water."

Alan stood and assessed the brutal damage someone had inflicted on this woman. The bloodied nose and bruised face indicated a severe beating, and the bloodied mid-section on her wrapper looked like a gunshot wound.

Alan ran from spot to spot, looking for anything to ease the woman's discomfort. Near a heap of discarded rubble Alan spotted an empty juice can. He ran to a small stream, rinsed the can and filled it with fresh, cool water. He found Eric still clutching the woman in his arms as she continued mumbling. Alan knelt close to the woman and cradled her head so she could sip the water. It appeared to Alan that the woman may have been here like this for one or two days without water or food.

The water seemed to sooth her. She sighed and burped. Her breathing relaxed. Eric tried to speak to her again in Hausa. She looked down, silent. Eric asked her in Pidgin English, "Na, *wetin yu name?"*

She steadied herself, tried to spit some blood, but it rolled over the rim of her lip and dribbled down her chin onto her blouse. Looking up with a squint she breathed in a gravelly voice, "Oneka."

Alan reached for her hand and held her cold fingers. He searched her eyes for signs of cognizance, as he spoke slowly, "Oneka. My name is Alan. Who did this to you?"

The woman looked over to see Alan. Her eyes brightened, she looked as though she understood his question, but gave a painful grimace in response.

Eric leaned forward and asked, "*Yu de tak kam tak?*" Looking to Alan he said, "I'm asking her if she speaks Cameroon Pidgin."

Oneka's eyes slowly rotated back toward Eric and she uttered, "*Savages dem. Boko 'aram ah de tink.*" Oneka caught her breath. "*Dem don burnt ma Hafsa. Dem killt bocu pipo.*" A tear coursed from a swollen eye as she spoke.

The reminder caused her eyes to close tight. Tears coursed down her dirt-smeared cheeks like a river cutting a valley in mud. After a moment, she continued, "*Dem don bring girl pikin hiya fo seka sey bad ting. Dem go, now.*"

"*Ah de sabi,*" Eric soothed, "those men do terrible things. *Una* safe now. They gone."

Alan and Eric were shaken, appalled at Oneka's egregious treatment. They glanced at each other with shocked stares, trying to comprehend the brutality of terrorists. Alan began to assemble pieces of a puzzle. The sacking of Hafsa, the taking of prisoners, this woman's testimony, and the French words spoken by Mona in the ransom videotape.

"*Whoside bad men dem go?*" Eric asked. Then to Alan he said, "Maybe she knows where the terrorist went."

Oneka took a lingering breath as though trying to gather strength to speak, "*Hear man say sout. A de sabi Yankari. Dem take girls and white woman.*" Her eyes closed momentarily and she let out a pained sigh, "*Dem take some 'portant minista who comot fo Cameroon.*" Oneka's hands trembled and her strained breathing rattled in her chest.

Alan physically wrenched at the reference to a white woman. He glanced at Eric, who nodded.

Oneka's eyes widened when she seemed to find a trace of energy, and said, "*White woman very fraid for life. Dem don go yestaday. Early. Ah be heeya fo most tu day.*"

Alan burst out, "Oneka, the white woman; did you see her?"

"Yessa. She merican. I tink se, Mona be dat woman ee name."

"Madam Oneka, Mona is my wife, *ma wuman*? I need to find her. Where is Mona?"

Alan's words seemed to take several seconds to register. Then a weak smile crossed Oneka's lips. *"Na, she won fayne wuman, dat Mona. She bin krai fo you."* There was a lengthy pause, as Oneka fought for breath. *"Man say dey go sout. Dey take ma student pikin an dat Mona wuman wit. I no know bout two teacher man. I tink sey, dey kilt dem."*

"Why did they do this to you, Oneka? Why did they take the others but beat you and leave you here?"

"Ah old-oh," she said. *"Boko 'aram no like teacha. Ah no be useful. Ah fight fo white wuman. Dem say dem go keel her if no get monee."* Oneka had a difficult time breathing and was unable to continue. Her pidgin became strained as her strength dissipated.

"Na so? yu sure dem go south?" Eric asked softly, and waited for the woman to gain her strength. *"Na, some army man dem tink Boko 'aram de go nort."*

Oneka looked up at Eric, shook her head painfully, and said, "Sout." Oneka slumped into Alan's arms. He sat on the ground and cradled her body as her rasping breath struggled for a moment, then ceased. Tears clouded his vision as he regarded the injuries inflicted by the heartless radicals. For fifteen minutes he held Oneka without moving, sobered by the realization that this courageous woman had known his beloved Mona. Alan searched for a pulse, and found none. Her breathing had stopped and vitality drained from her face.

Alan and Eric sat with moist eyes as Oneka's body grew cold, shocked by the animalistic behavior of fanatic humans towards others. "I find it difficult to believe," Alan said, "that people can be so cruel. What those people did to this poor woman makes me furious when I think that they are holding Mona."

"We can't leave this woman here," Eric said. "Her body will be torn apart by hyenas or other animals. Her family may want to come here to claim her body."

It took an hour for the two men to dig a deep grave using Alan's camping shovel. They waited longer but eventually placed Oneka's body in the ground. Alan carved Oneka's name into a piece of bark, wedged it on two forked sticks, and placed it near the grave.

There was an awful stench from beyond the border of the camp. It led Alan to the grisly discovery of decomposing bodies. He identified three sets of limbs, partially covered in dirt, branches and garbage. The stench was nearly unbearable, but Alan had to confirm that Mona was not among them. All three bodies were male. All three had head wounds.

Alan's emotions plunged and then soared as he surveyed the deserted camp. He could sense that his wife had been here. But, seeing the death and destruction left by Boko Haram made his stomach churn. *Where is Mona? Is she still alive?*

The wind gusted and blew dust on harmattan winds from the Saharan Desert across the abandoned campsite. Trees had no chance to filter out the minuscule grains of sand. Alan and Eric sought shelter in the car. Their ten-year old Peugeot wagon had only a half tank of gas. Their food supply was good for two more days, but their sleep-deprived bodies were nearly exhausted. "That woman, Oneka, said Yankari. Do you know where that is?" Alan asked.

Eric removed his cap and scratched his head. "Yankari is a river, but maybe she talks about Yankari National Park. It is a game reserve. Many people go there to see the forests and the wild animals." He pointed to a green area on Alan's map. "It is south from here. Maybe Boko Haram moves hostages there."

Alan heard Eric's description of Yankari, but he was too exhausted to respond. He leaned his head on the car head rest and closed his eyes. Warmth from the mid-day sun fostered an urge to sleep. The last thing Alan remembered, with eyes partly closed, was Eric's loud snore.

The earth trembled. A loud rumbling noise startled Alan and Eric awake. Both men jerked their heads around, frantically searching for the source of the intensifying clamor. *Crap. The terrorists are back. No time to run. Can't hide.* The two seemed hopelessly trapped as a large, Russian-made T-72 battle tank roared into the camp, its menacing main turret pointed in their direction. Running in the dust alongside the heavy tank were two columns of heavily-armed soldiers.

The soldiers surrounded the Peugeot, pointing AK-47 assault rifles at the passengers and shouting. The T-72 pulled within 20 meters and lowered the canon barrel toward the hapless vehicle. The shouting stopped. A cloud of dust raised by troops and vehicles swirled around the car. Alan recognized the uniforms and logo of the Nigerian army, and whispered, "Eric, I think we oughta show our hands and get out verrry slowly."

The two bewildered men stood beside their open doors as dust settled on them, their hands raised high above their heads, waiting for someone to speak. When no one spoke, Alan said to no one in particular, "Hi. I'm American. This is my friend, Eric." *Why did I say that? Guess I'm nervous? Why doesn't someone say something? Shit that's a big gun.*

The soldiers eased their stance slightly, apparently seeing no weapons. They parted for a U.S.-made Humvee, which rolled to a stop nearby. After another wave of red dust settled, a Nigerian officer climbed out, his eyes darting around the deserted camp. The soldiers parted to make way for him as he strode toward the Peugeot. Alan was nervous as he saw the officer look at him and ask, "Meester Aran?"

Alan stopped breathing momentarily. He gulped some dusty air and tried to speak but only said, "Hi, I'm an American." His mouth was dry and his eyes watered. When he was finally able to clear his throat. He said, "Yes, sir. My name is Alan Burke. How do you know my name?"

The officer smiled, looked at Eric and asked, "*wetin dey happen?*"

Eric looked confused, glanced at Alan, and replied in pidgin, "*Ah no no.*"

Turning back to Alan, the officer said in clear English, "Come, tell me what you find here. I surprise you alive still."

Both Alan and Eric breathed sighs of relief as the soldiers lowered their weapons. A number of soldiers shuffled off to survey the abandoned camp.

The officer introduced himself as Captain Hassan of the Nigerian Army, commander of an armored infantry unit. The captain demanded to know what Alan and Eric had found. The two told of the woman, Oneka, who was alive when they arrived but died from wounds inflicted by the Boko Haram. Alan described the bodies they had discovered in the nearby ravine.

The captain explained that he was in contact with the patrol in Hafsa and that Second Commander Ebi had informed him of two civilians who were trying to win the war by themselves. He also stated that it was against Nigerian law for civilians to interfere with military efforts, and it was also against the law for foreigners to enter his country without an official visa. "I should take you into custody, but I have an urgent mission to go north to find the Boko Haram. I cannot afford to have my men escort two fugitives back to Cameroon." He demanded that Alan and Eric go back to Cameroon immediately.

"How did you get here, Captain?" Alan asked. "Did you did not see the Boko Haram terrorists? They were here just hours ago."

"I am from Jos, from the west."

"The woman who we buried," Alan advised, "told us the terrorists took their hostages south."

"Ha. The meaningless babble of a dying woman." The captain brushed off the information with a wave of his hand and turned to go.

"Sir," Alan pleaded, "I respect your dedication to your mission, but if you attack the enemy, you chance harm or death to my wife and the other captives. These terrorists will kill them when they hear your army coming. Please, let me find them. Don't jeopardize their safety."

Hassan nodded his understanding, but said, "My mission is to eliminate terrorists. I am not authorized to change my mission." He turned to his men and shouted an order. Within twenty minutes the entire unit had deserted the camp, raising clouds of red dust.

After the soldiers were out of sight, Alan turned to Eric and asked, "The woman mentioned Yankari, the game reserve, is it north or south?"

They again located Yankari Game Reserve on Alan's map. It was at least a half day's drive south. "Let's go," Alan directed, "we don't have much daylight left."

Retracing their earlier course, they came to the intersection where tank tracks indicated that Hassan's army turned north. The south-bound road looked less inviting and tracks were less evident. After one kilometer on the south-bound road they began to see evidence that a large convoy had passed recently.

They spotted a farmer's hut just off the dirt roadway. Eric parked and approached carefully. Before he reached the grass and mud shack, he heard a grunt. A short, thin man wearing a waist cloth and a soiled T-shirt stood at the edge of a field of cotton stubble, partially hidden by tall grass. The farmer gazed at Eric and raised his palms skyward as if to ask, what do you want?

Eric asked in Hausa if the farmer had witnessed the terrorists pass by. The man shrugged. Eric spoke the few words of Igbo that he knew. No response. Eric tried English. Nothing. Realizing that even if he could speak all 521 languages used in Nigeria, this man would not respond. As a final attempt Eric addressed the farmer in pidgin and held out a sizable Naira currency note. *"You de talk pidgin?"* The man's eyes brightened slightly. With considerable sign language and creative pidgin, Eric was able to discern that an armed contingent had passed south the previous morning. The man pointed to an empty chicken pen. The terrorists had no compunction about stealing a farmer's hens.

It was time to contact Second Commander Ebi. Punching in the code numbers, Alan heard a loud crackle followed by a click and then breathing. "Yes." Came a clear response, "Second Commander Ebi."

"Sir. This is Alan Burke."

"Yes, I know. You using my radio."

"We met a patrol led by Captain Hassan one hour ago. He moved his tanks north, as you earlier suggested. However, I have reliable information that the insurgents went south, toward the Yankari Game Reserve. We just met a farmer who confirmed that a large company of armed people and equipment passed this way just over twenty-four hours ago."

"Thank you, *Mista* Alan. I will pass to central command. Please contact me when you find enemy. Oh, also, you should know, Boko

Haram advised the media that they give Cameroon and the U.S. forty-eight hours from today night."

"Thank God." Alan said, "we have a little more time. Thanks."

Eric steered the Peugeot cautiously south. Both men watched for indications where the terrorists may have turned off the dirt road to set up a camp in a sheltered area.

They passed several small villages, and a number of fields and pastures. There were no large farms in this part of Nigeria, and no large towns to provide markets for farm produce or fuel for their car. The Boko Haram had chosen their route well. Eric hoped that he would see a larger community soon since the needle on the gas indicator had dropped to less than a quarter tank and daylight waned.

At dusk they pulled off the road near a small river bordering the game reserve, and concealed the vehicle within the tree line behind tall grass. They snacked on English biscuits and bottled water. That night they slept fitfully, as unfamiliar jungle noises vied for attention.

CHAPTER 21
MIA

A mbassador Morrison returned to Yaoundé late Friday. He met with David Steinhouse and senior staff Saturday morning and had expected to meet with Alan Burke. Steinhouse informed the ambassador that he had not seen Alan Burke since Thursday. David said he was concerned that Burke was devastated over his wife's abduction and might be depressed.

Shortly after eleven a.m. David knocked on the embassy guest room door. "Alan? Good morning." After a short wait, "Alan, are you there? Time to get going, fella. Morrison would like to meet with you." Receiving no response, David asked his secretary if she knew Alan's whereabouts. She suggested that he was probably out having breakfast or taking a walk, and maybe it was fine to let him roam around Yaoundé to help keep his mind off his wife's situation.

David asked the Marine guards and the receptionist if they had seen Alan leave. The last person who saw him concluded that it was around ten Thursday evening when he returned to his quarters. Embassy security cameras showed him leaving the building at five a.m. Friday morning.

Morrison expressed disappointment that Alan was not available and suggested that something was amiss. An hour later he ordered Steinhouse to have the Marines search Alan's room. The guards looked for a note, anything that would indicate where Alan might have gone. They found most of his clothes either in his suitcase or hanging in the closet. Some of his papers were on the nightstand, but there was no sign of his passport.

Embassy staff visited local restaurants and hotels with photos of Alan. They interviewed expatriates who may have spoken with him. Finally, late Saturday afternoon, a shop owner not far from the embassy, said he had seen a man similar to the one pictured load food and equipment into an older car and drive away with a Cameroon man.

Secretary of State Lisa Townshend, who Morrison was obligated to keep informed, expressed alarm that her newest employee was missing. "I understand," she said, "that Burke may be under a lot of stress. I sympathize with his predicament, but if Alan is planning to do something rash, you must prevent it from becoming an international embarrassment." She instructed Morrison to continue searching for Alan and said she would bring this to the attention of the president.

Morrison sat at his sprawling desk staring at a huge pile of papers. Unable to focus on his work, he could only wonder where the hell Burke was. The red light on his phone set lit up. "Yes?"

"Sir, I have the Cameroon prime minister on the line. He sounds upset."

"Okay." *Great, this can't be good news.* "Thanks, Hazel. Put him on."

It was not good news. The prime minister angrily expressed outrage at the inappropriate behavior of U.S. Embassy staff. A Mr. Alan Burke had been stopped at a gendarme security checkpoint near Mamfe, close to Cameroon's border with Nigeria. It was understood that Burke intended to cross into Nigeria. The prime minister was furious that this was the same man who had stomped out of a recent meeting, acting like a spoiled child. "That man's impudence causes my president to question the maturity and stability of the American mission."

The more Morrison tried to placate the prime minister the more the man stormed his outage. The ambassador ended the call by agreeing to severely reprimand Mr. Burke for his rude behavior. He thanked the minister for the information.

He called Steinhouse into his office. "David, we've got a runner. It seems Burke has gone to Nigeria to search for his wife."

"Shit. Excuse my language, but I was afraid that guy was going to do something stupid. He seemed too interested in the coordinates for that Boko Haram camp. I'm sorry, sir, I should have locked him in a cell."

"Hey. Don't beat yourself up. Everyone has been put in a difficult situation. If there is blame, I think it should go to whoever allowed that woman to travel to Nigeria.

CHAPTER 22
CONSIDERING THE ODDS

Mona was awakened by her own scream. A horrifying nightmare about cold, sharp steel crashing through her cervical spine was too real. Her outburst was immediately penalized by a curse and a guard's backhand slap. She flopped against the side of the moving personnel carrier and slumped toward the floor. Something warm coursed slowly down her cheek. Life was a horrible nightmare. Fear numbed her from the pain. *Why don't they just kill me?* Blindfolded and hands bound she felt helpless with no idea where these men were taking her. They only removed her blindfold for a few minutes to eat, drink or use nature's toilet. She remained crammed on a seat in a corner of the vehicle, sweaty, smelly guards always nearby.

Battered and sleep-deprived, Mona felt disoriented. She had difficulty separating reality from her hallucinations. Her stomach convulsed, and she heaved bitter bile and water. She sensed her guards leap away to avoid vomit splatter. She heard them snicker at her. She cringed in fear whenever someone touched or came near her.

The heavy vehicle bounced along the unseen road for several hours. She could taste Sahara sands, thanks to the ever-present harmattan winds. She heard the now-familiar Hausa language being spoken by the boisterous men around her. Youthful voices suggested that some of her antagonists were boys. She wondered how such young men could become so radicalized.

Mona thought she heard the occasional cough or squeal of a young girl. Some of the girls had been spared, but they were being abused. She was saddened thinking about the horror they must be experiencing. *Where is Oneka? Were her screams of pain the last I will ever hear from her? I know Oneka was beaten for trying to help me. There were awful sounds like shouts, and screams, and gunshots.* At the time Mona had thought, *Am I next?* Her only way of clinging to hope was the ransom demand—as long as Boko Haram anticipated receiving ransom money she would be kept alive. She knew the official U.S. policy was opposed to honoring terrorist demands. When the U.S. finally refused to pay, her life would be worthless. The ransom demand stated ninety-six hours. *The hooded man said Sunday, midnight. Is today Friday or Saturday? I think it must be Friday. Damn it, Alan. You never should have let me travel alone. Holy crap. They're cutting off my head in two days. Are my people negotiating or not? I've gotta get out of here.*

Cowering against the side of the personnel carrier she caught a whiff of fresh, cool air. *It must be evening.* She lifted her hand and brushed it along the fabric that covered the personnel carrier. It felt course on the back of her hand, reminding her of circus tent material. She sought the place where air filtered in. It was a two-inch slit, probably caused by a tree branch, or a careless person. The fresh air was invigorating.

Her captors had given her stale bread many hours ago, and now she was hungry. *Not that awful, tasteless plantain. A cheeseburger and a mango smoothie would be great. I'd even appreciate a bowl of rice and yogurt.* Terrified that at any moment she could be struck with a weapon, or made to do unspeakable things, she struggled to be positive. *I wonder where Alan is right now. Is he doing anything to find me? What **can** he do? He could never find me. I've got to get a message to someone.* Mona fought depression as she considered the impossibility of her situation. *No one can help me but me. I've got to look for an opportunity. Daddy said to always think positive. There's a solution to every problem.*

When the vehicles stopped, road dust settled over everything. Mona could feel the gritty residue on her bare arms. Somewhere outside, birds chirruped. The birds bolstered her spirits. She had been a prisoner for four days, and the bird songs suggested freedom.

An hour later, a guard removed Mona's blindfold and shoved a banana leaf with *fufu* and fried plantain toward her. She ate greedily. Between mouthfuls of the starchy food she motioned for water. The guard grumbled as he retreated to get water and climbed down from the vehicle. Mona snatched a peek through the tear in the canvas wall. Her prison was in an open, flat area surrounded by dense forest. She could see pickup trucks with mounted guns, and armed men erecting at least a dozen tents. She could hear orders being shouted, tent stakes being driven, and smaller vehicles moving about.

The hours dragged on. The monotony and Mona's discomfort increased.

*   *   *

On Saturday, the fifth day of her captivity, she heard the commander's raspy shouting from outside her cramped prison. *I'm beginning to despise that voice.*

A beefy hand grabbed her arm and pulled her upright. The floor was uneven and strewn with objects she couldn't see. Her cramped legs were weak from lack of movement. She stumbled when her bare foot struck something on the floor of the transport. "Ow." It hurt, and she nearly fell but was kept upright by her guard who kicked the object away. *That felt and sounded like a rifle. Maybe these guys are getting careless.*

Her stomach heaved from fear, exhaustion and sleep deprivation. Near the rear of the truck a soldier removed her blindfold and indicated that she should climb down. She looked down at the ground and felt woozy. She slumped to a sitting position until the earth stopped spinning then reached for the handhold and descended.

Her clothes were disheveled, dusty, and stiff from dried sweat. She could not remember ever feeling this filthy and miserable. She straightened her tired and sore body and looked up to see Commander Edubamo's lewd stare. A rage burned inside her like hot magma ready to erupt. If she had the strength she would drive her fist into that ugly face. *Did I really think that?* Her angry thoughts surprised her. Despite all the polite manners her mother had instilled, she could feel the cornered tiger in her wanting to scratch and claw.

"*Yu foolish president no fit ansa ransom, Ah go make 'xample yu,*" snarled the commander. "*Everyman go see wey happen when dem no 'bey Boko Haram. Dem go see yu fyne head roll fo dust.*" Edubamo chuckled with a throaty rasp, and grabbed Mona's hair to force her to look at him. "But, *Ah* have special gift *fo yu.* Tomorrow, *bafo* we chop *yu* head, *yu go* see same *fo* head *fo* Cameroon minister." The commander chuckled and winked. "What *yu* think? *Dis* make *fo fayne sho fo* 'merica TV?"

Mona lost control of herself when she imagined the cold steel of the knife, her head rolling in dust. She vomited partially-digested plantain so violently that some landed on the commander's pant leg. Edubamo jerked back too late. His angry shouts in three different languages were unmistakably profane, and his violent gesticulation suggested that Mona had made her point.

As her tormentor stomped away, Mona sank to her knees. She felt her strength and her courage take a harsh blow. She had never envisioned losing her life in an African forest, in the hands of terrorists without ever having achieved the many dreams she once contemplated.

Mona spent another cold night secured to her seat, warmed only by the filthy clothes she wore and a moth-eaten blanket that a guard threw on her. On this her last night, she felt a slowing of her pulse, an almost resolute surrender to her destiny. Dreams of home became snapshots of happier times. She dreamt of her sweet mother and her courageous father. Mostly she thought of Alan, and that Thanksgiving visit. Unfortunately, every dream ended with a sad scene. Her mother and father seeing her on television, a prisoner of a terrorist group in some place in Africa that they had never heard of. Tomorrow they would see her executioner speak threats in mangled English, while he held a long saber high over his head. With a violent downward motion, he would remove her head, and her parents would see it roll in the dust.

As much as she wished that Alan would find a way to come to her aid, she knew it was impossible. She had no idea where she was, and assumed that she was doomed unless she could help herself. *How can I get a message to Alan to let him know that I don't blame him and that I still love him with all my heart?*

When the first traces of light filtered in through openings in the side of the large vehicle, Mona was already wide awake. During the night she had resolved to take charge of her situation. Yesterday's reminder of her pending fate frightened her into realizing that she was her only hope. The mental exercise of watching, counting, and scheming gave her a strong sense of alertness.

Sunday morning in mid-December the weather was dry and the fine dust blew through the torn canvas. The taste made her mouth dry and her thirst nearly unbearable. Her blindfold had not been replaced after her encounter with the sadistic commander last night.

The call of nature haunted her. Guards always escorted her and watched. It was embarrassing and humiliating. They made sport of their job of guarding her while her bound hands struggled with her clothes. But, it didn't matter, she had to go.

Mona made eye contact with the guard closest to her. By hand signals she indicated that she had to go. The guard rolled his eyes as if this were a major inconvenience. He grabbed her arm and pushed her toward the open rear of the transport. He snatched a rope, and formed a noose on one end. He looped it over her head and marched her some seventy or eighty meters from the center of the camp toward a thick growth of elephant grass and the dark, menacing forest beyond. The guard cut the cord on Mona's wrist, grunted and pointed toward the tall grass.

Thankfully, this man turned his back. The rope was to keep her tethered. This same vegetation was being used by the militants for their own toilet purposes. She found a reasonably clean, sheltered spot and surveyed for gawkers.

After she relieved herself, she sensed a slight earth tremble. She hesitated for an instant, wondering if earthquakes were common here. There it was again, accompanied with a distant rumble, like rolling thunder that increased in volume. She heard shouting from the camp. The metallic rumble was accompanied by screams and sounds of men's heavy footfalls.

The rope around Mona's neck tugged impatiently throwing her to her knees. She didn't understand the guard's panicky shouts, but his hysterics and gesticulations bespoke extreme urgency.

When the rope relaxed slightly Mona clutched the noose to relieve the chafing on her neck and was astonished to see that it opened enough to slip over her head. As sounds of pandemonium erupted in the camp, she quickly slipped the rope onto a rotting tree stump and shouted in a mock angry voice, "Coming."

Instinct took over. Mona couldn't see the camp clearly through the thick grass but heard shooting, and saw armed men rushing back to the camp from the tree line. Engines cranked and gunfire exploded. Her guard tugged on the rope and shouted again. Mona rose slightly and saw his silhouette through the tall grass. When bursts of automatic gunfire from the camp distracted him, she scrambled out of the tall grass toward the cover of trees.

She bent low and ran as fast as her enervated muscles allowed. She was breathless in seconds, her lungs screamed for air. She fell less than thirty meters from the stump. Turning, she saw the guard look back toward the noose end of the rope and give a strong tug. He screamed at the stump and pulled out a handgun.

Shit, thought Mona, *now he's going to shoot me.*

A nearby burst of automatic firearms distracted the guard's attention again. The roar of large engines and loud machinery was frightful. *That sounds like army tanks attacking the camp.* Mona was terrified, no longer able to know who or where her enemy was. Hearing loud bursts of canons, she decided not to be a target. Her guard was now running toward the stump-end of the rope, apparently not having seen Mona's scramble toward the trees.

She hobbled off into the darkest area and didn't stop until forest vegetation muffled the sounds of warfare. Near the edge of a stream she spotted a sturdy oku tree with several low branches. Placing a foot on a low branch she reached up and was able to grab a higher limb. Fear of recapture created a surge of adrenaline. Painfully, she pulled herself up. Limb by limb she struggled to climb, the rough, slimy bark leaving scratches on her feet, arms, and ankles. Once above the ground, she cradled herself into a wide crotch in the tree concealed by dense, leafy foliage. Out of breath and shaking from exertion and fear, she inhaled what she hoped was air of freedom.

She froze at the sound of pounding feet on the forest floor. Her pursuer, pistol in hand, was her toilet escort. He came into view with his head swiveling wildly from side to side. He ran out of Mona's line of vision then came back into view and ran through the stream and up the far bank. Two minutes later she saw the top of his head. Mona stiffened, thinking for certain that the soldier would look up and spot her.

Distant small-arms crackle and loud cannon blasts suggested that an army, likely the Nigerian Army, was attacking the terrorists' camp. *I'm glad I'm not inside that personnel carrier. God, I hope the other prisoners didn't get caught in the crossfire.*

Mona watched the guard search for signs of footprints, and assumed that his life depended on getting the hostage back to his commander. Many of his compatriots had trampled the wooded area, so much of the soil had been disturbed.

Two more Boko Haram militants suddenly entered Mona's view. They spoke in quick, excited bursts. They didn't carry visible weapons, and they looked like mere boys, shaking with apparent fear. They stopped abruptly, surprised, when they spotted Mona's toilet guard. The guard whirled toward them ready to shoot, but stopped as one of the boys called his name. The two militants looked confused when the guard shouted. They looked left and right, and began moving backwards. Harsh words became more heated and Mona's guard raised his automatic weapon and shouted angrily.

Crap. That sounds serious. I wonder if those two guys are deserting. I hope that jerk flees with them—I'd be safe.

The sudden loud clatter of an automatic weapon caused Mona to jump and almost lose her balance on the woody perch. The two deserters screamed in agony as their twisted bodies crumpled to the decomposing foliage. The smell of burned gun powder drifted up to her perch.

The distinctive-raspy voice of Commander Edubamo pierced the convulsive battle clamor. Through the oku leaves Mona saw that the commander was shoving another prisoner. She discerned a middle-aged African woman, her hands bound in front. She wore what may once have been an expensive suit. A colorful head turban matched the suit. Her face was strained in fear, and her body convulsed from exertion. *I wonder if that is the Cameroonian minister that Chioma spoke of.*

Edubamo shrieked angrily at Mona's guard while forcing his prisoner to kneel. The guard lowered his weapon and stuttered a nervous reply. *Is the commander furious that I escaped?* The guard's voice cracked in servility. With palms up, he pleaded with his commander.

In her awkward arboreal position, Mona's cramped body ached from lack of motion. Blood drained from her legs, coarse bark scraped her thinly clad legs and bare arms. While the men below argued, she moved ever so slightly to get more comfortable. Bits of bark and leaves fell to the ground giving away her hiding place.

The eyes of both terrorists spotted the falling debris. Squinting into the dark foliage they saw Mona's pale skin, which contrasted with the leaves and bark. Edubamo moved closer to the tree, pointed his pistol towards Mona and shouted. "Down. Now."

Mona's heart sank as her brief freedom swiftly vanished. She tried to comply with Edubamo's order, but her legs would not respond. Her strength failed her, and she feared falling. She clung to the trunk of the tree in a frozen trance, oblivious to the sounds of war in the distance, hearing only the pounding of her blood through her veins. She couldn't move. There was no hope in being Edubamo's captive. Her mind raced for a plan. *Maybe he won't shoot me if I am worth twenty million dollars.*

Edubamo's impatience tested his English, which became distorted. His shouting deteriorated into pleading. The man who had been ordered to guard her, said something, which seemed to make Edubamo angrier. He raised his pistol as if to fire a shot into the branches above Mona.

That gave Mona incentive to move. She slowly wrapped her arms around the trunk and swung one foot over to a solid branch to begin a journey down the tree. The last two meters were tortuous, as her upper body strength was exhausted and she couldn't trust her legs to support a jump. Traces of blood emerged on her arms.

The commander shouted an order, and the guard assisted Mona the last two meters. While maneuvering to get a grip on a lower branch she slipped and tore a sleeve on her shirt. When her feet touched the ground, she crumpled into a heap of sweating, shaking flesh. She heard shouting, and then a gunshot that numbed her ears.

Feeling no pain from the expected bullet, she cautiously turned her head. To her horror she saw her guard sprawled on the ground. Blood pooled and soaked into the moist soil under what was once his head.

Edubamo shouted, "Up."

With that, Mona realized that her life still had some marketable value. Had the ransom effort fallen through, she would now be dead. Though weak and exhausted, she was enlivened by her previous, albeit unsuccessful attempt to escape. In spite of that failure, she now gained some confidence that another opportunity would eventually present itself.

It took a huge effort to stand. She used the slippery tree trunk for support and inhaled deeply. Turning to her captor she said with a sneer, "I'm up."

Edubamo secured Mona's hands in front of her with a nylon tie. Loosening the belt of his former guard he connected the ties on the hands of his two prisoners.

Standing near the other woman prisoner, Mona sensed fear in her distressed breathing. An ugly bruise on her cheek and a spot of blood under her nose suggested rough treatment. The minister's size revealed a sedentary lifestyle, yet she appeared to be in fair physical condition. The woman's attire suggested she was the Cameroon official the girl Chioma spoke of.

Mona expected Edubamo to force her back towards the camp. Instead, he pushed his prisoners further into the intimidating forest. It was then clear to Mona that his men had lost the battle.

CHAPTER 23
BATTLE OF YANKARI

Trumpeting elephants jolted Alan from a troubled sleep. He leaped up and peered out the window to see traces of light-silhouetted trees on the eastern riverbank. He clambered out of the Peugeot, and spotted Eric by the water. From his perch on a rock, Eric appeared to have his eyes fixed on circles in the backwater where silver fish fed on hatching mayflies. Alan watched silently as the rising sun illuminated scattered high clouds. The air was cool and moist.

"Hey, Eric. You shoulda woke me. We gotta get moving."

"Shh." Eric stiffened, slowly stood, and turned toward the road two hundred meters away.

Following Eric's gaze Alan eventually perceived dark shapes headed toward the reserve. Vehicles with no lights. Slight vibrations and eventually engine noises. As the light improved, they could make out figures marching next to the vehicles.

"That could be the Nigerian Army," Alan said, "maybe my radio message to Obwale Ebi convinced the commander to turn his tanks around."

Alan rushed back to the car for Ebi's radio. Eventually Ebi's sleepy voice, sounding like he could use a hot cup of coffee, said, "Mister Alan. Where are you?"

"Good morning. I don't know exactly where we are, but we're near the Yankari Game Reserve. I just saw a large group of personnel and equipment moving in the direction of the reserve. Can you confirm that Captain Hassan's unit is moving toward the reserve?"

Ebi hesitated. "You must not use this channel. This transmission could be jeopardized. The intelligence you provided yesterday was confirmed with foreign satellite assistance. I close now. Return my radio. Out."

"Wait." But, the radio went silent. "Shit. He cut me off. Damn. I need to know about the ransom demand." *Crap! If Hassan attacks the Boko Haram, Mona could get caught in the crossfire*

The ground shook and the sound of machinery confirmed that tanks, probably Nigerian Army, were moving toward the reserve. Alan opened the boot and gathered items he had accumulated in Yaoundé. After tossing a rope, torch and provisions into a backpack he clipped a compass to his belt.

"*Na, whattee?*" Eric asked, no doubt exasperated yet again with Alan preparing to take off on his own.

"I've gotta get to Mona fast before that fucking army gets there. We can't use the road, so I am going cross country. You stay here. We'll need you to help us get back to Cameroon after I find Mona."

"Mr. Alan. Don't interfere with the Nigerian Army. You could get killed."

"Eric, if those fuckin T-72 tanks attack the camp they will blow the crap out of everything." Alan's panicked words came out high pitched. "The hostages will be toast. I've got to get there first."

"Then, I go with you."

"No. I need you here. This is my fight. I already dragged you into danger, and I can't ask you to risk more." Handing the army radio to Eric he added, "You should make another call to our friend in Hafsa. You gotta meet me here to get us back."

Eric threw the radio onto the back seat and stuffed snacks into Alan's backpack. "*Dey no bi bridge fo riva, but riva no be deep. Ah tink sey yu fit woka.*"

"You know, Eric," Alan smiled, "*Ah tink sey Ah actually sabi yu pidgin. Ah go waka fayne.*"

Alan saw Eric frown. He sensed Eric's resentment for being left behind. *I've involved him too much already. I can't let him get hurt.* Eric had family in Cameroon and Alan couldn't bear the thought of him getting injured, or killed. *Besides, with my backwoods experience, I can move faster alone.*

Positioning his spectacles squarely on his nose, Alan left his depleted cell phone behind and stepped onto the soft river bank. As he began wading across the shallowest part of the stream holding his backpack high, he said, "God, I hope there aren't crocodiles or piranha in here." It had been a while since he hiked and camped. He and his parents backpacked through mountains and deserts. They loved to climb with ropes and gear. They found joy in the great outdoors. Uniting with nature back then was fun. Today's trek was a matter of life-or-death.

Ignoring concern for jungle cats, Alan focused on locating Mona quickly. He followed his compass into the reserve, paralleling the access road. He hoped to get to where Boko Haram had set up a new camp. He must find Mona before the army found Boko Haram.

Too quickly the trail turned away from the main road. Alan had to traverse thick brush, and sometimes swampy ground to keep the road in sight. A canopy of tall trees in some places darkened the forest floor, making it difficult to see. Stopping occasionally to catch his breath, he listened for the army's noisy progress.

Obstacles abounded. *I wish someone had told me about the geothermal pools, and the hot, mucky water holes.* Alan half-expected to see wild animals sipping in the shallows of the pools. Parts of the reserve had dense stands of tall trees with interlaced foliage that restricted sunlight and prevented undergrowth, opening the ground for Alan to move faster.

In ten minutes, he was exhausted and drenched with sweat. With a clumsy step, he tripped and fell headfirst into hot mud and swamp grass. Panic swept over him. *Quicksand?* A loud clamor surprised him as unseen wildlife scampered away. He rose on unsteady legs and shook stagnant mud off his clothes and arms.

Hoping that he was tracking closer to Mona, Alan renewed his efforts. Branches raked his face and abraded his hands as he crashed through brush. When the tree canopy cleared, low vegetation snagged his boots causing him to stumble and fall. He rose again and again, always aware that every stumble lost time, and he might be losing the race with the army tanks.

Ah! There's the road. I'm not lost. While frantically sucking air he scanned the road from behind foliage. *Now would not be a good time to be spotted by either the army or the Islamic terrorists.* Either would assume he was the enemy. He saw no soldiers—no tanks. "Crap. Where is the damn army?" Alan was not exactly sure what he would do if he got to the Boko Haram camp before the army. Would there be time to locate Mona and the other hostages before the army arrived?

He plunged back into the forest and tried to increase his pace. The path that paralleled the road helped, but it soon wound snakelike up a steep incline. He grabbed tree limbs and brush to propel himself upward.

Automatic gunfire. Not far away. It sounded like a persistent crackle at first. "Nooo." Alan shouted in despair when canon fire erupted. He had missed his chance to save Mona's life. He plopped to his hands and knees, feeling horribly inadequate.

Colorful birds screeched as they hurtled past him, escaping the clash of human warfare. Several startled hartebeest sprinted for the dark, low ground. *Life. Life goes on. I can't give up now. Mona could still be alive, maybe injured.*

He stood, and jogged to the road. Seeing no movement there, he started to run toward the shooting with intensified vigor. His rubbery legs betrayed him. After a short distance he stumbled after a short distance, and rolled off the road. His backpack stopped his momentum, and he ended up on his stomach under a leafy black pine shrub. He gasped for air.

Forcing himself to get up, he was startled to hear heavy steps running nearby, away from the canon fire. He froze, and pushed deeper into the black pine foliage. Barely twenty meters from the road a man in camouflage leggings darted among the trees in the nimble sprint of youth. *He looks like a kid, dressed in terrorist garb.* His long black shirt, heavy military boots and the *shemagh* wrapped around his head gave away his alliance, but he carried no visible weapon. The youth disappeared quickly. Only the sounds of his retreating steps persisted. The surprising encounter with an enemy created a sickening chill, as Alan realized he had witnessed his first Boko Haram terrorist. *What the hell was that all about? Why is that kid running away from the fight? What would he have done if he had seen me?*

Artillery explosions diminished, replaced with automatic rifle bursts. Alan groaned, visualizing a destroyed terrorist camp. "God. Please Mona. Please be safe." He didn't want to think about the destruction that the tanks must be inflicting. His only thought was to get to Mona, whether she was alive or dead. He urged his body to move.

He stood up abruptly, and was shocked to stare directly into dark eyes peering through a *shemagh*. Panic froze Alan. He stared at a killing machine, a ruthless, religious fanatic, who had no qualms about killing women and children. The eyes of the man he faced told Alan that he was willing to die to reap his heavenly reward, and would not let this foreign infidel get in his way.

Both men were paralyzed by surprise. Alan hesitated, not sure if he should run or introduce himself. His options vanished swiftly as his antagonist raised a knife, shouted something in Arabic, and lunged.

Alan's left arm went up instinctively to ward off the attack. Fortunately, he avoided a deep neck wound, however, sharp steel sliced his hand as the attacker pulled back. He would die if he didn't respond with aggression. Pivoting on his right foot he swung his left leg high. A surge of adrenalin powered a blow harder than expected. His boot connected with the man's ribs. The swift turning motion, however, sent his spectacles flying.

An audible cracking rib and a scream of pain erupted from his adversary. Bent at the waist and sucking air, the man glanced toward Alan, who did not wait for retaliation, but raised his right knee hard into the man's forehead. The terrorist's head snapped backward and his body fell limply. Soft, low pitched groans signaled the end of the encounter. Alan satisfied himself that the man was alive but unable to fight. Wrenching the knife from his assailant's hand, Alan threw the weapon far into the forest.

Alan became acutely aware of pain and blood streaming from his left hand. He looked deep into the wound and blanched. Rummaging through his backpack he found gauze and tape to stem the flow of blood. To protect the wound from infection he found antiseptic. With tight windings he stopped the blood but not the pain.

Several meters away he saw light reflected off a lens and retrieved his glasses from the forest floor. Flexing his shoulders and arms he declared himself unbroken. He gently picked up his pack and placed it on his back. After taking a minute to catch his breath, he set off walking, then jogging, down the middle of the road toward the clamor of battle.

An armored personnel carrier blocked the road a half kilometer later. After explaining that he needed to see Captain Hassan immediately, the Nigerian soldiers drove him the rest of the way to the devastated camp, which was not on the main road but hidden on a maintenance road. There were no permanent structures, but dense foliage that concealed a park campground.

Acrid smoke rose from several burning vehicles. Blood-stained bodies sprawled grotesquely. Alan's eyes watered from the harsh odor of burnt ordinance and diesel fuel. Alan's heart sank in despair, as he saw no possible way anyone could have survived the evident havoc. He saw no prisoners.

Captain Hassan stood near his Humvee, holding a radio to one ear while dispensing instructions to his officers. Alan saw the frown as the captain turned and appeared to recognize him. But Alan was too furious to care.

CHAPTER 24
DEVASTATION

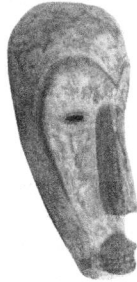

Alan ignored Hassan's dismissive scowl. The captain had previously ordered him out of Nigeria. "Humpf." He angrily scoffed at the captain's apparent disdain, and turned to look for any trace of Mona.

The army had beat him to the Yankari terrorist camp and had demolished it. Though the captain's frown suggested that the Nigerians didn't appreciate a foreigner meddling in military affairs, it had been Alan's prompting that had helped the army locate the terrorists.

The captain put down his radio, spat onto the dry earth and called, "Meester Aran. Why *yu heya*? Ah order you leave Nigeria."

The American shouted, "Sir, my wife is a captive of Boko Haram. I've got to find her. Was she here? I hope to God you haven't killed her."

"Ah, yes." The captain said. Hassan had focused on eliminating terrorists. Hostage safety was incidental. Hassan blinked, "My men tell me today morning of talk between Boko Haram, Cameroon and *yu presidant*. Please, come, sit my auto."

"No. Damn it. Where's my wife. I've got to find her. And, for the record, sir, my name is Alan Burke. Alan, with an L. My wife's name is Mona Burke. She could be here, in the camp that you have obliterated."

"Yes. Yes, I know, Meester Burke. Please sit. That is what I want to talk." Looking more closely at the American, Hassan added, "Gad. What happen? *Yu* seem like *yu* were in meat grinder. Look. *yu* hand."

Alan had forgotten about his wounds. At Hassan's reminder, however, he became acutely aware of the pain in his hand. He looked at the blood-soaked gauze, and felt a wave of nausea. Too anxious to tend to it he turned and walked toward the carnage. The captain followed. Alan scanned through the drifting smoke and swirling dust. He was mortified that he had not been able to find Mona before the army demolished the camp.

Occasional bursts of automatic weapons rattled as soldiers walked through smoking debris and weaved in and out of the nearby trees. Hassan walked in step with Alan. "Please know," he said, "there is more than one hostage. Of course, *yu* wife, Meesus Burke. But also, one minister from Cameroon. Maybe also some students and teachers from Hafsa. Ah sorry, but we not see any non-combatant as of now. Before you go search you must know that *yu* U.S. government tell today morning they are discuss ransom with the Boko Haram *fo* sake of *that yu woman*. This mean the enemy will keep her alive."

The word "alive" filtered into Alan's tired mind. "Are you suggesting," he asked, "that she was not here with these terrorists? You did not find any evidence of any of the prisoners?"

"Come. We search." The captain shouted to two soldiers, motioning for them to follow. He drew his sidearm and walked cautiously toward the center of camp. "Follow behind," he ordered waving Alan to stay back.

Alan saw shredded, upended or flattened tents, and smoldering vehicles. An abandoned pot hung over a burning campfire, its contents dripping from shrapnel holes and sputtering into the fire. Bodies with gruesome injuries revealed horrible ways to die. Alan noted that some appeared to have been very young men. One Boko Haram body that rested against a burned-out pickup truck could not have been eighteen years in this world. Alan couldn't help seeing the body of a child rather than that of a terrorist, and he groaned in sympathetic misery.

The sun burned through the small clearing, filtering late morning light on the destruction. Alan spotted a crushed canvas-covered personnel carrier under the freakish shadow of a large, partially shattered tree. A huge branch had fallen on the cab. The front wheels, axel and engine compartment had been smashed by canon fire. The rear of the transport vehicle was somewhat intact. Alan walked toward it, but a soldier quickly moved in front of him and cautiously approached from the side of the mangled vehicle expecting a fire fight. The soldier appeared disappointed.

The soldier signaled all clear, but Alan insisted on looking inside. He climbed the mangled ladder and stood on the pitched floor until his eyes adjusted to the dim light and drifting smoke. It was an eighteen-seat carrier with weapon brackets on the sidewalls. Several weapons were strewn on the floor.

A badly scuffed, colorful, woman's shoe caught Alan's attention. Its heel was missing. He sat down, overcome with emotion.

"*Yu fayne some 'ting?*" the captain shouted from outside.

Alan dropped his head into his hands and groaned. Ten days ago, he and Mona had dinner in a Paris restaurant. A beautiful evening. They were happily in love and excited to be starting a new adventure together. They danced for two minutes to a Taylor Swift song, but sat down when Mona said her foot hurt. He had checked her shoe. It was the same one he held now.

"*Ees hers?*" the captain asked.

Alan nodded, sensing that Mona was near. *Where? And where are the other prisoners?* His thoughts were cut short by shouts.

"*Meester* Burke. Come."

Five girls were huddled nearby, looking terrified as a soldier questioned them. The captain spoke to the girls in his native Hausa, using a soft, consoling voice.

Were these the Hafsa students Mona had referred to in her recorded French communique? Their clothes were probably the same school clothes they wore when they were abducted. They looked like they had not been fed well. Two of them were bent over in apparent discomfort, their eyes looked cavernous and they sat on the ground.

"What are they saying? Do they know about Mona?

The captain changed to pidgin, "*Na, yu* name *whatee?*"

Hesitating at first, one of the traumatized girls finally responded in a tremulous voice, "Chioma. *Ah..ah.. comot fo Hafsa.*"

"Yu from Hafsa," the captain said so Alan could hear. The captain queried further before turning to Alan. "They know of a white *wuman* who was captured. They *no no* her name, but one girl, Chioma, said maybe be Mona. That girl *say* white *wuman* American, and she friended language teacher named Oneka."

"Yes." cried Alan, "That's the woman we saw yesterday. Those savages murdered her. Ask the girl where Mona is."

Hassan was only able to learn that the American woman had been kept away from the others, "*Pikin* say when shooting start, they run to trees, there, left side. Two girls fall, maybe killed. They say there were four or five more *Hofsa pikin* in the camp but they no see them."

"What about the Cameroonian minister? Do they know where she is?"

Hassan questioned further. Chioma, who now spoke most confidently, shrugged her shoulders, saying that she spoke with a French-speaking woman prisoner, but never saw her face. "*Also,*" Hassan said, "*two men teachers from Hofsa were prisoners, but girl pikin not know where they be. Some hear shooting. Maybe man-teachers get executed. One girl know 'bout the Cameroon minister. They don tok pidgin and French small time. Girl say America woman was taken away two time. When they leave camp, bad men take her again. This one says she thinks America woman was here. She don hear guards talking about a white woman.*"

Chioma approached Alan. She touched his arm. Her eyes moistened as she spoke soft words Alan couldn't know. Alan's composure softened, but when she turned and walked away, he was too emotionally moved to ask what had just happened. Captain Hassan explained, "Girl say *yu wuman fayne person.*"

Alan's eyes watered and his shoulders drooped. Emotionally

drained, he felt stunned. That brave young girl just connected dots between him and Mona.

There was still the task of finding Mona. *Did Mona escape and is she hiding in the forest? Was she dead or wounded, lying somewhere in this rubble? Did her captors force her somewhere else?*

Pacing quickly from one burned-out vehicle to another, he searched for any trace of Mona. He called her name while his eyes roved the smoldering camp. Mangled metal, broken glass and lifeless, bloodied bodies of men and boys everywhere. Close to the side of the camp he came to an abrupt halt. "Captain." The bodies of two young girls lay close to the cover of the forest. Shrapnel wounds punctuated their bodies with blood.

Shaking in abhorrence and outrage, Alan knelt beside the two still figures. Flies buzzed. *Their parents will be devastated.* Deeply saddened at the sight of these innocent victims, he thought, *Will I find my wife like this?*

As Captain Hassan ended a radio conversation Alan asked, "Captain, what information do you have on the hostages?"

Hassan shook his head slowly from side to side. "Sorry, meester Burke, we get no news." After a moment the captain added, "Maybe is good. Maybe ransom demand still good. Maybe the American and Cameroonian hostages are live."

"Have you heard anything from Second Commander Ebi, at Hafsa?"

Hassan stared at Alan with a surprised look. "Yes, I talk with Ebi. *Yu* know heem? *Yu* have message for Ebi?"

"I need to know if he received a message from my friend Eric."

"Who is this Eric, and how *yu* know Ebi?"

"Eric is the Cameroon man with me yesterday at the terrorist camp. I asked him to contact officer Ebi. I need to know if Eric is safe."

Hassan shook his head in wonderment and barked into the radio. After two minutes he turned to Alan. "*Yu* Eric is well, as of one hour past. He saw men crossing the Yankari River. He *tink sey* they be Boko Haram."

Alan stared into the distance. Mona and several other hostages were unaccounted for. Some terrorists may have escaped. It is likely that the Boko Haram forced the captives to flee with them. If the ransom was being negotiated, it made sense that they would keep the hostages alive. Question is, where did they go? It would be a weird twist of fate if Mona was being spirited toward Eric's position.

Scanning the patches of tall elephant grass and the dark forest beyond, Alan saw a flash of light a split second before something impacted his side. A powerful blow spun him 180 degrees. Lying on the hard ground looking at clouds he slowly became aware that he had been struck by a bullet. Hot lead had pierced his left arm, and scraped his chest. The searing sensation hurt like hell. He felt something warm cascade down his arm. He felt himself being dragged, his boot heels plowing earth. When he opened his eyes, a medic was cleaning his wound.

Starbursts of burnt gun powder emanating from weapon barrels sparkled on the forest fringe as terrorists launched a barrage of deadly lead toward the Nigerian soldiers. Captain Hassan's men dove for cover and returned fire.

Alan gasped in pain when he tried to sit up. He brushed aside the alarmed medic and stood. He had to move. He wanted to believe that Mona was alive, and he still had a chance to help her.

The men he had seen during his race from the river were running away from the camp. They appeared to be Boko Haram but did not have hostages. The shot that hit him had come from the opposite side of the camp. Alan ignored his pain, picked up his crushed backpack and took several dizzying steps toward Captain Hassan.

Indicating the forest, Alan shouted, "I think the hostages are being taken that way."

"*Na so?*" Said Hassan, with a hint of sarcasm and a dismissive sniff.

CHAPTER 25
RACE TO THE CENTER

Four Boko Haram militants had retreated to the forest when their camp was overrun by the Nigerian army. Two terrorists concealed themselves at the edge of the forest to cover their commander's escape. Two others, one with a satellite radio, caught up with Edubamo. The commander immediately radioed the support center in Maiduguri, demanding to know the status of ransom negotiations. He was prepared to jettison the two women hostages who were becoming a burden. The rapid deterioration of his situation made it risky to keep them alive.

More than ninety-six hours had passed since he had made ransom demands. *Will Boko Haram make a final public threat before demonstrating to the world that the jihad is serious?* Keeping the prisoners alive would require help to escape the Nigerian Army. A deputy on the Shura Consultative Council confirmed that the captives still had ransom value. Edubamo knew well to follow the advice of his Islamic leadership assembly.

His leaders in Maiduguri directed him to the Yankari game reserve's visitor center, assuring him that an agent would transport everyone to a secure location.

Edubamo was therefore compelled to move further from his

intended destination, Maiduguri. A tenacious Nigerian Army was dictating his route, pushing him further off course. He seethed over this humiliation.

One captive had no shoes and the other was in deteriorating physical condition. The minister complained about sore feet. She had been beaten so often that Edubamo was aware that she might collapse. He removed the belt that coupled the two hostages. He was determined to reach the park's visitor center to meet the promised Boko Haram agent. The commander had no indication that the Nigerian Government had ordered the national park closed or that the entire park had been evacuated.

He shoved Mona with the butt of his weapon, attempting to prod her to move faster. He shouted in a harsh whisper, "*Waka. Quick-quick.*"

To the winded minister, he shouted, "*Go fo befo, una fat pig. Eef yu no wan dy yu fit woka quick, quick!*" One of Edubamo's men pushed the minister roughly. She stumbled and, while trying to catch her balance her colorful headpiece fell off. She reached to retrieve it, but the man kicked it aside and pushed her forward.

Edubamo's map showed that the visitor center was near the center of the national park. He estimated that it was less than two kilometers from his last camp. He could have made that distance in twenty minutes if not for the hostages.

CHAPTER 26
BIRDS IN FLIGHT

Mona struggled on bleeding bare feet, dreading a sprained or broken ankle. Her antagonists prodded her with rifle butts whenever she lagged. The forest air suffocated and left her gasping. Sweat soaked her clothes. She rested only seconds to catch her breath before being hustled deeper into the forest. She was intensely thirsty, but the muddy water in the streams she crossed was unfit to drink.

Mona made a valiant effort to step carefully to avoid falling. The one time she did fall, she was roughly assisted up by one of Edubamo's men who took the opportunity to place his hand on her buttocks to push her up. He squeezed, drew close to her and moaned. She pulled away sharply but heard him chuckle and whisper a comment to his comrade. She angrily vowed to keep her distance from the men.

Laboring ahead on painfully bruised feet, Mona looked for an opportunity to escape. She broke small shrub branches whenever she could do so undetected, and dropped leaves to provide a trail in the unlikely event that someone was looking for her.

Sudden crashing of branches startled her. The edgy militants raised their weapons but relaxed as a small herd of bushbuck burst

195

across the path and hurtled deeper into the dense forest. The men laughed nervously, as the harmless game disappeared. A tear rolled down Mona's cheek when the commotion had not been caused by rescuers.

Wet moss and rotting leaves provided a soft cushion of decay, and offered fleeting relief for Mona. For brief moments she felt the cool, soft moss ooze up between her toes and caress her sore feet. She could not hesitate long, for fear of another brutal nudge from a rifle butt. When dense foliage gave way to stony or rocky terrain, she had to step vigilantly as the commander shouted at her to hurry. She saw him motion to one of his men to help her. Afraid that he was suggesting that one of the men carry her, Mona shouted, "No." She wanted no part of that man's hands on her body. She would walk until her feet were bloody stumps before she would let one of these men touch her again.

Something ahead caught her attention. Ten meters in front was an asphalt footpath. She pointed excitedly and shouted, "Look." The three terrorists and the minister all gaped at the path. Mona observed that the walkway was a meter wide and continued in the direction they were headed. It passed steps to a game observation blind. The terrorists breathed a cheer. Approaching civilization, Mona felt a twinge of relief, hopeful that someone, a guard, an attendant, a helpful tourist, anyone might help her escape from this endless torture.

Another three hundred meters, circumventing huge rocks, a swampy lagoon and dense brush, the path terminated at the edge of a paved parking lot. Mona felt disappointment to see no parked cars, only baboons staring at her. Moving into a compound she saw numerous small chalets, but no tourists. A large structure sat to her left, and across an open area Mona saw an asphalt road passing through a tall, masonry archway. Mona thought it strangely desolate considering the time of day. A large sign read, WIKKI CAMP— YANKARI NATIONAL PARK TOURIST CENTER.

Edubamo's men cautiously approached the largest building with weapons ready. If there were no tourists there would likely be soldiers. If there were no soldiers or tourists, there might be no vehicles to commandeer. The terrorists cursed as they approached the visitor center and peered in through a barred window. On the front door was a sign written in several languages. The English version read, CLOSED.

Mona and the minister limped onto a wood deck. The captives were left alone for several moments while their captors searched for possible traps and an entrance to the shuttered building. Mona massaged her swollen and bruised feet.

The Cameroonian woman gave a wearisome sigh and plopped onto a wood bench. Unruly, mid-length, black hair had been exposed when she lost her colorful head piece. The soles of her shoes were separating from the uppers, and her suit was stained with dirt and sweat. She gasped for air, and slouched in apparent pain. Her fearful eyes glanced at Mona. Her limp shoulders and drooping arms confirmed her exhaustion. The minister's eyes, however, reflected a defiant demeanor. Mona looked into those angry eyes and sensed that below that fragile physical appearance was a strong, calculating character. *A woman doesn't get to be a minister in an African country without a lot of grit.*

"What's your name?" Mona asked in a commiserating tone. The minister's bewildered stare acknowledged the first attempt to communicate

The minister offered a faint smile and spoke in French, "Je m'appelle *Stany Ngey, le Ministre du Trésor du Cameroun.*"

"Stany, hi. I am Mona. Do you speak English?"

"*Un peu.*" A second later she added, "*Qui, small, small.*"

A Boko Haram militant sprung forward, pointed his weapon at the minister and roughly pushed Mona aside, indicating in a harsh whisper that they were not to speak. "*Ah go land yu slap.*"

The area appeared deserted. Mona heard Edubamo shouting in anger, and watched as he appeared to be searching for something missing. "*Whoside ma moto dey?*" He seemed very agitated that someone or something was not here.

Edubamo rounded a cabin some 20 meters from Moma when she saw him suddenly jerk his head up as if listening for a sound. He stood alert and cocked his head. Now Mona heard it too, a sound like the rattle of metal objects. The commander edged around the corner of the visitor center, and pointed his weapon toward a small structure fifty meters away.

Mona leaned forward and spotted a white pickup truck parked on the far side of that out-building. The sounds of clanging objects confirmed that someone was inside. She screamed a warning as loud as her voice could go, "Watch out! Watch out!" A hard fist knocked her to the deck. Her head spun in dizzy confusion.

CHAPTER 27
A TRAIL OF HOPE

Alan's head throbbed with every burst of gunfire. When the silence came, he slowly lifted his head to see a soldier run from the forest and report to his captain that the snipers had been neutralized.

"Did your men find the hostages?" Alan winced as he asked Captain Hassan.

Hassan sighed, as if annoyed. "No hostage. We *don* keel *tu* Boko Haram. That man who *shoot yu ee dead now.* Safe now. Go, see *fo yu wuman.*"

In spite of his wounds, Alan staggered toward the shadows of the tall baobab trees. Seventy meters into the forest, standing over the bodies of two bloodied militants, three Nigerian soldiers chattered in excited voices with animated gestures. Alan caught the words *kray die* and remembering what Eric told him in Yaounde, wondered if the soldiers mocked the deaths of their enemies. He feigned a smile and moved away.

Deeper into the forest, Alan searched, desperately hoping to see Mona. He only saw recently disturbed leaves and soil. The sound of the soldiers' voices faded. He was admittedly afraid to go further without the army. He scanned moss-covered trees and fallen branches, wondering again what flesh-eating predators lived in the reserve. In the muted light he spotted a shape on the ground that looked out of place. Moving nearer, he saw a camouflage uniform. *A body! I thought Hassan said there were **two** enemy guerillas, but that's not an army soldier. This one looks like another bad guy.* This guy was shot in the head at close range. Twenty meters away he was even more surprised to find two additional bodies. The bloodied remains wore the camouflage uniforms of Boko Haram.

Alan shouted in the direction of the three Nigerian soldiers, "Hey! Hey! Come. Help!" The soldiers followed Alan to the three bodies. Captain Hassan appeared behind them, the battle at the Boko Haram camp having been won.

A soldier shouted, "*Ee mon, ee no die* from *army.* Look," he said, pointing at a bullet wound in a dead man's head, "*Ee bin shot in ee head,* from close. *I tink sey, maybe ee be executed by ee own pipo.*"

Who shot whom? Why would the guerrillas execute their own men? As he stood there deep in thought, his eyes wandered to the green foliage and sturdy tree trunks around him. *What took place here! Where the hell is Mona?*

Alan stood aside as the soldiers talked excitedly, trying to piece together what they thought may have occurred here in the shaded forest just 300 meters from the demolished Boko Haram camp. Alan's eyes drifted as he also tried to make sense of the situation. He eventually focused on an object that didn't match the forest surroundings. *What's on that tree?* Moving closer, his eyes widened as he saw a piece of cloth. He gasped. The fabric looked familiar. Rushing to the tree he reached up to retrieve it. His eyes watered. It was the sleeve of a blouse. *Mona had been in this tree!*

The captain's eyes followed Alan to the tree and looked up into the thick foliage. Hassan saw the cloth and asked, "What is it?"

"It's part of my wife's shirt. She bought it recently, in D.C." He clutched the remnant, feeling a desperate closeness to Mona. "She may have climbed this tree. Look at the scrapes on the bark, and the small branches and leaves on the ground. Maybe she was discovered and forced down. She has to be near."

The forest floor was covered with decaying debris, hiding most footprints. Next to a camouflage-uniformed body there were scuffle marks indicating recent traffic, but there was no clear indication which way the survivors had gone. A soldier eventually found tracks in a nearby muddy stream. He indicated that four or five people had crossed it recently. At least one of them was barefoot.

The captain returned to his unit at the terrorist camp, and ordered two of his men to wait with Alan. He indicated he would return with additional soldiers and a radio.

The soldiers rested on downed tree trunks. One man called to Alan and motioned for him to join them.

Alan, too agitated to relax, was excited that Mona may be alive and nearby. He boiled with rage for her captors' treatment of her. *She must be terrified.* Based on having found her shoe he knew she was the barefoot one.

Rather than waiting for the armed protection, Alan walked to the small muddy stream to see the footprints. He couldn't resist following them. When he stepped across the mud, he noticed that there was a path of trodden-down grass, likely created by animals, but boot prints convinced him it was the path the terrorists had taken.

A soldier shouted, "*Wetin dey happen? Yu fit stay close. Listen well well.*" The soldier added, "*You fit bring much wahala. Ah beg, com out.*"

Alan didn't care if he caused a problem. On he went. When he looked back again, the soldiers were no longer visible.

The pulsating ache from his arm and hand sent throbbing reminders of his brush with death. His arms hung at his side and his fatigued legs shook uncontrollably. Then he shouted, "Sorry. *Ah go go me.*" He turned and trudged along the barely discernible path. The army soldiers waited for their commanding officer.

Tucking a loose end of his arm bandage into itself, he stumbled toward hope and fear. Near the boot marks in the mud exiting a small stream were the small, shoeless footprints. The edges of the wet dirt bordering the footprints had not yet dried and crumbled. The group had passed here about twenty minutes ago.

Adrenaline made Alan acutely aware of sound and movements. His fears stimulated a rush, and his pulse quickened. Every nerve triggered as he realized how close he was to the terrorists. He didn't want to stumble into another bullet.

Rounding a large boulder, he noticed several green leaves on the path. At first, they meant nothing to him, but when he saw a tuft of grass including its roots lying on the path, he realized that someone had intentionally left markers. It had to be Mona. She was signaling to him. His heart leapt with hope. *She is alive, and she is talking to me. Of course, Mona could not possibly know that I am anywhere within 500 kilometers, but I just know she is trying to communicate.* He could now concentrate on following a path of green leaves.

Alan's head throbbed. The searing pain down his arm kept him alert. At one point he plopped onto his knees until the dizziness passed. The loss of blood made him light-headed. He feared that he might faint or fall while running. The musty, hot air in the forest made breathing difficult. His only consolation was that he was in far better condition than he expected Mona was. She was barefoot. He wore hiking boots.

CHAPTER 28
MAINTENANCE MAN

Awoman's scream alerted Yankari Park's maintenance supervisor, Syed, that he was not alone. He stiffened when he heard the crunch of gravel. No one was supposed to be in the park.

He had ignored the order to evacuate. He was determined to finish a project, and he assumed the park service had overreacted, as the government often seemed to do. He needed this job. He had two wives and six young children to support. His days were long and the work was hard, but at least he had steady income. When the park manager threatened to dismiss him, Syed worked even harder.

He became further alarmed when he spotted a shadow moving across the maintenance yard. He had not heard a vehicle and wondered why anyone would still be in the park. The shadow seemed to be lurking rather than striding. Syed's concern increased when he saw the silhouette of a weapon. His blood pressure soared as he placed his hand on the long handle of a spade shovel.

Stepping over the clutter on the floor, he moved further into the shadow near the open door. Crunching gravel outside revealed the footsteps of someone moving cautiously a few meters beyond the thin wall.

A dozen thoughts ran through Syed's mind. His anxiety increased.

The warning from park officials about the evacuation and the possible presence of terrorist activity nearby now worried him. He thought of his family, his workmates, the sweet voice of the radio dispatcher, his bag lunch of roasted plantain and *fufu* on his workbench. Sweat from fear soaked his green uniform. His heart raced, and his breathing became loud.

The shadow of the crouching figure inched along the side of the building. Syed raised the spade over his head, unaware of his labored breathing. Unfortunately for Syed, the heavy breathing betrayed his position.

A burst of automatic gunfire shattered the silence. Hot lead and wood splinters rocketed through the tool shed wall. Fragments struck Syed's chest and throat. Seriously wounded, he collapsed to the dirt floor. Unable to get up, he could only stare at the corrugated tin ceiling. The feeling of helplessness frightened him. He sensed a shadow slide through the doorway. As he turned his head to see the intruder another shot rang out.

*   *   *

Mona and Stany Ngey recoiled at the loud gunfire. Mona screamed and buried her head in her lap, shocked at the violent act. Stany moaned and fell to her knees on the veranda, weeping. Mona reached out and grasped Stany's shoulder in a consoling effort. The minister recoiled from Mona's touch.

Shouting in Hausa, the two militants grabbed the captives and shoved them toward the white truck parked in the sun, near the tool shed. Across the open yard they saw the commander climb into the truck. The engine roared to life, and the truck kicked up gravel as it spun around and sped toward the visitor center.

Mona and Stany were roughly hoisted into the back of the pickup truck and forced to sit in the bed against the rear of the cab. The hot metal of the truck burned Mona's bare arms and feet. There was nothing to cushion them from hard metal.

One militant steadied his automatic weapon on the two captives. The other rushed to the front of the visitors' center and kicked open the front door. After much banging and crashing of glass, he rushed back carrying a wicker basket containing the contents of a ravaged vending machine. Mona glimpsed bags of curly potato chips, fig bars and energy bars. The man carried a half dozen bottles of water.

The truck turned toward the exit and rocketed across the parking lot. It picked up speed as it roared through the entrance gate. The force of the acceleration banged Mona and Stany against hot side walls with bruising force.

*   *   *

Alan stumbled to a breathless stop near a structure and peered around the corner of the visitor center building just as the pickup sped under an archway and disappeared into a mask of dust and foliage.

CHAPTER 29
ERIC

E ric Mbando waited near the Peugeot in frustration since early morning, feeling useless and abandoned. Alan had told him to stay with the car, but over three hours had passed since Alan waded across the river. He wondered if the American ever found the terrorist camp. *Did Alan beat the army to where the hostages were being held? Was he captured by Boko Haram, or worse?* Eric heard the percussion of canon fire and the angry sounds of battle not far away. He was scared, but still wanted to be with Alan. He kicked a stone in frustration, feeling powerless.

Sudden loud splashing startled him. Thirty meters downriver a man waded the current and scrambled up the near bank. Eric slipped behind a tree. Dressed in camouflage fatigues, the man appeared to be a militant. The intruder ran as though his life depended on speed. The man apparently had not spotted Eric's car, and, once across the stream, fled in the direction away from Eric. A jolt of primal fear paralyzed Eric when he realized that a desperate person might be willing to kill for a car in which to escape.

The Peugeot was visible from the river. Eric hurriedly pulled up some vegetation and cut branches to conceal the car. When the reflective metal and glass were obscured, he fashioned a club from a stout branch and hid. Two more men crossed the river ten minutes later. They also failed to notice the car. Eric wondered if Alan had encountered these men.

He waited in suspense for thirty minutes before deciding to use the military radio to call Second Commander Obwale Ebi's military unit.

Ebi's voice soon crackled over the speaker, "Yes?"

Giving his approximate location, Eric reported the army moving toward the game reserve, the sounds of battle, and the three militants crossing the river. He asked for any new information about Mister Burke and the hostages.

Ebi confirmed that Captain Hassan's troops had secured the Boko Haram camp nearly an hour ago, but he had no information about Mr. Burke or the captives. Ebi suggested that Eric contact Burke.

"*Na, how I fit call that man?*" Eric asked. "*I fit use una radio?*"

"No." shouted Ebi. "You must return that receiver to me *now, now.*" After a moment, Ebi continued, "*Call heem on cell phone.*"

Eric found Alan's phone and turned it on. A weak "beep" and it went dark and silent. *That's why masa left it back.* Eric returned to the boot to replace the phone when he noticed the thin, white cable. *Ah. The charging cable.* He inserted the charger into the 12-volt receptacle and threw the cell phone onto the passenger seat.

After another ten minutes his patience expired. If he abandoned this location, Alan wouldn't be able to find him. On the other hand, Alan could be dead now. In any case, it was unlikely that Alan would be able to find this exact spot. Eric made his decision.

He hurriedly pulled the foliage off the car. When the engine fired up the gas gauge barely registered above the E. The loud "beep." from the passenger seat meant Alan's phone was charging.

He maneuvered the vehicle out of the tall grass and crossed a field to the road. There he turned left and drove in the direction the army had traveled that morning. He stiffened as he cautiously motored into the unknown.

Two kilometers further he slowed when he saw a dense cloud of smoke. He was near the battle area. *I hope the Army won,* he thought. *If not, I could be foolishly driving into big trouble.*

Nigerian soldiers blocked the road, displaying weapons as they ordered Eric to stop. Speaking in a local dialect one soldier said, "Halt. This road is closed. You must go back."

Eric complied with the order, but exited the car and held his hands palms out to show that he was unarmed. He spoke in his mother tongue. Fortunately, one soldier understood. Eric explained that he was looking for the white man from the United States Embassy in Yaoundé. When that didn't appease the soldier's inclination to follow strict orders, Eric stated that he knew Captain Hassan and that the captain was helping him locate the American hostage of Boko Haram.

The soldiers allowed Eric to pass after searching his car. They cautioned him about possible snipers near the camp, which was not far away. Eric couldn't believe the destruction. *How can anyone survive this?*

Eric asked a uniformed officer what had happened, and said, "I must find Mr. Alan Burke." The man waved Eric off. Eric, in his civilian clothes seemed out of place at best, and possibly suspicious in a battle area.

A uniformed officer stopped Eric and demanded his identification. It took a while to convince the officer that he was not a murderer or a terrorist but was trying to help the husband of the American hostage. When he dropped Captain Hassan's name, another soldier remembered Eric from the first terrorist camp. That man pulled Eric aside.

"Cap'n Hassan *no be here. Ee don wok fo forest tu hour past. Ee follow 'merica mon.* He told Eric that Captain Hassan had left several hours ago with a detail of soldiers. Hassan and his men had followed Alan, who was tracking an unknown number of terrorists holding Alan's wife and the treasury minister hostage. Eric inquired about how he could get to Alan quickly. The soldier produced a map of the area noting that the terrorists were likely headed toward a visitor center several kilometers from their present position.

The map indicated that the main road went further into the reserve, but that one side road circled toward the visitor center. Eric left the destroyed camp immediately, found the side road, and sped toward the visitor center.

CHAPTER 30
THE CHASE

Alan walked on weary legs. The loss of blood made him light-headed. He sensed that he was scarcely minutes behind the terrorists, and he knew he might run into a trap. Gunshots not far away reminded him to be cautious. A well-traveled path suggested he was close to civilization. He wanted to shout relief, but he remained silent, knowing the Boko Haram militants were close.

Alan heard an engine race and tires crunch on gravel. He judged that he was within 500 meters of the gunshots and the loud engine. In fading light, he ran onto an empty parking lot. *Guess everyone's gone home already.* Rounding the corner of a building he saw the tail lights of a small, white truck as it sped past the entrance and into the shadows of the forest. He saw the word "ISUZU" on the tailgate of a truck and several indistinct figures in the open bed.

He stumbled onto the veranda of the tourist center and slumped onto a wooden bench. His head ached. His legs trembled with fatigue. He thought that the speeding truck had to be the terrorists but he had no way to pursue them. *I'll call the police.*

He jumped to his feet and staggered through the open door of the visitor center. "Help!" he cried out as he ran past the CLOSED sign. The shattered vending machine and packets of potato chips scattered on the floor caused him to stop. "What the hell?" he said. "Someone broke in, robbed the place, and sped off in that truck?"

No body, no blood, thank God. There's got to be a telephone in here. He looked under the service counter. No phone. He looked for a pay phone for visitors. Nothing. He forced the door to a back room. There, on the small desk was a phone. There was no dial tone. Grabbing a bottle of water from the broken vending machine, he went back outside.

The shed caught his attention and he ran toward it. He heard a groan of someone in pain. Lying on the shed floor he saw a bloodied man on his back, eyes open. The man's head slowly turned toward Alan with pleading eyes. The man made a pained effort to sit. A trickle of blood formed at the fringe of his mouth. "Do you speak English?" Alan asked, as he placed a rolled-up sack under the man's head.

A mixture of blood and spittle dripped from the man's lips as he tried to speak. "*Ah no fit tokah.*" After a short pause and some strained breathing, the man said something in a language unknown to Alan who winced and shook his head.

Spotting the name on the man's shirt Alan asked, "Syed?" The dying man nodded and screwed up his face in pain. Alan opened the water bottle and offered it. Syed sipped a little before turning his head away.

Alan then spotted the radio attached to Syed's belt and touched it. Syed nodded. With painful groans the man pointed a finger at the power button. A static-like buzzing indicated that the battery was charged and ready to transmit. Syed pointed to seven numbers in sequence. Alan entered each number as directed. A buzz followed by a distant click indicating a successful connection.

A man's voice came through the static, "*Allo, Syed.*" Alan didn't understand the Hausa that followed.

""Hi. This is Alan Burke. I am American. I don't understand Nigerian. Do you speak English?"

Several seconds of silence passed before a female voice said, "*Sah, I de talk small English. Who's side Syed dey?*"

Alan spoke in an exaggeratedly slow and loud voice, "Syed is here.

He is badly injured. He has been shot. He urgently needs medical help. Please call a doctor. Call the police."

Suddenly, a wide-eyed Nigerian Army soldier stepped into the open doorway with his weapon pointed at Alan. The soldier lowered his weapon.

Several more soldiers charged into the shed, followed by Captain Hassan. The captain scrutinized the scene quickly and said, "*Wetin dey happen?*"

"Sir." Alan pleaded, visibly relieved to see the Nigerian Army instead of Boko Haram. He held up the radio for Hassan. "Please talk to these people. This man needs medical help."

Hassan accepted the radio while instructing his men to give some help to the wounded maintenance man. The captain spoke in Hausa. Then he turned to Alan with raised eyebrows and palms up, pleading for an explanation.

Alan described the white Isuzu pickup truck he saw speeding out of the game reserve. The captain used his army radio to pass along the information to his superiors. He offered, "The army will set up road blocks on every road leading from here.

"What are you going to do," Alan asked after Hassan finished speaking with his superior.

"Ma unit already move out and proceed to Jos." Hassan replied. "My superiors instruct me to leave unit and take highway south following terrorists. Possible hostages with terrorists. Ma commanding officer may instruct me as he is get information from checkpoints. You must stay here."

"Captain Hassan," Alan pleaded, "I can't stay here. Let me ride with you. I've got to find my wife. I know she is alive. I feel it."

Hassan started to wave Alan off, but stopped, made eye contact, and said, "Get in Humvee bafo I change mind."

CHAPTER 31
WHITE HOUSE DEMANDS

Sunday, December 10, Secretary of State, Lisa Townshend anxiously hastened to the White House in response to the president's telephone call. Forty-four-year-old Townsend already had three solid years of exemplary experience as secretary. Aided by eleven years with the Central Intelligence Agency and excellent achievements in her post graduate studies, she was well-prepared for a diplomatic career. She was known by her colleagues for her professional approach, but she displayed a good sense of humor.

Lisa took long, fast strides into the icy December breeze that made the pedestrians on the capitol plaza draw their topcoats tight. The twenty-minute walk from the Harry S. Truman Building put a rosy sting on her cheeks and tangled her long black hair.

I wonder if there has been some major development. Word of Mona Burke's abduction by the Boko Haram has become a headline news story in U.S. newspapers, and Alan's desperate dash into Nigeria to find his wife is being wildly conjectured by many. I am aware that the kidnapping of an American by terrorists and the disregard of protocol by diplomats has angered the president.

POTUS had demanded a debriefing on the hostage situation. He sounded annoyed when he called Lisa. That made her uneasy. She had spent most of Saturday calling representatives of France, England, Nigeria and Cameroon to understand the positions of those governments, and discuss their assistance in solving the hostage dilemma. Now the president wanted to know what to communicate to the American public regarding the Boko Haram ransom threats.

"Good morning," the president said, "Then," with a curt command: "Lisa. Sit."

"Mr. President, I…"

"Madam Secretary, I want to know what the hell your employee is doing running loose in Nigeria. His assignment is in Yaoundé, Cameroon. What kind of idiots do you hire for state?" He paused briefly. "What's the deal with this hostage situation?"

"Mr. President, Alan Burke is under a lot of stress. He was dropped into a disastrous situation in Cameroon when his wife was kidnapped by Islamic terrorists. I…"

"Did you authorize this guy's wife to travel to Nigeria? Why didn't she travel directly to Cameroon with her husband?"

"Sir, I realize I may have exercised poor judgment in approving Mrs. Burke's travel to Lagos. I can't endorse Mr. Burke's abandoning his position, however, I understand why he may have made the decisions he made." Lisa shrugged her shoulders. "I apologize for the jeopardy my decision caused. He was ordered to take some time off. I imagine he just couldn't sit idle while his wife is in danger."

The president turned to the window and gazed outside, hands in his pockets. He was in the first year of his first four-year term. At sixty-five, he knew a second term depended on how well he handled international situations like this one. The job took every ounce of his energy and concentration, and it placed high scrutiny on every word he spoke.

He sighed and turned toward Lisa. In a more conciliatory tone he offered, "I'm sorry, Lisa. I am not blaming you. I understand the emotional pressure that young man is under. To be honest, I'm not sure what I would do in a similar situation. Nevertheless, we've got to bring his wife out of danger. What are you doing to get her back?"

Lisa explained, "Sir, Ambassador Tyler Morrison tried repeatedly to get Cameroon's government to support our surveillance assistance.

I tried to contact the prime minister yesterday to see what military intervention Cameroon is attempting. The prime minister seemed resistant to any interference from nations other than France. He appears to mistrust the motives of other countries.

"I don't understand," the president said, scratching his two-day facial stubble, "I would think their government would be doing everything possible to recover their minister."

"Sir, Ambassador Morrison told me yesterday that his embassy officials were becoming frustrated. Everyone, not only the prime minister, is pissed about Burke entering Nigeria illegally. The USAID mission director is on Morrison's case, demanding to know why one of his drivers is AWOL."

"I don't care about the USAID driver. Why doesn't the Cameroon president use the personnel and equipment they requested, and that we provided last year, for just this type of crisis?"

Lisa outlined her conversation with Morrison. "Mr. President, according to the ambassador, the Cameroon government harbors trepidation about dealing with Nigeria. They are reluctant to engage Boko Haram terrorists who, they suspect, are more heavily-armed than the Cameroon Army.

"Then why don't they allow us to help them? Our military personnel are in the area."

"It's complicated, sir. Gender differences? The abducted minister, Stany Ngey, is a woman, and some leaders are not as deferential to a female minister. Many women do not run for high-level government positions because of fear of chauvinism. Further, the minister is Christian, and Ngey works in a heavily Muslim-influenced area. The minister was from Cameroon's Western Region, born into the Bamileke Tribe."

"What else, Lisa? I am not convinced."

"I feel, sir, that Cameroon's reluctance to challenge the Boko Haram could also be the result of religious affiliations. Western influence in the nation's education system, religious and social attitudes is hated by Boko Haram. Cameroonians are a very patient, non-warlike people, and they know that Boko Haram is better armed than the Cameroon army. Finally, we can't forget there is the issue of respecting national borders.

"Right," stated the president, "everyone but your embassy staff respects national borders." After a minute, he added, "Okay, work with Nigeria through Great Britain."

*   *   *

Lisa flew to London that afternoon to meet with the British prime minister. Great Britain had historical ties with Nigeria, and Townshend hoped that they could help influence a peaceful resolution. As a potential bargaining tool, several ISSL terrorists were incarcerated in British prisons.

Lisa understood Cameroon's reluctance to work with the U.S. Embassy, and advised Ambassador Morrison to bide his time, and temper his frustration by keeping the Cameroon government informed of the U.S.'s actions, and keeping his door open. They spoke several times every day during the crises.

"The ransom deadline has come and gone." Lisa told Morrison. "We have not seen further video of the captives since the previous Friday, and neither the U.S. nor the Cameroon government has received additional threats. We believe Boko Haram has extended their deadline. We want to believe that the hostages are still alive."

CHAPTER 32
ROAD RAGE

M ona Burke and Stany Ngey caromed off the truck sides as it hurtled south, away from Yankari Park. Painful bruises on their arms and legs were partially obscured with road dust. The terrorists had crudely tied their hands to the truck walls. Their wrists wore raw from rope abrasion. They both winced in pain with every jounce of the truck.

Mona coughed up Sahara dust. She had inhaled a lifetime supply, but she noted that the armed guard bouncing on the fender well nearby also struggled to breathe. The ordeal began to weaken Mona's resolve, but it may have also altered her moral convictions. She prayed for the strength to kick the guard over the edge of the truck when he was off balance. She realized, however, that getting rid of one terrorist could jeopardize her life even more.

Outside the city of Jos, the pickup truck pulled into a dimly-lit fueling station. Mona heard an urgent, whispered discussion between Edubamo and a sordid-looking man who glanced at the two women in the rear of the truck bed and pointed down the road. Mona thought she heard references to Abuja.

The commander turned the Isuzu onto a larger road and accelerated. It was now dark enough to require headlights. The air cooled, and Mona used the shelter of the cab to stay out of the wind. Earlier she had noted the setting sun, and calculated that they were headed southeast. She wondered if they were anywhere near Abuja. She would like nothing better than to see the driver who brought her to Kaduna and beat her. *What was his name? Oh yes, Bennett. Bennett Ngu. I'd kick him in the nuts for deceiving me and starting this horrible nightmare.*

Edubamo accelerated the truck through a manned customs inspection station. The uniformed agents waved their arms furiously, and shouted for the driver to stop. Laughter from the cab emphasized the commander's contempt for law. Mona hoped that the customs officers would not shoot at the truck. Hopefully they would radio authorities. *I should have shouted for help when we neared that checkpoint.*

After several more hours the engine strained as the road steepened. Mona noticed the cool air and smells of heavy foliage. She had no idea that they were near Nigeria's Cross River National Park. The pickup's engine growled on the uphill climbs when Edubamo downshifted. On the downgrades the Boko Haram guard was jostled about, especially when the commander braked around curves. At times, Mona thought that the guard, who had a bad habit of leering at her and Stany, might lose his grip and tumble over the side.

Time passed in monotonous bouncing with the cool wind blowing her hair into hopeless knots. Grit blanketed the prisoners, and their eyes watered from the dust. Mona and Stany each held firmly onto the truck frame to lessen the pain of the ropes on their wrists.

A lighted sign on the side of the road indicated that they were in Nigeria's famous Cross River National Park. Mona remembered reading about the gorillas. *I read about this park. I hoped to visit it one day, but not like this.*

Mona guessed that it was past midnight. There was scant traffic, but Edubamo's driving had become erratic. The truck occasionally brushed the road's edge only to be jerked back to the lane. Alarmed, Mona visualized additional ways to die. *Tied to the bed of the truck I would surely be crushed if the truck rolled over.*

*   *   *

Behind the wheel, Edubamo slapped his face to keep alert. At this speed he knew that a wrong move or a tire blowout would be disastrous. His fingers ached from his intense grip on the steering wheel. Tension in his neck was painful and his back needed a rest, but there was no time to stop.

The man in the cab with Edubamo cursed loudly, and jabbed his finger toward the windshield, pointing at something on the road ahead.

Edubamo braked, lightly at first, then with great urgency as bright lights abruptly flashed directly at them from less than a kilometer ahead. Moonlight reflected off gray metal. The commander recognized a military tank and several other vehicles forming a roadblock. "Shit." He shouted a litany of profanities in several languages, and pumped the brakes until the truck's tires gripped the pavement. *Why an army tank?* Then, realizing that the Nigerian army had likely been alerted from Yankari, or from the customs station they had sped through, he chose to turn and run.

"The army knows we have the hostages," the commander reasoned out loud, "they can't shoot at the hostages." He brought the truck to a controlled stop, spun the wheel sharply to his left and pressed the accelerator to the floor. The Isuzu's tires screamed as the truck spun into a 180 degree turn. The rear end fish-tailed around the anchoring weight of the front engine, throwing the terrorist guard completely off the back of the truck.

*　　　　　*　　　　　*

Mona and Stany gasped as they saw the man's terrified expression when he flew over the side, his fingers desperately reaching for traction. In the nanosecond before he took flight, his panicked scream was louder than the engine's roar. The man landed awkwardly and bounced before rolling to the shoulder of the road into a lifeless heap. Mona cringed in sympathetic agony, even though Edubamo had unwittingly accomplished what she had earlier wished for.

*　　　　　*　　　　　*

Edubamo did not stop. Military vehicles were closing fast. He pressed the accelerator, fighting the wheel to keep the truck from going into a sideways skid. He ordered his companion to fire his weapon at the pursuing vehicles.

*   *   *

Mona screamed as the man leaned out his window and fired a burst from his AK-47. The explosions were deafening, and the hot shell casings ejected into the truck bed. She shouted at Stany to put her head down, realizing that the army soldiers might return fire, and that she and Stany could be caught in the crossfire. *Please don't shoot back!*

An intense spotlight blinked on from a pursuing vehicle, directing a blinding light on the truck's rear window. At first, Stany and Mona instinctively ducked and shielded their heads and necks. Then Mona realized, *I've gotta make sure they know we're here.* She sat upright, closed her eyes against the powerful light and exposed her head and shoulders to the military vehicles.

The terrorist in the passenger seat held his automatic weapon in his left hand and shot from the passenger window. Apparently reacting to Mona's movement, he reached further out, swung the barrel of his weapon and struck Mona. She flew against the back of the cab, hitting her head on its unyielding metal frame. The concussion made her body slump to the floor of the truck, tethered only by the rope on her wrists.

CHAPTER 33
ERIC, THE HEART OF THE MATTER

E ric's car barely had gasoline fumes to burn by the time he reached Yankari Park visitor center. Police, army, and ambulance vehicles, all with flashing emergency lights, indicated that something serious had happened. Several emergency medical technicians were pushing a gurney with a body on it. *I hope this ambulance is not here for Mr. Burke.* Jumping from the Peugeot he approached the EMTs, afraid Alan had been brought down by terrorists.

An officer asked Eric what he wanted. Pointing to the body bag he asked, "*Ah fit looka?*"

It was not Alan. Eric still shook with fear of the worst. He asked a uniformed officer what had happened. "I must find Mr. Alan Burke." The man waved him off. Eric sensed that his civilian clothes seemed out of place in a crime scene. *Maybe Alan ee wuman here.*

The officer demanded Eric's identification. It took a while to convince the officer that he was not a murderer or a terrorist but was trying to find the husband of the American hostage. When he dropped Captain Hassan's name, a soldier remembered Eric from the first terrorist camp. That man pulled Eric aside.

"Cap'n Hassan *no be here. Ee don pass fo road tu hour past.*"

"How fo that *'merica man*, Mr. Alan Burke?"

"*Na, ee fit ride wit cap'n.*"

"*Weh side ee de go?*"

The soldier said that radio reports suggested south, and gave Eric directions to get to a main road. He explained that the leader of the Boko Haram unit was the feared Commander Edubamo. He had murdered a national park worker, stolen a vehicle, and looted the visitor center. They knew nothing about hostages. One officer started to describe the murder scene but was interrupted by an officer, who had just received a message that the stolen vehicle sped through a check point on the highway headed toward Cross River National Park nearly 100 kilometers south of Yankari.

"How do I get there?" Eric asked immediately.

Eric, worried about running out of petrol, asked where he could find a fuel station. The man shook his head, "*No be fo heeya.*"

Eric asked a policeman who had just completed a transmission on his radio. The officer brushed him aside with a wave of his hand. Eric searched for a compassionate person but finding none, maneuvered the Peugeot so that it blocked the park's only exit.

An ambulance attempted to leave the center twenty minutes later. The driver stopped within a meter of the Peugeot and repeatedly blasted his horn. When the Peugeot didn't move, the ambulance driver climbed down and stomped to where Eric leaned against his vehicle with arms folded. The driver shouted expletives and demanded that Eric move his car. Eric pretended to not understand the man. When the ambulance driver persisted, Eric pointed to the open fuel tank door and shrugged his shoulders.

This started a round of shouting from impatient drivers. Several soldiers offered to push the car out of the way. Eric said. "*Na, how Ah fit move from dis place? Ah no de get petrol, and Ah de fear for terrorist mon.*"

Finally, a soldier jumped off the back of a personnel carrier, dislodged a twenty-liter gas can and helped Eric pour ten liters into the Peugeot's tank. The engine whirred several times, sucking fuel to the carburetor. Blue smoke shot out the rusted tail pipe as the French-made engine fired up. Eric moved the car to let the ambulance pass.

After other vehicles sped through the gate, Eric followed. He headed south toward the Nigerian state named Cross River.

He was less than five kilometers from the visitor center when Alan's cell phone, still tethered to the charging cable, buzzed. He parked on the shoulder, and saw that the screen read: Len Watson.

He pushed a button and timidly said, "Hello."

From five hundred kilometers away, Len Watson said, "Hello, Alan?"

"No sir. This is Eric. I have Mr. Alan's phone, but he is not here."

"Eric. Hi. This is Len. Len Watson, from Kribi."

"I know, sir."

"It's good to hear your voice. Where are you, and where is Alan?"

"Sir, I am in Yankari National Park. I am driving to find Alan. I think he is with an army captain, and they are following Boko Haram terrorists, who have taken Mr. Alan's wife and another hostage. I don't know, but the army thinks the terrorists are headed south, towards Cross River State."

"Eric, I am at the lodge at Cross River National Park, in that state. We were just warned about Boko Haram terrorists. I want to help but I'm not sure what to do."

"I don't understand, sir. Why are you in Nigeria?"

"I am a guest speaker at a seminar. I've been in Nigeria for two days, attending the Central African Wildlife Preservation Seminar. It's part of my work, to write and speak about preservation of timber and wildlife. I will be here for two more days. I heard about the kidnapping of Alan's wife on Voice of America. I called your boss, Richard Alquist, at USAID this morning. He told me Alan left the embassy last Saturday, and they think he is in Nigeria.

"Yes sir. Mr. Alan wants badly to find his wife. I am hoping to find Alan."

"Be very careful, Eric. I'm sure you know that Boko Haram terrorists are very nasty fellows. You could get yourself killed. By the way, your boss is looking for you. I guess you failed to let him know you were not going to report for work."

"Yes sir. I didn't take permission. I only want to help Alan find *ee wuman.* I didn't know I would be gone so long." After a short pause Eric added, "But, sir, I must go quickly. I need to catch up Alan."

"Okay, Eric, but please stay in touch. I'll call Alan's phone if we get news about Boko Haram movements."

The road ended abruptly at a T junction. Eric screeched to a stop. *Left, or right?* A faded sign pointing left read BENUE. Another read KANO and pointed in a northerly direction. *The Boko Haram operates out of Maiduguri, and that is way north.* Eric glanced at his watch, spun the steering wheel, and pressed the gas pedal to the floor.

CHAPTER 34
CHASING EDUBAMO

Commander Yusuf Edubamo spotted the Nigerian tank and sensed the trap. *Damn! The army had roadblocks everywhere.* Going north toward Maiduguri had not worked. After Hafsa, he had driven south, toward Abuja, to outsmart the Nigerian Army. But every road was blocked, and now his plan was imperiled, as the army persistently cut off highways going north. His alternative was to hand his hostages to a contact in Abuja, but at his petrol stop he had learned that the army had blocked the road beyond Jos. He did not want to lose the hostages. He was not afraid of the infidels' bullets. He was not afraid to die; however, he would enjoy taking as many lives as he could. He would continue south, circle back, and enter Abuja from the south side.

Edubamo's escape had become more problematic when he saw his own man fly off the back of the truck. *Too bad. He was a good fighter and a trustworthy soldier. No matter. He is now in a better place.*

Edubamo concentrated on outrunning the army. He watched for additional roadblocks. As he rounded a sharp turn, the headlights of the pursuing vehicles disappeared for several seconds, giving him thoughts of a desperate strategy. He passed a number of smaller dirt service lanes entering the main national park road.

Edubamo timed the disappearance of lights in his mirror as he rounded sharp curves. At the first opportunity, he spun the wheel of the Isuzu without touching the brakes and slid sideways for several meters before darting off the pavement and accelerating onto a narrow dirt track. Dense undergrowth immediately eclipsed his vehicle, absorbing the glow from its headlights. He downshifted and coasted thirty meters, killing the headlights.

He saw flashes of light as three vehicles zoomed by the service lane. He spun the vehicle around, kicking up a cloud of gravel. His prisoners rolled into each other and against the sides of the truck bed. After several seconds, Edubamo pounded the steering wheel, "Fuck you army imbeciles. Catch me if you can," he shouted in a bitter, raspy voice.

*　　　　　*　　　　　*

The ropes securing Mona and Stany to the truck kept them from flying over the side. The rough jerking motion created tension on their bindings and raised painful sores on their wrists. In desperation, Mona used her teeth to bite the knot. To her surprise, she was able to loosen the binding a little on her right hand.

*　　　　　*　　　　　*

Edubamo waited two seconds with lights off at the main road. Seeing no cars coming from either direction he turned on the headlights, and steered onto the pavement in the direction he had just come from.

Five hundred meters down the road was another small road to the right, with a sign that read CORP YARD. He brought the truck to a sliding stop, taking the turnoff as a likely shortcut to get to what he thought was a village named Corpyard. The dirt road looked slightly more promising because of multiple tire tracks. His prisoners again suffered as they were bounced around mercilessly.

Edubamo maneuvered the truck over the ungraded dirt lane at high speed. He knew the army would come back, block-off the area, and search every square meter of the forest until they found him. He needed a road that led out of the park. He thought he had found it.

*   *   *

In the bed of the pick-up truck, Mona and Stany fought desperately for handholds. Had these hills not been the home of wild beasts, and had their hands not been secured to the truck bed, Mona would have considered jumping off when it had slowed. The dark forest may conceal dangerous snakes and flesh-eating cats. More important, the man sitting in the passenger seat still held a loaded weapon. Mona did not want herself or Stany Ngey to be targets.

Mona bit the loosened knot that bound her right hand and freed the rope. She worked the crude knot on her left hand, and, in spite of the bouncing and rolling in the dark, she freed that as well. The terrorists in the cab appeared to be oblivious to her movements. Relief was immediate.

While the commander and his passenger seemed fully occupied navigating the narrow, road, Mona hoped they could not see her or the minister. Holding on with one hand, she reached to the spot where Stany's hands were secured. Then putting both hands to work on the knot, she hoped that she would not get thrown over the side. Stany, apparently realizing what Mona was trying to do, used her shoulder to steady Mona. It took several minutes but both knots came free. Stany sighed in relief and massaged her abraded hands. She patted Mona's shoulder to acknowledge her appreciation.

*   *   *

Edubamo cursed with rage when the small dirt road ended in a construction site. A dead end. There were no buildings, only an old Caterpillar bulldozer and multiple piles of crushed rock and sand. Three deer dashed across the open area and disappeared into dark vegetation. Edubamo drove the pickup around piles of construction materials, searching frantically for an outlet. Maneuvering the pickup in a wide circle with the bright headlights he saw, other than the

229

reflection off the eyes of a huge Cross River gorilla, nothing but dark, forbidding jungle. He considered charging cross country into the darkness, but the foliage was too dense to allow the truck to pass.

Reluctantly, he turned the vehicle back to the direction he had come and stopped. He killed the engine and sat, exasperated, deciding what to do next. The only sounds were the tick, tick, tick of the cooling engine. His subordinate glanced out the rear window to assure himself that the two prisoners, their potential bank roll, were present in the truck bed. Two forms were visible in the darkness, but, from his angle their hands were not visible.

Edubamo had no choice. The highway was the only avenue of escape. Eventually the army would flood the area with soldiers. It was nearly midnight. *Darkness is my only friend.* He decided to take the chance of finding another way out before the army spotted him.

*   *   *

Mona heard Stany's labored breathing and painful moan, and she touched Stany's shoulder. Stany jerked away. "It's okay Stany, it's me. Did I touch a bruise?" Mona whispered, "Are you okay?"

Stany seemed to sense Mona's concern and reached out her own hand to touch Mona's arm. She whispered, "Okay."

Lying on the cool bed of the truck Mona heard the silence broken by the screech of an owl, the chirping of crickets and the distant wail of an unidentified animal. They had been running since early morning when the Nigerian Army had attacked the terrorists' camp. Mona's mind raced, frantically seeking an escape. She sensed that the Boko Haram were desperately looking for a way out, and that something climatic was about to happen. *These guys are going to kill us because we have no more value, and now we're slowing them down. If they don't kill us, the Nigerian Army probably will by trying to save us. We've got to find a way out of this.* Every option was dangerous. She felt a twinge of despair.

I am responsible for getting myself into this untenable and deadly situation by insisting on going alone to Kaduna. Mona also knew she could not abandon Stany Ngey. *I need to help her escape as well.*

Her biggest concern was the man in the passenger seat with the automatic weapon. Her hands were free and she knew she could run, but that weapon had a long reach. Having observed the minister's distress during the race to the game reserve, Mona didn't expect that Stany would be able to run very fast, or far. And, this forest could be teeming with wild animals.

She sensed Stany's intense gaze, and heard her voice crackle with fear when she asked, "*Wuna fit ron?*"

She reached over to grab the minister's arm. In the filtered light from the back window of the truck cab she saw both fear and determination in Stany's eyes, and asked in a whisper, "Can you jump?" She couldn't remember the French word for jump. She repeated, "Jump? You *fit* jump?" She mimed jumping using her fingers.

Stany's gaze intensified, eyes focused intently on Mona. Mona sensed a strong emotion, as she felt Stany's hand excitedly squeeze her shoulder. Mona perceived strength and determination in the minister's grip.

Mona had read of the fate of other women who were imprisoned by the terrorists. They were often raped and made to bear the children of their captors, and if they refused to submit to sharia law, or when they were no longer useful they would be summarily killed. Stany lived in a world where people understood the likely fate of Boko Haram captives.

Mona heard Stany's deep, quivering sigh. Stany nodded her head and said, "*Oui.*" She grasped Mona's arm tightly and whispered. "Okay, w*una fit yumping.*"

Mona's spirits lifted at Stany's response. In the moment of camaraderie between the two women, Mona was encouraged that they would work together. She experienced a trace of hope seldom felt since her capture nearly eight days ago. Mona now considered a plan that would take advantage of their captors' preoccupation with their struggle to escape, and which would not overly endanger her and Stany's lives. She also had to consider the fact that both she and Stany were exhausted. An additional concern was their location. They were in a dense forest that teamed with wild, possibly dangerous creatures.

Mona understood that the terrorists' main objective was to avoid the Nigerian Army. She also reasoned that she and Stany might still be alive only because the ransom demand had not been officially denied. Because the truck had turned 180 degrees, and hearing the angry cursing from the cab, she deduced that the driver had made a grave mistake by taking a road that dead-ended. She assumed that he was now deciding the next best plan for escape. It was very likely they would encounter the army patrols again, and that there may be more shooting.

Before she could act, the engine started. Tensing for an opportunity to jump off the back of the truck, she heard Edubamo grind the gears shifting into low and jerk the truck forward. The headlights were off. At twenty-five kilometers per hour they moved toward the paved road. When the truck stopped near the pavement with the lights off, Mona realized she had to act now.

Mona grabbed Stany's arm and whispered in French, "*Allons.* Come on." Mona scrambled over the tailgate and landed on crushed gravel further bruising the bottoms of her bare feet. Edubamo suddenly punched the accelerator, turning the wheel sharply to the right. The truck's tires slipped on the gravel but squealed loudly onto the tar. Stany followed Mona, but the sudden forward motion of the truck propelled her off the tailgate. She rolled over the tailgate and landed awkwardly, partially on the gritty road surface and partially on Mona. Dust and gravel shot from the tires, covering the two women with painful pellets of stone and grit. Darkness, combined with the cloud of dust, concealed their movements, and the racing engine covered their noisy escape.

*　　　　　*　　　　　*

Edubamo and his passenger, apparently intent on studying the road watching for military vehicles, sped on. The commander turned on the headlights and accelerated. The pick-up's tires screamed on the pavement as the truck accelerated to top speed in seconds.

Choking, and blinded from the dust and dirt, Mona was pinned to the ground by Stany's heavy body. Mona reached for her companion, who was sprawled motionless. Mona cried out, "Stany. Stany." She pulled herself free and crouched near the still figure. Stany was covered with gravel and dirt. "Stany. Are you okay?"

The minister twitched, and moaned softly. With apparent great effort she rolled onto her side, and spat road dust. She coughed and, with a painful effort, mumbled, "*Je vais bien.*"

Mona sighed relief and assisted Stany to a sitting position. Mona couldn't see the numerous bruises and scratches on Stany's arms and legs, but could see the way Stany held her head and moaned that she was in bad shape. The minister was unable to put weight on her legs, but Mona encouraged her to move. "Come. Quick. We've got to get off the road before they return. Lean on me ." A loud squeal of tires on pavement caught both women's attention. Brilliant lights lit up the forest from several hundred meters down the main road to the right. The treetops all around them took on a brilliant white glow, as though they were on fire. Mona stared in astonishment as she heard loud crashing noises and an amplified voice echo through the forest.

CHAPTER 35
DEMISE OF A TERRORIST

E dubamo had accelerated the Isuzu to its top speed, and had barely covered three hundred meters when the forest lit up with a blinding light. From several hundred meters ahead and behind him super-bright floodlights blinded both jihadists. The Nigerian Army had been lying in wait. Startled, Edubamo cursed as he lost control of the Isuzu, which crossed the road and leaped a drainage ditch at high speed. The passenger side glanced off a tree and directed the truck front-first into a sturdy Musanga tree. The violent impact lifted the rear of the vehicle a meter off the ground. Edubamo flew forward, crushing his chest against the steering wheel, forcing air from his lungs and cracking several ribs. His head struck the windscreen. He lost consciousness, and his body slumped against the driver's door.

Slowly he became aware of loud, crackling sounds of a megaphone. He felt something warm and sticky on his head. A loudspeaker blasted unintelligible sounds. He shouted to his passenger, "What does it say?" Turning painfully to his right he saw his trusted ally slumped against the dash board slowly collapsing toward the floor, the barrel of his weapon shoved grotesquely into his neck.

Edubamo tried to assess his situation. Anger more than fear controlled his emotions. His door wouldn't open. Searing pain shot through his chest. Desperate to fight until his last breath, he again forced his shoulder against the door. It held firm. He leaned his head out the window as bright lights moved toward him. He struck his rifle butt against the door until it creaked open a crack. He pushed his head and shoulders out, and screamed in pain as he rolled onto the moist ground. He remained prone, trying to muster the strength to stand.

The loudspeaker blared demands that he surrender. He cursed the Nigerian Army for their persistence. Remembering his hostages, he reasoned, *they won't shoot. They are afraid of hitting my prisoners.*

The Nigerian soldiers were not shooting at the truck. They stopped twenty-five meters away. Rocket-propelled grenades, or canon fire from their T-72 tank, could have obliterated the pickup truck. Instead, the military focused their bright spotlights on it and demanded Edubamo's surrender.

*   *   *

Army sharpshooters pointed long-rifles at movement on the ground next to the open driver- side door. As the figure rose to his feet and staggered backward toward the trees a rifleman found him in his scope's crosshairs. The first bullet brought Edubamo to his knees. A second shot removed a major portion of Edubamo's skull. For a moment the forest was silent, except for the rhythmic cooling ticks of the truck's hot engine.

*   *   *

The roar of a high-powered vehicle shattered the solemn stillness. A military Humvee skirted the flanks of other army vehicles and pulled to a stop near the upended Isuzu. Two figures jumped out. One, in an army captain's uniform, brandished a pistol. The other wore civilian clothes. Two blood-soaked bandages reflected intensity in the man's steely composure.

Captain Hassan grabbed Alan's shoulder, and pointed his weapon in the direction of the smoking pickup truck. Alan pulled away from the captain and rushed forward.

*   *   *

Alan had a bad feeling as he approached the Isuzu. From the bright lights he saw there was nothing in the bed of or under the truck. He approached the passenger door and yanked it open. He jumped back, startled, as a body rolled out of the cab and onto the ground. He watched as soldiers inspected the remains of Edubamo and his still companion.

Alan searched around the truck for bodies that may have been propelled over the cab on impact. There was no sign of Mona. Alan pounded on the hood with his wounded left hand and shouted Mona's name in frustration. To Captain Hassan he said, "I can't believe this. Mona is not here and these two animals are not talking. We chased these jihadists a thousand kilometers, but Mona's not here!"

"Come." Hassan said, "your wife may still be alive. We will find her."

"Right," Alan looked up with tired eyes, "I will find her."

While Hassan instructed his men, Alan spoke to the soldiers who had chased Edubamo. His best pidgin was barely good enough to get curious nods. Finally, one of the officers approached Alan and asked what he was doing. The man told Alan in clear English that he had been in a vehicle that chased the Isuzu and that he had observed at least one woman, maybe two, in the back of the pickup.

Now we're talking. That had to be Mona and the minister. She must have either been dropped some place by the terrorists or had escaped.

With the officer's help Alan encouraged the captain to lend them his Humvee. They drove to the place where the officer first saw the woman in the back of the truck. Using a floodlight, they searched the road and ditches. Alan shouted Mona's name. When they neared to the place where Hassan waited, the driver of a Land Rover flagged down the Humvee.

The Land Rover had four gold stars displayed above the windscreen. The occupant was a heavy-set Nigerian man dressed in a formal military uniform displaying four gold stars on each collar. He introduced himself as General Rasaki, and asked for Captain Hassan. The officer driving Hassan's Humvee spoke to the captain in Hausa, and directed the general to Hassan. Then the general pointed to Alan and said in English, "Who are you?"

Alan said, "Alan Burke, American. I work for the U.S. State Department. My wife was taken hostage by Boko Haram. I need to find her."

The general simply nodded and ordered his driver to go.

"Is that the man in charge of counter-terrorism?" Alan asked remembering the article he read on the airplane.

"General Rasaki. He *be big mon fo* new counter-terrorism unit. He go see that Boko Haram mon *bin* capture or die."

"Let's search in the other direction"

Just three hundred meters beyond the army vehicles Alan saw the first side road. It was on the left, and the driver slowed so Alan could scan with the floodlight. He called out, "Mona! Mona!"

A movement in the brush near the road caught his eye. He froze, startled to see a human hand raised to shade a face, and he lowered the light. He called again, "Mona?"

Mona waved an arm weakly over her head. Alan leaped from the Humvee and rushed to the spot. It was her. "Mona." he shouted with joy. Before he reached her, Mona started to wail. She was kneeling on the ground next to a black woman. Both were bruised and bloodied and covered with grime. Alan knelt by Mona and she fell forward onto his chest, shaking uncontrollably, allowing her emotions to flood.

Alan and the officer carefully carried Mona and Stany Ngey to the Humvee. Neither woman could walk. Both had cuts and bruises over much of their bodies. Mona appeared to be near shock, her mumbled speech was incoherent. Alan thought he saw a tortured smile fade quickly from her bruised face. Though relieved to finally find his wife, Alan was chilled to see her battered condition.

The Humvee stopped near Captain Hassan. "These two women

need medical attention," Alan shouted as he jumped from the Humvee. Alan's spiked emotions were near panic. The Captain immediately called for medical assistance.

"Good," said General Rasaki, "I'm happy you are found." Looking at the black woman he asked, "Are you the Cameroonian minister?" When she stared at him, confused, he asked in French, *"Êtes-vous le ministre du Cameroun?"*

Tears flowed down her cheeks, illuminated by vehicle lights. *"Oui. Je suis Stany Ngey."* she answered in obvious pain. Her pleading gaze moved between the general and the captain. She said, *"Aidez-moi, s'il vous plaît."*

Mona understood Stany's expression of distress, and implored in a raspy voice, "She needs help. She's hurt and starving, and she wants to go home."

"These women need medical attention," the general agreed, "We must get them to a hospital now. We will also need to debrief all the parties in Abuja."

"Sir, it is late," Captain Hassan noted, "The hospital in Abuja is far. Can we get them airlifted tonight?"

General Rasaki considered their location and said, "We are not far from Cross River National Park, and there are medical staff in Kanyang station. We can take them there now. I will arrange an airlift to Abuja."

When soldiers moved Stany from the Humvee to a stretcher, she reached out with a trembling hand and pressed Mona's shoulder. Mona put her own hand on top of the minister's. Stany gave a sigh of relief. When Stany spotted the mangled Isuzu she gasped. Squeezing Mona's hand, she said, *"Merci."* They shared weary smiles of joy.

"Please sir," Alan persisted, "can your medic at least give these two women some fluids before they pass out? They're in bad shape."

CHAPTER 36
IT AIN'T OVER

A soldier hurried through the snarl of men and military vehicles and approached the captain. *"Massa, we de git won man dey fo road. Ee want fo tok wif yu. Ee don sabi you fo Boko Haram camp. You want we bringum?"*

"Na, whoskyne moto ee git?" asked the captain.

"Ee git some ol katsangkat, suh."

"Yes. Na Peugeot 404 be dis man ee moto," the captain said pointing to Alan, *"bringum."*

The soldier left to get Eric. Hassan said, *"Mr. Alan. I very happy yu wuman ee fayne-o. Yu most fortunate man fo get such brave wuman. I go gi yu small time to greet, but then we fit finish we wok."*

"What work are you talking about?" Alan said.

"Numba wan, I need yu report. Then, *I fit* arrest you for entering Nigeria without propa visa."

"So." Alan was mildly annoyed. "What are you going to do, evict me, and make me go back to Cameroon? I'm ready. Let's go now. Please take my wife and me to Yaoundé, immediately."

General Rasaki interrupted. "No. We must bring your wife and the minister to Abuja where qualified physicians will treat their injuries. Debriefing should only take two or three days. You will be

241

allowed to accompany her after you are processed through immigration.

"What? What debriefing?" Shouted Alan. "Sir, with all due respect, my wife has spent the last eight days as a prisoner of the worst terrorist organization in the world. She has been starved and beaten. She needs medical attention now, and she should not be transported hundreds of miles to be interrogated by military soldiers. You can get your damned debriefing when her wounds heal."

"Mr. Burke. I understand your frustration, and I sympathize with your wife's condition." Then the general added in an accusatory tone, "I understand, sir, that you are a U.S. diplomat assigned to the embassy in Yaoundé, Cameroon. Is that correct?"

"Yes," Alan answered indignantly, "that's correct."

"Then, Mr. Burke, you are aware that the United States Government is very interested in the successful return of this American hostage. Likewise, my Nigerian president needs to provide your American president and your secretary of state, who I believe is your boss, with a complete report of what happened and how the issue is resolved. Do you agree?"

The general was correct. Yet Alan remained defiant. There was no way he was going to let this general take Mona to Abuja. She needed immediate medical attention. "No, General. I don't care who needs to know what happened. I need to get my wife to a hospital immediately."

"Mr. Burke, we will get your wife to the best hospital in Nigeria, but we cannot get there at this hour. We are close to a national park facility that has a small medical unit. If you agree to stay out of trouble, I will not deport you just yet. Our army medical personnel will attend to your wife and to the minister. A helicopter will be there in the morning to fly everyone to Abuja."

Mona raised her head when the general mentioned Abuja. she angrily said, "Abuja? If I have to go to Abuja there is one man I want to hunt down. I will take the entire Nigerian army with me and have that bastard arrested."

"What are you talking about, Mona?" Alan said, "Who do you know in Abuja?"

Fury flashed in Mona's eyes, "The man who got me into this damn mess. I'll never forget his name. Bennett Ngu. That man tricked me and handed me to Boko Haram. He is responsible for the bruise on my chest and the blood on my head. He turned me over to that fucking monster over there that they just stuffed in a bag. He is evil, like all of the damn terrorists."

"Madam," said the general, "I know that name. The Counter Terrorism Unit knows where to find him. If you press charges we may be able to detain him for a very long time."

"Okay captain, if we have to go to Abuja let's go now? We chased across eastern Nigeria all night from Yankari to here. It's nearly three a.m., and my wife is injured and exhausted. She needs medical attention now. Take us to that hospital you say is the best in Nigeria."

*   *   *

An African man dressed in civilian clothes approached Alan who turned in surprise as the man softly said, "Mr. Alan?"

"Eric. Wow. How did you get here?" Alan gingerly offered his hand, but winced in pain, and swung his left arm over Eric's shoulder in a mighty hug.

Eric stepped back to survey the bandages on Alan's arm and hand. Smiling, he said, "*Masa, na whatee? Wa hoppen fo yu? Yu seem like wounded soldier mon.*"

Before Alan could begin to formulate an answer, Eric's eyes went to the injured white woman. "This *na yu wuman?*"

Alan responded in kind, "*Na, ma wuman this.*" Turning to his injured wife he said, "Mona, I want you to meet Eric Mbando. He is from Cameroon, and works for USAID. He has taken leave from his duties, without permission mind you, to help me find you. He has been a great help and. he will probably be in a lot of trouble when he gets back to Cameroon."

Mona painfully lifted her hand to greet Eric. "Hi. Whatever you did to assist, I appreciate it." Turning to Alan she said, "I see that your pidgin is coming along." She added with a devilish smile, "It seems better than your French."

Alan brushed off the insult with a smile, and turned to Eric. "How did you find me? Where is that old clunker you stole?"

"Borrowed," insisted Eric. "And it will be returned." He summarized his radio conversation with the army officer in Hafsa, his search for Alan at the game reserve, and the long overnight trip to get to this roadblock.

"That is unbelievable." Alan said, "I thought you would be back in Cameroon by now."

"I could not leave you in the jungle. I am glad the big lions did not eat you in Yankari."

"What?" Alan shouted. "Now you tell me there are lions in that game reserve? *Wondaful.*"

Eric gave Alan his cell phone. "Sir, Mr. Len called you. He is at Cross River National Park."

When the words finally sunk into Alan's tired brain he exclaimed, "You mean Doctor Len Watson? Our Kribi tree doctor friend? Len Watson is in Nigeria? Come on. What would he be doing here?" *What an unlikely coincidence that Len is in Nigeria, just a short distance away.*

Alan told Eric that the general was taking them to the national park headquarters as soon as Mona was treated.

"Good. I can take you there. The Peugeot is just behind those military tanks and trucks, and it still has small petrol. Can we leave now?"

The booming voice of General Rasaki cut in, "Mrs. Burke, the Cameroonian minister, and Mr. Alan will ride with me." Apparently, the general was not about to let the former hostages out of his sight. "You can follow us there if you like, but if you are driving a vehicle that is not registered in Nigeria, you may be stopped by the police."

*   *   *

At half past four Tuesday morning the general's Land Rover pulled to a stop in front of the government inspection bungalow at the park's research station in Kanyang. The sun had not yet kissed the morning mist but barely cast a dim light east of the park's tall strombosia trees. The air felt cool and moist, and dark, menacing clouds gathered in the northern sky.

A facility caretaker accompanied them to an infirmary where a registered nurse admitted Mona and Stany Ngey. Both women discovered bruises and fractures they had not noticed until the tension of their captivity and escape dissipated. They now felt pain they had previously refused to acknowledge.

Mona complained of nausea. Her stomach was nearly empty, but any food she attempted to consume would not stay down. Her body temperature climbed, her breathing and her pulse became rapid, and the color of her skin paled. She appeared to be in danger of going into shock. The army medical technician cautioned Rasaki that the national park was ill-equipped to handle Mona's dehydration. Alan was beside himself, and pleaded for the general to get Mona to a hospital immediately.

The General requested an air force chopper to be sent from Abuja immediately, but was told that bad weather kept the army's helicopters grounded.

News of the delay distressed Alan even more. He occupied himself by running after ice, water, tea, soup and fresh fruit to comfort Mona. He visited a shop looking for clean clothes. Mona attempted a smile when she saw the underwear printed with the park's logo.

Mona's temperature continued to climb. Alan massaged her head with a cool towel. She opened her eyes and gave Alan a weak smile before drifting off again.

The facility's medical staff complained, "We can only try to keep her temperature under control and keep her comfortable." The small infirmary had only three beds, an x-ray room, and a cabinet with limited, basic medical supplies for emergencies such as snake bite, poison ivy, animal bite, or exposure. Staff included only the registered nurse and a young paramedic.

While Mona battled a fever, the nurse replaced the soiled wrappings on Alan's arm and hand. His left hand was infected, and was now painfully swollen.

Staff treated the numerous injuries Stany Ngey had received. She suffered a broken arm and a sprained ankle when she rolled off the moving pickup. She would need ten days before the ankle could support her weight. The paramedic stitched several of Stany's open wounds, and placed a cast on her broken arm.

After waiting with Mona for a while Alan stepped outside, found a chair, and called Mona's parents in Pottawattamie County, Iowa. They were desperate for news about their daughter. Relieved to learn that Mona was alive and safe, the Morgan's erupted with joy. The parents wanted to speak with her, and demanded that Alan bring her home immediately.

Next, Alan called his boss, the U.S. ambassador to Cameroon. Tyler Morrison first expressed relief that both Alan and Mona were in safe hands. He then went into a tirade of admonitions. The ambassador was outraged that Alan did not obey protocol, nor keep the embassy informed of his movements. He yelled into the phone, "Do you have any idea how embarrassing it is to be shouted at by the president of the United States?

"Why the hell didn't you communicate with us to work out a less dramatic solution? Not only that, but because of your damn Nigerian venture, the Cameroon prime minister's all over my ass. On top of that you had the audacity to kidnap the USAID driver/mechanic. What were you thinking?"

Alan absorbed the verbal abuse patiently. He knew that he couldn't have done anything different. The governments of Cameroon and the U.S. seemed to be incapable of action, with everyone trying to be politically correct and afraid of interfering with Nigeria's sovereignty. His ears burned as he listened. When Morrison slowed to take a breath, Alan asked, "Do you want to call the secretary of state, or should I?"

That did it. Now Tyler sounded even more pissed. Alan knew that a subordinate should not call his supervisor's boss, but he was fed up with protocol. The ambassador sighed loudly, and said in a condescending tone, "Dammit Alan, as I said, I am glad that you and your wife are both safe. You must have gone through hell. I don't understand some of your decisions, but we'll talk about that later. For now, just give me a quick summary of where you are now, where you have been, who you are with and what happened. **I** will call the secretary. I need something substantive to tell her. And keep to the facts. Remember, she debriefs the president within the hour."

Even the short version took Alan ten minutes. He ended by stating that their plight was not over. Mona was in danger of going into shock, and the three of them were to be flown to Abuja for medical care and debriefing.

Tyler Morrison warned, "Don't talk with anyone until someone from the state department is present. I won't be able to attend, but the U.S. ambassador to Nigeria, or Secretary of State Townshend must be present."

Ambassador Morrison then asked for an evaluation of the condition of the Cameroon treasury minister so he could update her prime minister. *Tyler will enjoy giving the prime minister the news.*

Alan called Len Watson next. There were more important calls to make, but, after the scathing lecture from his boss he wanted to hear a friendlier voice.

Len expressed relief to learn that Alan and his wife were both safe. "Is it okay if I pop by the infirmary to say hello and meet your wife?"

Finally, Alan called Mona's employer, Benjamin Warner, of Adams, Benson & Chang. Maryland time was six hours behind local time, so the law firm's senior partner was at his home, likely sleeping. Alan left a brief message to let Ben know that Mona was safe but suffering from injuries and dehydration.

Lack of sleep caught up with Alan. The cell phone fell out of his hand. His head bobbed forward and he drifted off.

Len Watson arrived an hour later. Alan wiped some sleep drool from his mouth and struggled to focus. The two men greeted and gingerly shook hands. Alan gave Len the two-minute version of his story before they checked on Mona.

Soft light reflected off the perspiration on Mona's forehead. The bruise on her face was a rainbow of colors. The paramedic informed Alan that Mona's temperature still hovered between 102- and 103-degrees F.

Len was shocked at Mona's physical condition. He asked Alan to step outside the room with him. There he told Alan, "Your wife looks terrible. Her life could be in danger if we can't get her metabolism back to normal soon."

"Yes, I'm aware," Alan said, "the chopper is delayed, and the medical staff say that this clinic does not have the correct medications to treat her. They are low on saline drip, and struggling to get liquids into her. They are trying to keep her comfortable until she can get to a full-service hospital."

Len appeared to be deep in thought. Finally, he said. "I have an idea. Remember what I told you about how some of the forest tribes depend on certain trees for their healing power? If I could just find fraxinus excelsior we could make our own drugs."

"Can you put that in layman's English? What is fracky excelsior? I don't want you trying anything experimental on her."

"Sorry, mate. fraxinus excelsior is an ash tree. The leaves and bark can make a medicine that could help lower your wife's temperature and improve her breathing. Hmm, I don't think Ash grows in this part of Africa. But wait. There are other plants. Yes. I have it. The soursop grows here. I've seen it in the park. There is also the polylalthia longifolia tree, also known as the masquerade tree. The fruit and the leaves have tremendous healing powers. I once attended a symposium where a tree expert taught the healing powers of plants. Let me make a quick call to Doctor Medford to confirm."

Alan was not amused. He didn't particularly want a forestry expert experimenting with tree juices on his wife. Yet, hope springs eternal, as the English poet Alexander Pope wrote. Alan would try anything that seemed safe and had promise of bringing his wife back to full health.

Within the hour, Len had staff running throughout the grounds of the Cross River National Park searching for a soursop, or a masquerade tree. A groundskeeper spotted a healthy specimen bordering a parking lot. Following the advice of Doctor Medford who read from an on-line medical journal, Len scribbled down the steps to prepare a potion.

Mona's temperature remained high. Nine days of this wild odyssey had been extremely stressful. As the morning progressed, she would wake frequently in a state of delirium, her body wet with perspiration but shaking with chills. She tossed her head from side to side and moaned.

Alan placed a cool towel on her forehead. Mona's eyes opened but she was too weak to speak or smile. She gently squeezed his hand.

"Honey," Alan said, "please hold on. You've been through a lot, but you've got to hold on. We'll have you in the best hospital in Nigeria soon. Okay?" His voice seemed to have a positive effect on Mona as her mouth curved into a faint smile. Alan squeezed her hand. "Listen, sweetheart, a friend of mine wants you to try a local remedy to give you some strength. Will you try it?

Mona made the slightest of nods before turning her head away to cough.

Ten minutes later Len came into the room with a small vial of a greenish-looking liquid. Len said he wasn't sure whether he should have Mona drink the potion or rub it on her body. After consulting with Alan, it was decided to have her taste it first.

Alan tenderly lifted Mona's head. Her clothes were damp with perspiration. He asked for more dry towels then passed the vial under his nose before bringing it to Mona's lips. The concoction smelled like newly mowed wet grass. He looked at Len with a raised eyebrow as if to ask, Are you sure this is a good idea?

Len looked concerned, but confident. He shrugged his shoulders.

Placing the vial to Mona's lips, Alan said, "Okay, love. Please take a sip. This has healing powers."

Mona sipped a very small amount, made a sour face, and softly mumbled, "Horrible." She pulled away from Alan's supporting arm and lay her head on a dry towel. Soon, she smacked her lips. Rolling her tongue over her upper lip she breathed a soft, "More."

Alan was surprised to hear that, and looked at Len with a quizzical expression. Len only shrugged and smiled.

Mona took a longer sip, swallowed, and relaxed on Alan's arm. She consumed the remainder of the green liquid, smiled and laid her head back. Her breathing became rhythmic, and her whole body seemed to relax. Alan worried when it appeared that she had fallen into a deep sleep. He looked at Len for assurance that this was normal. Len only shrugged.

Mona slept soundly for a full hour without moaning or moving. Alan watched her closely. Len stayed nearby, watching for any indication that his idea was working.

Mona's eyes opened and slowly focused on Alan. "Who's that?" she asked, glancing in Len's direction.

"Hello, Mrs. Burke. I'm Len Watson. I've either just cured you or poisoned you, and I'm waiting to see what you do next."

Alan laughed and said, "Honey, this is Doctor Len Watson. He's the tree PhD I told you about. He picked me up at the Douala Airport and showed me around some projects in the southern part of Cameroon. He just made a medicine from a sourpuss tree."

"Soursop. Soursop." injected Len, forcefully.

"Yes, that tree. It has medicinal properties. If it works he'll be a hero. If it doesn't I'll kill him. How do you feel? Do you think we can make our helicopter flight to Abuja?"

"I feel groggy. And I need to brush my teeth. That stuff tastes like I imagine dog pee would taste."

CHAPTER 37
RUDE AWAKING IN ABUJA

Alan held Mona's hand Wednesday afternoon as the French-made Air Force AS332 Eurocopter sat down on the expansive national park lawn. Two men in white coats descended the stairs and scooted under the rotating air foils. A soldier unloaded two wheelchairs.

The doctors found Mona sitting upright munching on a dry English biscuit. They checked her scrapes and bruises, her badly injured feet, and swollen eye, and prepared her for the flight to Abuja. She managed a weak smile as they asked routine questions to determine if she was capable of travel. Her feet bulged, swollen and swathed in bandages.

Alan helped answer the doctor's questions. When the doctor asked about the prospect of moving her today he said. "Absolutely. We want to get her into a first-class hospital as soon as possible."

The doctors connected Mona and Stany to intravenous solutions to safeguard against dehydration and severe cramps. They replaced the cast on Stany's fractured arm and treated her sprained ankle before lifting her onto a wheel chair. The doctors cleaned and replaced the dressings on Alan's arm and hand and injected antibiotics for the infection. General Rasaki then ordered his men to wheel Mona and Stany to the chopper. Both had IV's attached to their wheel chairs.

Eric informed Alan that he had made peace with his USAID office in Douala. His supervisor granted several additional days leave so he could travel to Abuja, then transport the Burkes to their post in Yaoundé, Cameroon. Eric began his drive to Abuja the minute the NAF chopper lifted off. He agreed to meet Alan at the hospital in Abuja.

The blades of the helicopter whirled and the engine roar became deafening. The aircraft shook. As it lifted off the ground Mona reached for Alan's knee. The noise and vibration unnerved her, so Alan attempted to distract her. "What happened to your left shoe," he shouted?

"How did you know I lost a shoe?"

"I found your right shoe on a bombed-out APC." Alan watched Mona's face change from surprise to one of sadness. Looking into Alan's eyes she said, "I still can't believe you were right behind me."

"I thought you knew. Weren't you leaving that trail of leaves so I could follow?"

"I am so glad you did, Alan. I wished it, but didn't think it possible." After a pause Mona added, "There are other hostages besides Stany and me. I hope they are okay. There is a woman teacher who helped me, even though her village had been sacked and she had little hope. Her name was Oneka."

"Mona, honey. I'm afraid Oneka didn't survive. Eric and I found her badly injured. She died in my arms. Oneka told us where to find you. She seemed like a lovely person. Honey, I'm so sorry."

Mona turned toward the window. Her body shook, and Alan knew she was crying. He placed his good hand on her shoulder.

Forty minutes later the military chopper skimmed the rooftops of military buildings and landed at the Nigerian Air Force Base. A crowd of fifty spectators and well-wishers watched from afar as medical staff gently lifted Mona and Stany off the aircraft, and placed them into a waiting ambulance.

*　　　*　　　*

U.S. Deputy Chief of Mission, Gertrude Williamson, from the U.S. Embassy in the Nigerian capital stood nearby as Mona was settled in the ambulance. Williamson introduced herself and asked Mona about her condition. A U.S. Marine took their photograph to be sent to Washington, D.C., as confirmation of Mona's escape from the Boko Haram. Alan held an IV for Mona as they were transported to Abuja's Maitama Clinic.

The hospital was immaculately clean and seemed efficient. In minutes Mona was relieved of her clothes, some of which she had worn nine days, bathed, cautiously shampooed, and placed on clean, white sheets. Doctors replaced her IV and sutured the wound on the side of her head.

Medical staff also checked Alan's arm, and cleaned and dressed the infected knife cut on his left hand. He had lost a great deal of blood and so was given a transfusion. The pain became pronounced as it replaced the urgency of finding Mona. He also became acutely aware of how close he had come to never making it beyond the instant that bullet came centimeters from reducing his heart to mush. The doctor gave Alan pain medication, advising him that it could make him drowsy. Alan refused an offer to be assigned a room because he wanted to be ready to assist Mona. He insisted on staying nearby, but doctors shooed him off to a waiting room. Within twenty minutes Alan felt the painkiller's effect. He dozed off in a waiting area and was soon snoring at a volume uncomfortable to other visitors.

The medical staff made it clear that Mona would recover much faster if everyone would clear out of her hospital room and not linger in the hallways. Reluctantly, the embassy's deputy chief of mission, General Rasaki, and other officials and journalists were shooed away.

*   *   *

General Rasaki had hoped to debrief Alan while Mona and Stany were being treated and resting. It was the general's responsibility to issue a report to his high command, requiring the testimony of everyone involved in the abduction and rescue. The general hoped for the opportunity to claim honors for success against Nigeria's primary enemy. However, since Alan could not seem to keep his eyes open, the general left a note for him stating that he would be in the conference room nearby.

*   *   *

At 9:30 p.m., Mona stirred. One eye slowly opened. She could hear a machine humming behind her, and that monotonous beeping sound that told her that her heart was performing just fine. Her other eye slowly opened. It was dark outside her window, but a soft glow from a lamp illuminated the IV tube that ended in her left arm. There were the usual hospital sounds, distant voices from somewhere down the hall, but otherwise it was quiet.

She wasn't sure what awakened her, but she had a strange feeling there was someone else in the room. She looked up. There was someone else, and he wasn't a doctor.

CHAPTER 38
BED PAN HEROICS

E ric loved driving. The sound of the tires on the road, the feel of the wind rushing by, and the gentle purr of a well-tuned engine were beautiful melody. He did his most creative thinking when there were no passengers to entertain, no tedious security checks, and no particular hurry to get anywhere fast. Perfect, with a little background makossa music.

Eric was a cautious, attentive and efficient driver. He was the best. Employers praised his efficiency. He never had an accident and was always where he was supposed to be, on time. He was thoughtful and courteous. He planned his trips well and always had his vehicles clean well-maintained, and ready for the road.

Alan's cell number and a hospital address were in his pocket. Shortly before nine p.m. Wednesday he saw the distant lights of Abuja. He stopped the car near a roadside cigarette stand. Stretching his tired joints and muscles he meandered to the stand and asked for English biscuits. He engaged the shopkeeper in casual talk using the local dialect and paid for the biscuits with Cameroon CFA. Though not the currency of Nigeria, the shopkeeper accepted it with a smile and asked in pidgin, *"Husay yu komot? A tink say yu komot fo Cameroon, no bi so?"*

Eric devoured half the biscuits while visiting then abruptly asked, "*Ah fit borrow yu cell? Fo jus wan call?*"

The man smiled again and showed Eric a cell phone. "*Tree hunert CFA.*"

Eric laid three hundred CFA on the grimy counter and dialed Alan's number. He waited as the phone buzzed repeatedly.

*   *   *

Alan awoke to violent shaking. One eye popped open. General Rasaki bent over Alan shaking his shoulder. "Whaa…" From somewhere deep within a scary dream the general's voice and an irritating noise penetrated Alan's consciousness. He jumped so fast the general jerked back to avoid a collision. Disoriented, it took a moment to recognize Rasaki, whose face was inches from his own.

"Mr. Alan. Your pocket is buzzing. You may have an urgent telephone call. Please wake up."

Alan slowly reached for his cell phone. "Heh… Hello?"

He heard a familiar voice. "Mr. Alan. This is Eric. I am just now arriving Abuja. How is madam? Is she getting proper treatment?" After a pause, Eric continued, "Where can I find you?"

Alan confirmed that Mona was getting good care and was currently resting. He gave Eric directions to Maitama Clinic.

Eric arrived at the medical facility twenty-five minutes later. He rushed to the reception desk. "Mrs. Alan Burke?" he asked, "Mr. Burke and his wife came here this afternoon. Mrs. Burke was captive of Boko Haram. She came with the Army's General Rasaki. I am friend with the Mr. Burke."

"*Ah. Yes,*" said the receptionist, "*I know that wuman pikin. She be admitted at tree forty-seben taday. She de fo Room 432, on top floor. Doctor not allow to git visitor, but Ah jus allow her fren to go, so I guess it be okay fo you visit her also.*"

For a reason Eric was later hard pressed to explain, he asked, "Who was that?" Eric asked, "Was it Mr. Burke?"

"*Oh, no. Meesta Burke,* na *ee be America man. Na, he be white man. Dis*" *some Nigeria man. He no want gi ee name but we insist to see ID. See here, on log, he name be Ngu, Bennett."*

Eric froze. *That name is familiar.* He had heard that name recently. Something was not right. His eyes widened in alarm when he remembered General Rasaki saying Ngu was well known to his anti-terrorism force. Eric asked, *"Husay meesta Burke ee dey?"*

"A don hea he dey fo waiting room."

"Madam, Ah beg, call security. That man be Boko Haram. Eric dashed to the elevators, leaving a stunned receptionist staring after him. He pushed the elevator button, but as the seconds ticked away he bolted for the stairs. Two steps at a time. His short legs and eighty-four kilos tired him quickly. He was out of breath before he reached the third floor. Bent over at the waist he drew deep breaths.

A man dressed in blue scrubs stepped into the third-floor landing. He looked surprised to see a stranger hunched over and sucking air like a jet engine. "You okay?"

"Yes sah. I jus.. need.. to get.. my wind."

"My good man, you ought to take the lift. You might injure yourself dashing up these stairs."

"Yes suh. Thank you suh. Ah go go me," he puffed. Ten seconds later he was at the fourth floor. Still puffing hard, he charged out a door and skidded to a stop on a tiled corridor frantically looking at numbers on the wall. Spotting a woman in a pink uniform he ran to her. The nurse's aide shrieked in surprise. Eric asked, *"Ah say, Miss, husay room 432 de?"*

Wide-eyed in terror, she stepped back. Finally, nodding at Eric's apologetic look and his upturned palms, her shaking hand motioned left.

He started in that direction but stopped abruptly and turned back toward the aide. "Na, which way to waiting room?"

She pointed in the opposite direction, and said in perfect English, "At the very end of the hallway."

"Thank you, miss."

He realized that it was critical that he check on Mrs. Burke's safety before searching for Alan. There was not enough time. Turning on his toe, he sped toward room 432.

As he passed room 430 he slowed and tip-toed. He heard a masculine voice coming from 432. He hoped it was Alan, or maybe a doctor, but needed to be certain. The door was closed. The handle rotated, but the door would not give. A doctor could be doing a procedure. Mr. Alan may have wanted privacy with his wife. But what if Ngu is in there?

He knocked on the door and shouted, *"Missus* Burke. Are you inside."

An immediate woman's scream for help spiked Eric's adrenaline. He took a half step back and lunged forward plunging his right shoulder into the door. The aide, who had followed Eric, screamed, "Hey! What are you doing?"

Eric shouted at the aide, "Please, get security, now!

The solid-core door had not budged. Eric's right shoulder ached from the impact, so he backed up a step and accelerated his muscular weight forward, slamming his left shoulder against the portal. He heard the sound of splitting wood, and the jam moved several centimeters. Objects inside the room slid and crashed onto a hard floor. Eric pushed harder and the door opened further.

Eric heard pandemonium erupting at the nurses' station. He shouted for someone to call the police. A nearby nurse screamed.

The barrier to Mona's room opened enough for Eric to see a man holding a knife. He gulped noisily seeing the Islamic terrorist face-to-face. He still couldn't see Mona. *Have I made a grave mistake?* Mesmerized by the intimidating knife moving from the man's left to right hand and back made his stomach churn. He had no experience in defending himself against weapons. Eric was terrified of being cut, however, his blood ran hot whenever he witnessed someone being bullied or injured by an aggressor. No one was there to help. It was up to him to act.

Movement to his right revealed the woman he had met yesterday. Mrs. Burke looked terrified. She was off the bed, an IV tube still attached to her arm. Her feet appeared to be tangled in the bed sheets and her hair flopped crazily across her face. In a hoarse voice she shouted, "Look out. He's got a knife."

The knife flashed right and left as Ngu crouched cat-like, and inched forward. Eric's mind raced as he desperately looked for a way to defend himself. By blocking the doorway he had cut off his aggressor's escape. *Not a good idea.* When the man flung a chair aside and took a menacing half-step toward him, adrenaline took over.

The steel-framed chair that Ngu had used to brace the door lay just inside the room. Eric used one foot to draw the chair between him and Ngu. Except for the overturned bed stand, it was the only large object between him and the man wielding the fearsome five-inch blade. As Eric reached a hand for the chair, Ngu let out a shout and charged with the knife straight out in from of him. Mona's blood-chilling scream seemed to distract Ngu, who slipped awkwardly. His body twisted and his right leg failed him. But, a Boko Haram terrorist would happily cut Eric into tiny pieces before letting him cut off his escape.

Mona continued screaming. Ngu's stumble had allowed Eric time to grasp the backrest of the steel chair. He now had something to hold between himself and the lethal-looking blade.

Ngu straightened and scowled, his eyes darting wildly as if measuring his options. Eric sensed indecision in his attacker.

Then, a familiar voice from the hallway gave Eric's spirit a boost.

"What the hell's going on Eric? Mona? Are you okay?" Alan, still a bit groggy from the pain medication, stopped just outside 432. A heavyset, uniformed man appeared next to him.

The terrorist's plan to defiantly re-take the American woman as a hostage had developed a little hitch. Ngu limped a step backwards and glanced between Mona, Eric, and Alan, who now poked his head over Eric's shoulder, observed the knife, and exclaimed, "Holy shit!"

If the terrorists were able to re-capture the American woman, it could prove the superiority of Boko Haram over the West. Judging from the venomous stance of his adversary, Eric knew the terrorist's only option was to kill anyone who stood in the way of his mission.

Bennettt Ngu's eyes glanced toward Mona. He edged to his left and reached for her hair while making sure Eric kept his distance. Mona pulled away, causing Ngu's hand to grab air. The miss caused Ngu to look for her again. In that instant, Eric raised the chair above his head.

Alan, pushed his way into the room and kicked the bed stand aside. He shouted at the intruder as he moved next to Eric, "Who the hell are you?" What the hell do you think you're doing?"

The chair whistled through the air at the end of Eric's strong arm. One leg of the chair struck Ngu's wrist. The weapon spun free and clattered to the floor.

Ngu dove for the knife, as Mona jumped out of the way. Quick as a mongoose on a cobra, Eric jumped over the fallen bed stand and stomped his heavy boot on Ngu's hand. Ngu cursed in pain as Eric stomped again, then drove his knee into Ngu's back. Eric put all his weight on the prostrate terrorist and shouted for help. A bulky security guard arrived at that moment and plopped his full weight onto Ngu.

"Careful. *Ee de git knife under ee hand.*" Eric struggled to push the knife away from Ngu's reach.

Alan rushed forward and kicked the knife out of Ngu's reach. Then he went to Mona and moved her out of range of the flailing arms and legs.

Ngu's crushed right hand was incapable of grasping the knife, but the jihadist would not surrender to infidels. He twisted his body in the opposite direction and swung his left elbow into the side of the security officer's head. The officer moaned, went limp, and rolled onto the floor.

Eric was losing his advantage as he frantically struggled to stay on top of Ngu. Alan pounced on Ngu, who fought like a cornered wolverine with arms and legs flashing, fingers poking and scratching, and using his head as a weapon. Ngu twisted his body and rendered a knee to Alan's groin and a hard blow to Alan's head. Alan's momentum waned.

A mighty clang startled everyone. Ngu's body relaxed slightly, and he moaned. A second clang sounded and Ngu's struggle stopped.

Eric rolled onto his side and pulled his trapped arm free. He looked up at Mona, who was leaning against the hospital bed with an impish smile on her face. Calmly, she said, "I'm glad this hospital still uses stainless-steel bed pans."

Alan pulled himself from the pile and crawled to a corner, where he struggled for breath, his face pale.

The room began filling. Several astonished medical staff stood helplessly by while another security guard bound the hands of the semi-conscious Ngu.

When General Rasaki forced his way into room 432 he saw a scene that included Mona Burke leaning against the bed holding a bloodied steel bedpan. One security guard was on the floor moaning and rubbing the side of his head. Alan Burke grimaced in a corner looking pale and miserable. Eric sat on the floor puffing hard, and a second security guard sat on the prostrate form of a handcuffed man. Medical staff looked on in dismay.

Mona smiled a devilish smile at the general and said, "Relax general, we have everything under control."

Alan turned to Eric and, between winces of pain, said, "Eric, you are some incredible driver. How is it that you always seem to be in the right place at the right time?"

"Sometimes luck is better than being good. I was fortunate to be here when this man tried to take *yu wuman.*"

CHAPTER 39
YAOUNDÉ, OR BUST

General Rasaki escorted Bennett Ngu toward the door and said, "Ah, Mr. Okeke. We finally meet."

Surprised, Alan said, "What? I thought his name was Bennett Ngu. You know him by another name?"

"Yes Mr. Burke. The man you call Ngu also goes by the name of Pail Okeke. He is wanted for murdering six police officers. I have been hunting him for months."

Mona blanched and slumped against the hospital bed. Gaping at her husband in astonishment she said, "Alan, I believe that is the name of the man who was supposed to meet me at the Lagos airport."

"What? You mean a murderer was assigned to be your protector? I don't believe this. How could...? This is insane."

Even with handcuffs on his wrists and chains on his legs, Ngu was defiant. He called on Allah to perish the infidels around him and spat toward the woman who had given him a throbbing headache. As the general was about to march him out the door, Mona said, "Wait. I need to ask him a question."

"Of course, Madam."

"Mr. Ngu, or Okeke, or whatever your name is, what is your relationship with Albert Achebe?"

Bennett scoffed and spat out, "*Ah no know that name.*"

"But you told me at the Abuja airport that Achebe's office told you to meet me. Explain that."

"Who is Achebe?" General Rasaki asked.

"Albert Achebe is an attorney, my contact in Lagos. My employer referred him. Achebe was the only person who knew I was traveling to Abuja and Kaduna, but somehow, this man was conveniently at the airport in Abuja to drive me to Kaduna. I was suspicious of him because I couldn't understand who sent him. Now I wonder about Achebe."

Ngu looked away, avoiding all eye contact.

"Don't worry, Mrs. Burke," General Rasaki said. "You will give me the address for this Achebe fellow, and we will visit him," Rasaki said. "There may be a sinister relationship with a terrorist organization, or it may simply be an unfortunate coincidence. I am in charge of Nigeria's Counter Terrorism Special Forces. I investigate civilian connections to the Boko Haram. It is difficult to know everyone's loyalties and hidden alliances. As an attorney this Achebe is in a position to be very useful to the terrorists. He could be an active agent for Boko Haram, or, possibly his communication or security systems could have been breached."

*   *   *

The general pulled a few strings to help Alan get a Nigerian visa the next day. Alan was finally able to move freely in Nigeria. General Rasaki had made it clear, however, that Mona, Stany Ngey, Alan, and Eric must be debriefed before they would be allowed to leave Abuja. Alan complained that he needed to begin his new job. Eric groaned and said he badly needed to get back to his family and his USAID job. Mona said, "I just wanna go home."

Secretary of State Lisa Townshend flew to Abuja to personally interview Mona and Alan. The secretary's report would go directly to the president who scheduled a press conference for that afternoon.

International radio and television reporters wanted to question Mona about her capture, treatment, and escape. Both CNN and CBS *Sixty Minutes* requested exclusive thirty-minute interviews with the Burkes. The media portrayed Mona as a hero for using her wits to expose the position of the terrorists.

Alan wanted to leave Nigeria and find a place to heal. Mona expressed concern about possible retaliation from Boko Haram. Alan realized that if Ngu had the audacity to enter Mona's hospital room, she would not feel safe anywhere in Nigeria. She mistrusted everyone. "I want to go home," she repeated.

Mona's doctor advised her that she was vulnerable to post traumatic stress and to be alert for signs of depression. Alan grasped her hand and said, "Mona, we don't have a home in Cameroon yet. Moreover, the ambassador is not too happy with me. It might not be very convivial to be there right now."

"I can't go there," Mona said, "not now. I just couldn't handle that. I need to go someplace where I can get my feet back on the ground, no pun intended."

Alan hugged Mona and said, "The most important thing I learned from this experience is that I love you much more than I need my diplomatic career." Then he looked Mona in the eye and said, "Okay! let's go somewhere quiet. Maybe a resort in Europe. I know a great beach in Goa. How about Hawaii?"

Mona smiled at Alan for the first time since they split up in Paris. She hugged him and whispered, "Yes. Yes."

The State Department granted a sixty-day leave of absence for Alan, with the caveat that he and Mona fly directly to Washington, D.C. That was fine with Mona, who wanted to visit the law offices of Adams, Benson & Chang. She had some hard questions for her employer. She was curious about how information about her travel to interview US-Toys landed in the hands of Mr. Ngu.

Eric was to drive his friend's Peugeot back to Yaoundé. Alan was saddened to part company with the man who had risked his life to help find Mona. Even if he never returned to Cameroon, Alan knew he would not forget Eric's steadfast determination and loyalty.

"Maybe we meet one day in Douala," Alan told Eric, "and I will toast you with the most expensive import beer."

"No need," Eric replied with a smile, "I don't drink beer. Anyway, I should thank you. You helped me rescue an important minister for my country, and you helped me defeat the people who killed so many of my countrymen."

Mona hugged Eric, and gave him a small wrapped package. "Thank you for keeping my man safe," she said tearfully, "and thank you for saving my life. Please travel safely."

Alan shook Eric's hand and embraced him, saying, "Thank you for staying with me. I could not have made it without your help."

"Remember, sir," Eric replied, "it takes two hands to tie a bundle."

When Eric walked toward the Peugeot, Alan used his new, favorite pidgin phrase to wish Eric a safe trip, "*Waka-fayne.*"

*   *   *

During their mandatory first stop in the U.S., Alan and Mona were ushered into the office of U.S. Secretary of State Lisa Townshend. She welcomed them and praised Mona, who still walked with crutches, for her courage and perseverance.

Turning to Alan she assumed a severe stance, with one hand on her hip, the other pointing at Alan's chest, a slight frown creasing her forehead. "But, you, Mister Burke," she said sternly, "Your antics have been most reproachable. You abandoned your official post as a deputy program officer at a time when the ambassador to Cameroon needed you most. You illegally crossed the Nigerian border without a proper visa, and you violated State Department protocol. Those are serious offenses for a U.S. diplomat."

Alan looked shocked, but meekly said, "Madam Secretary. You are correct. I admit that I abandoned my post and violated rules of protocol. I did it knowingly, and my only excuse is that I couldn't stand by and do nothing to help my wife. I…"

"Alan. Stop." Lisa Townshend said, smiling. "I understand. You did what you had to do. I can't chastise you for doing what I hope anyone would do to protect his family." She held Alan's gaze for a moment, then said, "I have no intention of demoting you. In fact, I want to suggest something else. A new position just opened up in the U.S. Consulate General in Barcelona. It requires fluent Spanish, but you can consider that opportunity while you recover. We'll talk more about it in two weeks."

*   *   *

Alan and Mona flew to Mona's hometown of Council Bluffs, Iowa, where Mona recovered quickly under her mother's care. By the end of January, as the snow piled high above the cornstalks, and temperatures dropped below zero, Mona looked across the drifts and said to Alan, "Honey, I'm ready to tackle the world. Let's move to a warmer climate.

"You know, Honey," Alan said, "I learned a lot this past few months. Mostly, I've come to appreciate how special you are. You are so strong and self-reliant. I love you so much. I also have a new respect for the goodness in people like Eric. He may appear to be a simple driver-mechanic, but he has a heart of gold and an inner strength that amazes me."

"You were very fortunate to find him," she said. "But, you know, I'll bet that there are others just like him all over the world. His kind stand tall when they're needed."

"I never realized how committed some terrorists are to their cause. I still cannot understand the zeal that drives Boko Haram to kill non-believers, but I now sense how committed they are to sharia, and how hate can drive people to violence."

"Please, Alan, the thought of terrorists gives me goose bumps," Mona said. "History is filled with religious fanatics who placed their ideals above the lives of others."

"But, Mona, the most important thing I learned," Alan said as he reached for her hand, "is that I never want to be away from you again."

"Alan, don't let the African experience stifle our careers. I support you fully."

"I know now I can make a difference in international work," Alan said. "I want to get back into the game. I feel toughened by the recent experience, and I have a strong conviction that I can use my skills to help make this world better." After a pause he added. "But I won't go anywhere without you. If you are not interested in working overseas we won't go. Are you with me?"

"Yes Alan," she replied. "I learned a lot about myself in Nigeria. I want to be with you wherever you go. I gained confidence in my abilities, and I am not afraid to work overseas. Let's get back to work."

APPENDIX

KAMTOK DICTIONARY
Some key pidgin words and phrases used in this narrative

Cameroon Pidgin Words & Phrases	Translation
Ah	I
Ahbeg	Please, I beg
Ah bin see ee	I saw him/she/it
Ah dey fayn or *Ah fayn-o*	I'm fine
Ah di wok	I am working
Ah go go me	I will go
Ah go land yu slap	I will slap your face
Ah nehva wok	I haven't worked
Ah no gree	I don't agree
Ah no no	I don't know
Ah no sabi	I don't understand
Ah wan chop	I want to eat
Ashya,	Hello, goodbye, sorry for your trouble, excuse me
Bif	Meat (any kind of wild game)
Bin bi	Past tense

(example: Ah bin wok)	(example: I did work)
Born House	Birth Celebration
Bringum	Bring it, (bring him, her, it, them)
Brohda (*Mbrohda* in French)	Brother
Bush meat, Bif	Wild game
Chop	Food or to eat
Comot	Come out from, come out of here
Comot fo road	Make way
Cuttin grass	Hedge hog
Dantite (*carte d'identit* in French)	Identity card
Dem	Them
Di	Progressive aspect
Di man ee wuman	The man's wife
Don dong	Perspective aspect
Ee	He
Ee big pass me	He is bigger than me
Ee rohn go pass me	He runs faster than I can run
Fit	Can, able to (past tense = bin)
Fofu (foofoo, or foufou)	Food made from cassava root and green plantain
git	Get, got, has, have
Go	Future tense
Gi mee	Give it to me
Go fo befo	Go ahead, begin
Ha now, how fo yu?	Hi, how are you?
Hus kayn news?	What's new?
Huside ma dash dey?	Where's my tip? My extra?
Kain ting, kayne ting	That kind of thing
Kam	Come
Katsangkat	Peugeot car model 404 (French for four hundred four)
Krai dai	Wake, death celebration
Lak	Must, (also means to like)

Listen well well	Pay attention
Ma	My (example: Ma pikin = my children)
Mos	Must, ought to
Na so?	Is that so?
Neba or neva	Never
No bat neyws	No bad news (in response to *hus kayn news?*)
Ohs	Us
Open eye	Bossy
Oshiya	Sorry, excuse me, sorry for your troubles, greeting
Papa dem	Older men
Pikin	Child
Pipo	People
Put han (as in put hand)	Help
Quickly quickly catch monkee or softly, softly catch monkee	You must be fast and smart to accomplish your goal
Sabi	To know
Sofly sofly catch monkee	Proceed gently and we will achieve our goal
Soso	Continually
Stick dem	Trees
Tif, Tif man	To steal (verb) Thief (noun)
Tight frien	close friend
Vex	Upset
Una, wuna	You (plural)
Wah	Our, we
Wahala	Trouble, problem
Woka fayne	Take care, have a good trip, as in walk fine
Wan	Want to. May also mean 'one'
Wan an no fit taye bundle	You cannot tie a bundle with just one hand
Wetin dey happen?	What happened? what's going on?
Wey	Who
White mimbo	Palm wine, raffia alcohol
Wuman	Woman, wife

ACKNOWLEDGEMENTS

An author can dream and play with words, but others help make the words tell a better story. Thanks to my critique group: Jil Plumber, Dita Basu, William McGinnis, Marjorie Witt and Wendy Blakeley for their patience and encouragement. Thanks to my editors: Bill Tilden, Lyn Roberts, Kymberlie Ingalis, and Elisabeth Tuck for guiding me through numerous iterations and correcting my unusual application of the English language. I appreciate the contributions of the readers: Holly Hand, Mavis Sonnier, Abraham Ndofor, Marcia McCord, Eric Mbangowah, and Rachael Mariko Kerkhoff Slotemaker, who stirred my imagination with their ideas, and uncovered shortcomings in continuity, mechanics and logic. Ndofor and Mbangowah gave credibility to my use of Pidgin English. Thanks to Bobbee Campbell and Troy Wilson who contributed images of their Cameroon and Nigerian artifacts, and to Matthew Kerkhoff whose computer skills helped produce the map of Nigeria and Cameroon.

ABOUT THE AUTHOR

Ken Kerkhoff writes both fiction and non-fiction drawing from his overseas experiences. While living in Cameroon, he developed appreciation and love for the gentle-but-proud Africans who accepted his family with warm cordiality. Ken writes about the generous, peaceful, hardworking Africans who strive for a better life for their families. Affected by recent terrorism and civil disruption that frustrates the people's dreams of a once-bright future, Ken offers this book to highlight his concern for people he holds dear.

Growing up on his parent's Minnesota farm, Ken developed a yearning to challenge the world beyond the fences. His first book, *Paper Boat, Discovering India With A Master Storyteller*, confirms a lust for travel and adventure. Ken's writing blossomed when his home town newspaper published his weekly letters home from India.

Ken lives and writes from his home in California, where he also crafts with wood, gardens, travels with his wife in their RV, plays softball with the Walnut Creakers, and fly fishes whenever he can.

Made in the USA
Las Vegas, NV
10 April 2021